Nicole's Revenge

Nicole lay on her bed in the darkness. From below she was sure she could hear muffled cries – the tantalising sound of a woman reaching her climax. She pressed her hands over her ears, but her cheeks burned and her mind was filled with tormenting pictures of the woman in the lewd leather harness, licking her lips as she gazed at Jacques. Nicole was ready to drive the ivory phallus deep within her, longing to feel its caress, but she would tease herself for just a moment longer...

Nicole's Revenge
Lisette Allen

BLACK LACE

Black Lace books contain sexual fantasies.
In real life, always practise safe sex.

This edition published in 2005 by
Black Lace
Thames Wharf Studios
Rainville Road
London W6 9HA

First published 1995

Typeset by SetSystems Ltd, Saffron Walden, Essex
Printed and bound by Mackays of Chatham PLC

ISBN 0 352 32984 X

Nicole's Revenge

It is September, in the year 1792, and France is in the throes of violent revolution. The king is a prisoner in his own capital, and the country is run by the National Assembly which bends to the rule of the bloodthirsty Paris mob. The guillotine is in regular use, and the powerful armies of Austria and Prussia threaten the French borders. Foreign ambassadors have been swiftly withdrawn by their governments, and those aristocrats who have not already fled Paris are either imprisoned or deep in hiding; for flight from the city is impossible now that the gates of Paris are shut tightly on the enemies of the people . . .

Chapter One

As dusk fell across the city the rain stopped at last, leaving the streets chilly and damp. The lamplighter had done his work, and at uneven intervals the overhead lanterns swung dimly on their ropes, casting a lurid glow over the shabby façades of the tall, overhanging tenements that leaned in on the narrow alleyways.

The cobbled paths of the Faubourg St Marcel were dirtier than ever, since no-one now was paid to clean them. After the rain of the afternoon, a dirty rivulet of water trickled down the gutter in the middle of the road, sluggishly taking a pile of rubbish with it. There was a stale smell of wine and tobacco and city dirt upon the air, and people were strangely subdued as they sat out around their doorsteps, muttering in low voices, casting anxious glances down the street.

Perhaps their silence had something to do with the ominous murmuring noise in the distance. More than a murmur, it was like an echoing rumble of thunder, menacing, chilling to the blood. The Paris mob was out on the streets tonight.

A sudden commotion from the wine shop down the road caused everybody's head to turn. Always a popular gathering place, citizen Gaspard's wine shop was

3

this evening almost surrounded by a crowd of roughly dressed men in wooden *sabots* and red woollen caps stuck with tricoloured cockades; the *fédérés*, conscript soldiers from the provinces. Some sat on upturned wine barrels, leaning forward eagerly; others, local men, peered over their shoulders, calling out, shouting encouragement, their tankards of rough wine held high. The reason for their amusement was soon evident.

Two of them were holding a female prisoner, an *aristo* to judge by her clothes, and were laughing openly at her distress. They'd caught her trying to scuttle off home with a loaf of stale bread, under cover of darkness; the bread lay in the gutter, and she cursed them openly. Slender and tawny-haired, her amber eyes ablaze, the girl struggled fiercely in their grasp, even though she must have known that escape was hopeless. Her gown, with its crumpled silk skirts and worn lace fichu, was a sad relic of past finery; her hair had been pinned up, but now it cascaded round her shoulders, and she looked at her captors with all the contempt in the world.

Meanwhile more and more men were clustering eagerly, anxious for sport, till she was completely surrounded. One man, slouching back against the wall, took his blackened pipe from his mouth and grinned at his companion.

'Our fine neighbourhood tribunal has done well tonight, citizen. Looks like we've caught ourselves a little *aristo*, slinking out under cover of dark.'

The other man chuckled, pushing back his filthy red cap from his low forehead. His eyes were alight with lewd excitement. 'Not an *aristo*, Jean; but the leavings of one! This fine lady was a dancer at the Opera. Regard her well, my friend, look at her face, her figure, her lovely legs. No wonder the comte de Polignac chose her for his own!' He leaned forward through the ring of onlookers and tugged at her skirts, revealing one shapely, slender leg up to the thigh; a groan of appreciation went up from the onlookers, and she kicked out viciously, until someone twisted her arm behind her back, and she shut her eyes tightly against the pain.

'The comte is in prison?' asked Jean, unable to take his eyes from this stunning beauty that the dark alley-ways of St Marcel had so unexpectedly thrown up for their delectation.

'*Merde*, no!' The other man spat into the gutter and swigged more wine. 'The vile traitor got away to Austria, they say. But he's left his little *poule* behind, for our pleasure! I remember seeing her riding in his carriage; her name is Nicole, Nicole Chabrier. See how she dances now!' And, stepping forwards once more, he reached out his tobacco-stained hand to twist his fingers in the captive girl's glorious, tawny-chestnut hair that gleamed so enticingly in the glow of the street lamp. She whirled round, in spite of the strong arms that imprisoned her, those wonderful amber eyes spitting scorn.

'Take your hands off me, you vile, drunken scum! Go and drown yourself in your cheap wine – that's all you're good for!'

Someone clicked softly, dangerously between his teeth. '*Aristo*,' he murmured. 'Death to all aristocrats.'

The girl caught her breath. No-one guessed how desperately she was fighting down her fear.

'You dare to call me an aristocrat?' she said in a low, vehement voice. 'When my family slaved for gener-ations in the Normandy fields? Working and dying for the great nobles, who never even knew they existed? I'll swear, you *cochon*, that each one of my family worked harder in one day than you've ever worked in your life!'

'But you found easy pickings when you came to Paris, eh?' sneered another, coarse-faced man. He hitched his breeches higher, openly fondling himself beneath the coarse homespun fabric as he did so. 'I'll bet that warming de Polignac's luxurious bed was a lot easier than labouring in the fields! You miss the comte, do you, wench?'

5

The girl stopped struggling then, and, tossing back her beautiful hair, said, very steadily, 'If Gerard de Polignac came back tomorrow, I'd have great pleasure in throwing him into prison myself.'

There was a sudden silence, almost of disbelief, as if the ragged onlookers couldn't take in what she'd just said. Some of the men drew back slightly, giving her space, and it was then that she saw him.

In the pool of darkness well beyond the streetlamp's dim glow, a dark-haired man leaned almost nonchalantly against the grimy wall of the tenement, his arms folded across his chest. He was tall, taller than the poor *sans-culottes* who inhabited this warren of alleys and courtyards, and almost respectably dressed, in a dark, sombre coat and high, mud-spattered leather boots. He wore no hat, even though it had been raining; and his long black hair was tied back at the nape of his neck. She could see little of his face, because it was in shadow; but what she did see made her shiver suddenly.

Someone sitting on an upturned winebarrel broke the silence contemptuously. 'What shall we do with her, *mes amis*? Throw her into the Conciergerie with the rest of the *aristos* and the poor, quaking priests?' He took a long swig at his beaker of rough red wine. The wine shop owner was doing good business, and many of the men were openly drunk.

Another called out, 'Later! But first, fellow citizens, let's have some fun! She claims she was a ballet-girl at the Opera. Well, then, let's make her dance!'

Someone, a *fédéré* in a short red jacket, chuckled, 'String her up from the lamp-post. She'll dance as well as she's ever done in her life, I vow! Let's see for ourselves what de Polignac's *poule* can do.'

The tawny-haired girl Nicole twisted violently in her captors' arms to see the soldier who spoke, and spat at him, full in the face.

'*Morbleu!*' The ruffian thus anointed leaped towards her and grabbed her by the shoulders, hurting her.

6

Somehow she wrenched herself free again and clawed at his face, fighting like a wildcat, so that there were murmurs of amused admiration from the avidly watching men. There was something about her that forced their respect, because she was so wild, so beautiful, so full of spirit.

Almost reluctantly, four of them stepped forward, brawny arms braced, to pull her off their suffering soldier comrade.

Then, they stopped. A sound echoed through the still night air which they'd all missed, engrossed as they were with their captive; no-one had heard it approach except the man who still stood unseen and alert in the shadows. A drumbeat, getting louder, rhythmic and menacing; and along with the drum, the sound of a hundred pairs of feet dancing to its beat, the sound of a hundred ribald voices raised in the coarse words of a song. Then the street was suddenly filled with the tide of people, more women than men; a flood of red caps and tricolours and ragged clothes; whirling, singing, stamping, infecting all in their path with the wild fury of the Carmagnole.

It was the Paris mob in full flow, filling the street, engulfing the crowd of men outside the wine shop so they had no identity, but were just part of this seething mass of humanity, dancing hand in hand with the women, posturing, clapping, baying for blood. The girl Nicole, stumbling and sobbing vainly to get away from those stamping feet, suddenly felt strong arms seizing her, pulling her back into the darkness away from the heavy wooden *sabots* of the prancing women. Looking up into the dark, shadowy face of the man she had seen watching her from the darkness, she struggled anew.

'Let me go, damn you!'

But this man was wide-shouldered and strong, more formidable by far than those half-starved peasants who'd held her earlier, and her struggles were in vain. She shivered visibly as she heard his cool, cultured

7

voice saying softly in her ear, 'You'd rather be out there dancing with them, my Nicole?'

She sagged back against his chest, sickened, and he held her by the shoulders as she gazed trembling at the lurid scene that unfolded before her eyes.

The mob had parted to make room for some young, gaudily-clad women who were carrying stuffed straw effigies of the king and queen. They were shrieking with laughter, thrusting the two figures against one another in a parody of copulation; a young, striking looking woman called out, 'No, that's no good! Didn't you know our Marie-Antoinette prefers the tender embrace of her own kind?' Grinning, she pulled a young female friend towards her and they embraced openly; the crowd shouted encouragement, until a drunken man leaped forward and pushed himself between them shouting, 'You forget her Swedish lover! Our queen was eager enough for him, wasn't she?' And he grabbed the first woman to himself, ripping at her gown and bending his head to savour her exposed breasts; the woman leaned back in his arms, sighing with pleasure, and before Nicole's horrified eyes the man loosened his trousers and began to copulate with her vigorously, there in the street.

She slumped back in her captor's arms, glad of his support, sickened by the sight. And yet, somehow, the heat of their open lust was starting to course through her own blood, making her limbs strange and melting. Even though she was repelled by the degrading sights she saw, she couldn't drag her eyes away.

They were raiding the wine shop now. The poor owner, Gaspard, after protesting feebly, had turned tail and fled before the mob's jeers; men were rolling out barrels of wine and brandy, and smashing them open until the wine ran like blood along the cobbles. Still the drum beat, still they danced on, swooping and kicking in glee, spinning in pairs and dropping to the ground, drunk with lust. A girl stood on an upturned wine cask, posturing in a strange, erotic dance of her own; a man pulled her to the ground, and kissed her hungrily. Those who didn't have beakers were bending down to lick up the wine as it ran down the gutters; a woman on all fours, lapping at the wine as it gushed from a hole in the side of a barrel, was seized avidly by a soldier, who lifted up her skirts and slid into her from behind as she moaned her delight.

Nicole trembled in the stranger's arms, unable to tear her eyes away from this dark, primitive celebration, feeling excitement as well as fear at the sight of these vivid, earthy people, revelling in their sensuality, without fear or shame. Oh, what had driven them to this?

People like Gerard de Polignac, she thought bitterly, and all the other aristocrats who had for generations crushed people like them under their red-heeled shoes as if they were the scum of the earth. That was who!

For these poor people, it was a celebration of new-found freedom, of life, of love. And she found it wildly erotic. The beat of the drum, faster now, matched her own fluttering pulse; she felt the heat churning in her stomach, the melting at her loins as she watched the ecstatic coupling of a man and woman only a few yards away. She felt her nipples tingling and tightening, and bit on her lip to fight down the heated sensations that threatened to overwhelm her. The man was behind her, firm and strong; his hands lightly caressed her almost bare shoulders, and she leaned weakly back against him, feeling the hard, sinewy strength of his body, breathing in the cool male scent of him. His hands slipped to encircle her narrow waist, and rose, so slowly that she thought she was imagining it, until she felt the soft caress of his palms against her stiffened nipples beneath the lace of her fichu. She shut her eyes, feeling a sudden wild surge of passion. His loins were hard against her hips. Oh, if only she could have this man now, this mysterious stranger! If only he would draw her down into the shadows and make love to her with wild abandon, touching her with those long, lean fingers that were circling her breasts and driving her almost to the dizzy edge of rapture! Already, her breathing was short and laboured with the approach of ecstasy. She shut her eyes to avoid the sight of the mob, but there was no shutting out the fierce sensations of pleasure that were arrowing down to her loins from the sensitive buds of her engorged breasts. She could feel his lips against her hair, feel his warm breath on her cheek . . .

Then a harsh, drunken voice called out, 'Hey! We'd almost forgotten de Polignac's whore! Where is she?'

Someone else shouted, 'Yes, let's have de Polignac's wench! Let the noble citizens of Paris see her naked! If she was good enough for him she's good enough for us, eh, *mes amis*?'

Nicole felt the fear ricochet through her heated body. She whirled desperately to look up into the man's face. She saw him then properly, by the light of the swaying lamp above them; saw that he was grim and harsh-featured, with narrowed eyes that were almost black. Gripping her by the wrist none too gently, he grated, 'This way. I have a *fiacre* waiting.'

And before she had time to draw breath, he was pulling her away from the baying mob, dragging her through the maze of courtyards and stinking alleys, until at last they reached the Rue Mouffetarde and he bundled her into a small carriage. Here, unbelievably, all was quiet. Nicole, furious with herself because she was unable to conceal the fact that she was openly trembling, turned defiantly to face him. 'Quite an adventure, monsieur! But now, I would be very much obliged if you would take me home!'

Calmly he signalled to the silent, sombrely-dressed coachman to move off, and said, 'Home? You have no home now, Nicole Chabrier. The mob will scent you out. They'll hunt you down relentlessly, because they don't like it when their prey escapes from under their noses.'

She gripped her hands in her lap. 'Then I'll leave Paris! Stop this carriage and let me out this minute!'

'I assume you've no papers. You'd never get past the barriers.'

She slumped back against the seat, knowing he was right.

He went on remorselessly, 'And what possessed you to be out on the streets on a night like this? In those clothes?' He gestured almost contemptuously at her shabby finery.

She retaliated furiously: 'I have no other clothes, monsieur! And I was looking for food; I haven't eaten properly in days. What was I supposed to do? Starve?'

He shrugged. 'It would be nothing new in Paris these days.'

There was a chilling silence. She gazed, anguished, into his cold, impassive face. He had a lean, almost aristocratic look about him, with a strong jaw and a hawk-like, high-bridged nose, every feature accentuated by the thick, glossy black hair that was drawn back from his wide forehead. His mouth was wide and thin, cruelly sensual; she remembered how much she had wanted him, as he silently fondled her in his arms, and felt faint. He was only a few years older than her, not yet thirty, she would guess; and yet there was a cool self-possession about him that spoke of a world of experience, of things that she could only begin to imagine.

'You obviously despise me,' Nicole said in a low voice. 'Why did you trouble to rescue me?'

He paused a moment, smoothing an imaginary speck of dust from his dark, close-fitting breeches. Then he said, 'You meant what you said, back there? About giving de Polignac up to the people if he should ever dare to return?'

'Oh, yes,' Nicole said bitterly. 'I meant it. I would turn him in, and any aristocratic friend of his, with the greatest pleasure!'

'Then I think, Nicole Chabrier, that I might be able to give you the chance for revenge.' He raised his hand to silence her as she gasped aloud. 'It might take some

11

time, and I can't make promises. But I think somehow that you're just the kind of woman I'm looking for.'

She gazed at him, astounded at this stranger's arrogance. Who did he think he was? Judging by his sombre but elegant clothes, he was some provincial *bourgeois*, a lawyer perhaps, elected as a deputy to the National Assembly. He must be from the south, from Provence, because his skin looked brown from the sun . . .

Her mind whirled inconsequentially. She felt trapped by this strangely assured, calm, frightening man. Trapped, and yet deeply aroused. She was still hot from the feel of his hard body pressed close to hers, from the insolently casual way he had caressed her breasts. She glared at him defiantly, but inside she knew it was a hopeless defiance. He was right; she couldn't go home again to her poor lodgings in St Victor. She was marked down now, as Gerard de Polignac's *poule*. They would hunt her down with ruthless efficiency, the bloodthirsty Paris mob; cut her to pieces.

But she wouldn't let him know her fear. Tossing back her long tawny hair, she said contemptuously, 'I suppose you've picked me up for your own amusement, have you? Well, you can think again, monsieur! Because believe me, I'm not about to make the same mistake as I made with Gerard de Polignac, especially not with some petty provincial lawyer!'

He smiled. 'I picked you up because I admired your courage. Nothing more, Nicole. Believe me, I have no need to entice women into my bed.'

She swallowed hard. She believed him. He would be fighting them off, this one. But she wasn't going to flatter his vanity. 'You have a high opinion of yourself, don't you?'

'Forgive me, citizeness Nicole.' His dark eyes glinted wickedly. 'But I was rather under the impression that it was *you* who wanted, shall we say, something more, only a few moments ago . . .'

His voice trailed away in wicked implication. He was

almost openly laughing; she could see the glint of his evenly-spaced white teeth against his sun-darkened skin. He knew, then! This devil of a man; he knew that she'd pressed herself willingly against his hard body, knew that she'd been on the brink as he caressed her breasts so subtly while they watched that bestial crowd!

Nicole smiled at him very sweetly. 'Don't flatter yourself, my provincial *bourgeois!*' The *fiacre* was slowing down as they approached the river; springing to her feet, she reached for the door and flung it open, ready to jump.

She stopped, the blood draining from her face as she heard a terrible, curdling scream in the distance. Slowly it died away. Then, hurtling down the street towards them, was a gang of men, bearing flaming torches aloft, shouting and yelling. Their shirts were red with blood.

The man pulled her roughly back inside the carriage and slammed the door shut as the coachman swung aside into the Rue St Jacques. 'They're murdering the prisoners,' he said grimly. 'Turn your face to me, and whatever you do, don't look out again. There's nothing we can do; we'll be out of their way in a moment. That's it, Nicole. Look into my eyes, and try not to listen to them.'

She felt sick as the whirling mob surrounded them. She tried desperately to do as he said, to look into his calm, strong face, not to listen. They were slowed down now, by the people outside; a rough, brutish face leered in through the window, and she stifled a scream. Someone wrenched open the door, shouting obscenities; the man reached across quietly to take her hand, and faced the intruder.

The rough peasant who'd flung open the door gaped openly. Then, to Nicole's utter astonishment, he said, 'Citizen Jacques. It's you. A thousand apologies!' And, closing the door firmly, she heard his voice commanding the mob to let the *fiacre* through.

Nicole couldn't believe it. Who was her rescuer? How did that awful man know him? Why did he have the

13

power to drive quietly through the streets of Paris, on a night like this? They had called him Jacques, and that was all she knew about this man who held her life in the palm of his hand.

Beyond questions, almost beyond weariness, she slumped back in her seat as the coachman wheeled the hired carriage through the darkened, deserted streets of Paris into the St Germain des Prés *quartier*. Empty, boarded-up churches stood like grim relics of a past age at every street corner. This was the quarter, Nicole knew, that used to be favoured by the great noblemen of Paris. Now, their mansions stood shuttered and dark on either side of the spacious streets and squares. Their owners had fled long ago – hunted *aristos* like Gerard, comte de Polignac. Or, if they were still within the walls of Paris, they had more sense than to live in these great, ostentatious mansions, a symbol of their decadent power.

Her eyes drifted shut, but suddenly she sprang up in her seat, because the man was leaning over her, with a piece of soft black velvet in his hands. And as she gazed up at him, still dazed, he began to gently bind it around her eyes. 'One of my rules,' he said calmly.

Nicole struggled, trying to push away the frightening, engulfing darkness. 'No!'

'Yes.' For a moment he gripped her hands as she fought, and she was terrified by the steely strength of him. 'I'm afraid so, Nicole. For your own safety, you see, as well as mine.'

'No,' she repeated numbly, 'no . . .'

'Do I have to tie you up as well?'

The threat was like a silken blade held to her throat. Faint with fear, she submitted, and all was darkness until she realised that the carriage had stopped.

With almost tender hands, the man removed the blindfold and she blinked dazedly, realising that the carriage had pulled to a halt before a small side gate set in a high, shadowy stone wall. The man called Jacques was already climbing out, dismissing the carriage quietly; he bowed Nicole through the open gateway as if she were some great lady; except that his mouth was twisting crookedly, as if in some secret amusement. The moon shone fitfully through the lowering clouds and Nicole, gazing around her, gasped in astonishment at what its feeble light revealed.

Even in this near-darkness, she could see that the high wall concealed the secret of a truly palatial residence; the imposing town home of a marquis, perhaps, or even a duke! The gardens that surrounded it were almost choked with flowers; the air was heady with the aromatic scents of late summer as full-blown roses and faded lavender bushes sprawled across the overgrown gravel paths.

And the mansion itself had the strange, dreamlike quality of belonging to another age, a long-vanished era of peace and tranquillity, with its tall, imposing facade and its high, shuttered windows that gazed blankly down on the overgrown gardens. In front of the house was a wide gravelled courtyard, overgrown now with weeds; there was a graceful flight of stone steps leading up to the great main door. A colonnade to the side of the main building revealed extensive standing for the former owner's carriages; some of them stood there still, their paintwork sadly worn and dull. There would be no privately-owned horses now to draw them; they would have been commandeered months ago by the Insurrectionary Commune, for the army.

Suddenly Nicole caught her breath, because she thought she'd seen a face, a pretty, youthful girl's face surrounded by a cloud of dark, curly hair, peeping out of the shadows at the side of the house. She started forward, but almost instantly the face was gone. Jacques' hand was at her arm, gripping her. 'What is it? What did you see?'

'Nothing.' She laughed weakly at herself. 'Nothing at all. Unless it was a ghost.'

He led her slowly towards the steps. Yes, perhaps it was a ghost; the daughter of the great nobleman who had once lived here, and filled this fine mansion with his family and servants. A sense of unbearable sadness swept over her, that such a beautiful place should be so abandoned and neglected.

Jacques silently took her arm to lead her up the wide, moonlit steps; and suddenly Nicole, almost over-whelmed by it all, shook him off blindly. 'Is this some kind of joke, citizen Jacques?' she whispered. 'To bring me to the mansion of a great lord?'

'On the contrary,' he replied levelly. 'This is perhaps one of the safest places to be tonight. You would rather be out there, with the mob, Nicole?'

She was silent; there was no answer to that. With yet another key, he opened those big front doors. They creaked back on their hinges, opening into utter dark-ness; there was a smell of dust, and cobwebs, and faded, long-ago finery.

Jacques withdrew a flint and steel from his pocket, and carefully lit some half-burned wax candles in a silver candelabra. They flared up with a startling bright-ness, and Nicole gasped.

They were in a beautiful, spacious hallway, lined with faded silk hangings and ornate gilt mirrors, relics of a previous age of luxury. Doors led off enticingly; and at the far end a wide, graceful staircase curved extrava-gantly up to the higher floors. Despite the dust and the cobwebs, Nicole's eyes lit up in wonder. 'Oh, it's beautiful!'

He had been watching for her reaction; he smiled approval. 'I thought you would be pleased with it,' he said softly. 'This house has certain interesting secrets. You see, its former inhabitants were very fond of pleasure.'

Nicole stared blankly up at him. 'You mean dancing? And food?'

He smiled enigmatically. 'Not quite. But I may have a chance to explain later. You will forgive me, Nicole, if I leave you alone in the house? Just for an hour, no more. I have a few errands.'

'What errands?' She was suddenly frightened at the thought of being on her own, remembering the Paris mob out there on the streets, hearing again those terrible screams.

'Some people I have to see, including some other visitors I'm expecting. And then there is the small matter of supplies; food, for you and I.'

'You'll find nothing at this hour!'

He grinned crookedly. 'My stomach sincerely hopes you are wrong.' And he moved towards the door.

'You'll leave me here, all on my own?' A note of hysterical desperation was starting to creep into Nicole's voice; she could hear it, and despised herself for it. She fought her fear down frantically, and added, in a lower voice, 'How do I know you'll come back?'

His dark eyes gleamed as his hand reached for the door-handle. 'You mean you *want* me to come back, Nicole?'

'I'd be perfectly happy if I never set eyes on you again!' she hissed at him, her hands clenched at her sides. 'Arrogant provincial upstart!'

He watched her assessingly. 'I'll come back all right, don't worry. Here, if you're anxious, have this.' He reached into his capacious pocket and drew out a gleaming, dangerous-looking pistol. 'You know how to use it?'

She caught her breath, and reached out tentatively. It was cold and heavy as she took it in her hand. 'Of course I do!'

'Good. Then I'll be back soon.'

And he was gone, out into the darkness. The doors closed heavily behind him, and Nicole felt suddenly bereft. Then she started to laugh, rather shakily. Here she was, all alone in this great, forlorn mansion, with only a cold pistol for company! Back at her miserable lodgings in St Victor, the landlady would be wondering where she had gone, but old Madame Rimaud wouldn't waste any sleep over her missing tenant. Too many people went missing in Paris these days.

17

Citizen Jacques – who *was* he? She shivered when she remembered the way he looked at her; half-assessing, half-amused. He was strong and dangerous, a real man indeed, not like the painted and powdered fops who used to inhabit Versailles. Her skin felt heated when she thought of him; she suddenly imagined his lean, muscular body, dark from the Provençal sun, and a tremor ran through her. She remembered his mouth, wide and wickedly sensual. His kiss, she knew, would be devastating; and as for the rest of him . . . She tingled deliciously.

Fool, she told herself bitterly. Little fool! Men were never what they seemed, nor gave what they promised. Remember Gerard.

Her mysterious citizen Jacques had saved her from the mob. What she must do now was play along with his crazy schemes, use his mysterious power over the rabble, and then get the hell out of Paris. But what exactly had he said? *'I think, Nicole Chabrier, that I might be able to give you the chance for revenge.'*

To get her revenge on people like Gerard and his mincing friends, she would risk anything. Anything at all that the mysterious citizen Jacques might suggest.

Slipping the heavy pistol into the deep pocket within the folds of her skirt, she picked up a lighted candle, and started to explore.

Beyond the hallway was the great *salon*. As she entered it, she caught her breath in wonder. It was beautiful, high-ceilinged and spacious, with heavy chandeliers and ornate carvings and yet more mirrors reflecting its aged splendour. The full-length, high-arched windows were shuttered, though, and a thick layer of dust coated every surface of the beautiful gilded furniture. A few years ago, thought Nicole sadly, this *salon* would have been filled with laughing, glittering people, dancing and talking inconsequentially. Now, those long-gone people were spirited away, to England or Austria. Or they might be dying, out on the streets or in the prisons, at this very minute.

She remembered the men running down the street, their shirtsleeves stained in blood, and the horror of it all shook her anew. France. Oh, France, she thought sadly. What has happened to you?

Four years ago, Nicole, aged nineteen, had left her mean little Normandy village for Paris, full of ambitions and dreams. Not for her some peasant clod of a husband, and a lifelong struggle for existence. She was going to be a great actress and dancer, was going to marry a great lord! And now, here she was, homeless, friendless, utterly dependent on the dark, mysterious man she knew only as Jacques. Again, she felt the flicker of warning, was aware of a strong impulse to flee before he got back. But she fought it down, because to attempt to pass through any of the barriers was absolute madness, especially without papers. The National Guard would be on particular lookout tonight for any Royalists, and they might even have special orders to look out for de Polignac's woman.

Besides, she wanted her revenge . . .

Slowly, aimlessly, she wandered on, finding a shallow flight of steps that led down to the big, stone-flagged kitchens, and all of a sudden she realised how voraciously hungry she was. The man had said he'd bring food; she hoped he wasn't lying, because the thought of some good, crusty bread and creamy yellow cheese made her mouth water. She hadn't eaten since yesterday, and that had just been a dish of vile bean stew in a backstreet café. She was absolutely ravenous.

Some bottles of red wine lay in a dark recess; she pulled one out, causing the dust to fly. Suddenly realising that she was thirsty too, she found a knife and levered the cork out carefully then drank deeply of the rich, comforting liquid. She felt herself come to life again as the wine heated her, remembered who she was; Nicole Chabrier, talented actress of the *Comédie Française*, ballet-dancer at the Opera! She walked, humming, out of the kitchens and swept up the great curved staircase, the bottle in one hand, candle in the other.

She imagined she was a great lady, sweeping up the steps in all her jewels and finery; she could almost hear the rustle of the silk, smell the rich perfume, hear the whispers, the excitement as people watched her graceful ascent.

She smiled to herself, wandering almost happily along the vast gallery that linked the upstairs chambers, peeping into room after room.

Then, she found the bedroom that must have belonged to the great lady of the house. It was furnished with a great, high bed with a richly embroidered canopy; the walls were hung with silk, and the cabinets and cupboards were of exquisite design, inlaid with laquered porcelain. There was a high, mirrored *bureau de toilette*, on which the abandoned silver brushes and scent bottles still sat. Almost breathless with excitement, like a child in a fairy-tale, Nicole put her candle carefully onto a small gilded table in the corner and sipped slowly at her wine, once more feeling its warmth race through her.

This was wonderful, all this finery, and all hers, even if only for one night! In a sudden outburst of exuberant delight, she began to fling open drawers and cupboards, pulling out gowns, fichus, lace shawls by the handful. And then, in a chest by the bed, she found the undergarments, folded so delicately away: the silk chemises, stockings, bodices; all the wonderful clothes that were fit to be worn next to a fine lady's white, delicate skin!

She lifted them out of the drawer almost reverently, placing them against her cheek, marvelling that such luxury still existed in this city where no-one dared wear anything except homespun or coarse cotton, for fear of drawing attention to themselves. She delved deeper into the drawers, finding faded nosegays of lavender, a packet of letters wrapped up in ribbon, and – what was this? A large, intricately carved walnut box, placed right at the back of the drawer . . .

She sipped some more wine thoughtfully, scarcely

aware of its heady potency. Then, catching her breath in strange excitement, she lifted the lid of the box. It was beautifully lined, with padded pink silk; and inside it, ranged in meticulous order, were half a dozen smooth, cylindrical ivory implements, of varying lengths and thicknesses, all lying in pristine condition in their silk cushions.

Nicole's eyes widened; then she laughed aloud to herself. Of course, she'd seen objects like these before, because some of her friends, dancers at the Opera, had shown them to her when she had not long been in Paris. They'd laughed at her rustic innocence, encouraging her to admire their fine phallic shape, telling her in whispered giggles and innuendos how they could be used to imitate the loving of a man. But the thought of the refined, courtly inhabitant of this palatial room, a duchess, perhaps, coarsely pushing an ivory penis up between her fine legs, was just incredible!

She frowned. What had Jacques said to her, just before he left? *'They were fond of their pleasures, Nicole. You'll see.'*

She suddenly realised, then, that her own secret parts were moist and pulsing as she fingered the smooth, thick ivory of the biggest of the implements. Then, she caught sight of herself in one of the tall gilt mirrors that adorned the walls, and saw that her cheeks were lightly flushed with the wine; her lips were full and tremulous, and her thick-lashed amber eyes were dark with arousal. She shook back her long tawny hair from her face; it cascaded loosely down her back, making her look wild and wanton; a *poule* indeed.

She realised, then, that her dress, the last remnants of the finery that Gerard had bought her, was sadly worn, and hideously muddy from where those hateful men had grappled with her outside the winebar.

Slowly, her eyes shining with suppressed excitement, she started to unlace her bodice and chemise, and let it all slip to the floor. Then she looked at herself again.

In the soft candlelight, her skin was smooth and

21

golden. She'd lost weight in the last few months because food was not plentiful in Paris, especially for a lone girl who'd lost her protector; but her rosy-tipped breasts were still high and firm, and the slight loss of flesh from her face suited her, accentuating the high, wide cheekbones, her small but determined chin. She reached for the wine and drank deeply, more deeply than she should, she knew, but it warmed her, and her dark thoughts were crowding in on her.

She fingered her bare breasts slowly, drawing out the long, rosy crests and feeling a wild tingle of excitement suddenly surging through her blood. A slow flush rose anew in her cheeks; her lips were parted moistly. Damn Gerard. Oh, damn him, for discarding her.

When she'd first met the comte de Polignac, she'd been dazzled, because he was tall and fair and handsome, with exquisite manners; he dressed beautifully, and spent extravagantly, a totally different species from the peasant youths who'd tried to press their clumsy attentions on her back home.

Nicole had always refused their crude advances, determined not to sink into the racking, grinding poverty of the other women who bore child after child without being able to feed them properly. She'd scorned the local youths, and the girls who submitted to them so quickly; she'd glimpsed them often enough, coupling like animals in the hayfields or in the barns, anywhere they could find, but she'd always known they weren't for her. Once one of them had pounced on her and shown her his big, ugly penis, and she'd laughed scornfully at him, telling him to find someone of his own kind. After that, the peasant lads had scorned her for having ideas above her station, and Nicole had quietly continued with her plans to get away for good.

She'd been in Paris scarcely six months, and was just beginning to be noticed as an actress, when Gerard began to call on her. The first night, when he took her to supper after the theatre, she could hardly speak for

22

excitement, because she knew that this was what she deserved.

Gazing now into the mirror at her naked figure, she caressed her firm breasts very softly, revelling in the exquisite melting sensations that were rippling through her. Then, with a little smile on her face, she began to pull on some fine silk stockings, gartering them with silken bands halfway up her slender thighs. A white silk bodice was the next item to take her fancy; it was cunningly boned and shaped to lace up below her breasts, not across them, so that it pushed their bare, creamy curves up even higher, emphasising the thrusting ripeness of her jutting nipples. Suddenly she felt wildly excited, and it wasn't just the wine, oh no, it was this whole place; the danger, the mystery, the forbidden luxury.

And the thought that soon her mysterious rescuer would be returning . . .

She ran her hands voluptuously over her slender hips, seeing in the full-length mirror how her thighs, her loins were fully exposed between stocking-tops and bodice. The soft mound at the apex of her thighs was pulsing sweetly, running with juices so that the finely curling triangle of tawny hair was slick and shining.

Gerard had loved her secret hair, had knelt to breathe in its scent while he ran his white, beringed hands all over her body. That first night, when he'd undressed her, he'd watched her in a silent paroxysm of delight; Nicole, wanting him desperately, had held out her arms to him, wanting to feel him deep inside her, but he'd come to his climax even as he lay down beside her, spurting over her soft belly, rubbing his slender white penis in his own sticky seed and groaning softly to himself.

Nicole had been desperately disappointed as the melting hunger inside her turned into a relentless, gnawing ache; but she told herself she was happy because he was happy, and she loved him. Or so she thought at the time.

23

Gerard, comte de Polignac, was a selfish lover. Nicole realised that soon enough, from the stories of other men, other affairs, that she heard from her friends at the Opera. Her physical pleasure meant little to Gerard; but at the time Nicole didn't mind, because she was so besotted with his aristocratic good looks. To want more, she told herself, would be to want what those peasant girls had in the hay; to be little more than rutting animals.

She felt her eyes drawn down once more towards those startling ivory penises. Several of her friends, she knew, possessed artificial toys like these. Her best friend, Anne-Marie, a young actress with whom she used to share lodgings before Gerard found her a luxurious little apartment of her own, had told Nicole laughingly how lonely, love-starved women kissed such objects before they went to sleep, called them their lovers. Once, at a drunkenly riotous party after the theatre, a woman had demonstrated how they were used, pulling up her skirts and slowly, lasciviously driving the big shaft up inside her flesh while her face contorted with pleasure. People had laughed and applauded, and Nicole had blushed in the shadows.

Feeling dizzy now with need, Nicole picked one up in her trembling fingers. It was very long, and thickly-circumferenced; the very sight of it frightened her, made her mouth go dry, and yet excited her wildly. Its head was round and smooth and tempting. Tentatively, she stroked its coldness against her engorged folds of secret flesh, letting it slide lightly along her honeyed crease; she jumped a little and sighed aloud, because it was good, so good! Catching her full lower lip between her teeth, she slid the ivory up into her pulsing wet hole and felt her inner muscles clutching desperately, begging for more. She paused, taking deep breaths to steady herself, and caught sight of herself in the mirror.

She could see her secret flesh embracing the ivory shaft; could see how her flesh lips were dark, slick, plumply engorged. She allowed one fingertip to lightly brush her little bud of pleasure; a mass of exquisite sensations soared into being, just waiting to explode. But not yet! She wanted to savour it all, to tantalise and tease her own sensitised flesh; to relive all the wildly sensual experiences of this unbelievable evening; the bestiality of the mob, as they crudely pleasured one another out there on the street; her own bitter humiliation and terrible secret excitement as she watched them copulate so openly, while she shamelessly allowed the man Jacques to pull and stroke her nipples with his wonderful, knowing fingers until she was on the very brink of cataclysmic release, there in a total stranger's arms.

Clenching her teeth, feeling her breath coming short and shallow with her excitement, she reached down to slide the big ivory penis in higher, higher. Oh, it was such bliss! And her pleasure was miraculously heightened by being able to stand here before this full-length mirror, able to see for herself the glorious contrast of clinging white silk and lewd golden flesh, able to see her full, pouting breasts, her moist, secret parts that were juicy and ripe for love.

Her eyes dark with burgeoning desire, she began to play with her tingling, hardened nipples, pinching them and rolling them as they thrust out obscenely above the tightly-laced white corset. She bit back a soft moan of longing, knowing that she could drive herself into an explosion of the sweetest possible pleasure at any minute, but determined to savour for as long as she could this delicious agony of suspense. Her inner muscles clutched tightly, lasciviously at the thick ivory shaft, almost pleading with her to slide it vigorously up and down until she reached her shuddering, glorious climax. She shut her eyes and thought suddenly of the dark-haired man Jacques, remembered the way he'd looked at her, touched her so knowingly. Biting her lip, she imagined suddenly that it was *him*, thrusting his penis deep inside her, darkly male and powerful; and the thought of him, obscenely pleasuring her most

25

secret parts, made her almost swoon in a paroxysm of delight.

No! She didn't want this to end, not yet. The ivory phallus was clenched firmly in her vagina; throwing back her long, thick hair and smiling triumphantly at herself in the mirror, she walked across the room to pick up her bottle of wine and slake her thirst. She walked with a swagger, swivelling her naked hips, imagining how plumply ripe her bare bottom cheeks must look beneath the tight white bodice, revelling openly in the tight, cold caress of the ivory penis between her legs, a luscious promise of pleasure. On a sudden impulse she went to pick up Jacques' pistol from her pile of discarded clothes, and weighed it in her hands, feeling strong and powerful.

Too late, she heard the soft footsteps outside the door. By the time she'd whirled round, he was leaning nonchalantly back against the closed door, his arms folded across his chest. And he was laughing, damn him, laughing at her, so that she could see his white teeth gleaming in that dark, dangerous face.

'*Morbleu*,' Jacques breathed, 'a sight for sore eyes indeed, my little Nicole . . .'

Chapter Two

No longer wearing his dark coat, Jacques was dressed simply in a white silk shirt and ruffled cravat, with skintight black breeches and long leather boots enclosing his muscular legs. His dark hair was tied back smoothly from his starkly handsome face. He looked, thought Nicole wildly, absolutely devastating. And he was laughing at her. She was going to kill him! Without hesitation, she levelled the pistol at him. The wine she'd consumed flooded through her, making her utterly reckless. No – better than killing him, she'd humiliate him; she'd make him beg for mercy, this infuriating citizen Jacques!

Standing there defiantly in her scanty bodice and stockings, the ivory penis still tight between her damp thighs, she pointed the pistol at his chest and hissed, 'So, monsieur. You find me funny, do you?'

'Funny? Oh, no,' he said, shaking his head helplessly. 'As a matter of fact, *chérie*, I think you're the most wonderful thing I've ever seen in my life.'

Nicole smiled grimly. It was quite clear to her now what she had to do, how to start getting her revenge for the humiliations she had suffered, all her life, at the hands of men. Slowly she sauntered towards him, aware of her firm, high breasts trembling softly above the tight bodice she wore; with a sigh of satisfaction she observed the secretly swelling bulge at his groin, where his breeches fitted snugly across his lean hips. She would teach this man a lesson he'd never, ever forget!

'Take your clothes off, citizen Jacques,' she said softly. He hesitated; Nicole lifted the pistol higher, in a threatening gesture, so that his dark eyes narrowed to black slits, following her every move.

'Move, damn you!' she hissed.

With a soft, expressive shrug, he unknotted his white cravat and began to unbutton his billowing shirt, pulling it slowly out of his breeches. His mouth quirked apologetically and Nicole, the breath catching at her throat, realised that already his concealed manhood was pushing and straining at the taut fastening of his breeches. Her quivering inner flesh clutched helplessly on the thick ivory stem between her legs. Oh, how she wanted him! But she would humiliate him first. That was what she wanted, more than anything, to utterly degrade this arrogant man, to have him grovelling at her feet.

One hand pointing the pistol, the other on her naked hip, she planted her stockinged legs firmly apart, knowing that her own soaking, secret flesh folds would be tantalisingly revealed to his stare.

'Kneel, citizen Jacques,' she purred. 'Kneel, very slowly.'

He did as she said, his face expressionless, and as he knelt there with his thighs slightly parted, his unbuttoned shirt fell open, revealing a glimpse of thickly ridged chest muscle tapering down to a flat, hard stomach. His body skin was tanned and smooth, except further down, at his belly, where a line of soft black hair arrowed hypnotically down to his concealed groin. It was a sight that made Nicole's mouth go dry.

He was beautiful. And strong, she realised suddenly; dangerously lithe and strong. Not heavily, coarsely muscled like the peasants of the Normandy fields, but with the whiplash, sinewy strength of a frighteningly

28

fit man, not an ounce of fat or flab on his body. Though what did sheer physical strength matter, she reminded herself triumphantly, when she had the gun?

Nicole licked her full lips, relishing every second of her new-found power. 'Now,' she said huskily. 'Release it, citizen. Release your manhood.'

He frowned.

'Or are you afraid to?' she whispered exultantly. 'Afraid that I'll laugh at you for your poor inadequacy?'

Compressing his thinned lips, he unbuttoned the straining placket of his breeches very carefully. And Nicole gasped aloud, the colour flaring to her cheeks, as, freed now from constraint, his rampant member jerked upwards against his belly.

Inadequacy, Nicole reflected rather faintly, was not a happy choice of word.

His penis was magnificent. Already darkly engorged, it was long, and thick, and silky smooth. She could imagine what it would feel like, against her fingers, her lips. The wine-heated blood coursed tumultuously through her veins; and her nipples tingled deliciously, while her inner muscles spasmed warningly round the ivory stem. She knew that if she wasn't careful, she would climax at any minute, and it was too soon, because she wanted to make him suffer.

She watched him avidly, saw him easing the fastening of his breeches from around the velvety pouch of his heavy testicles. Just then his palm accidentally brushed the thick stem of his penis, and it jerked hungrily, a tear glistening at its swollen tip.

Nicole, seeing it, laughed scornfully. 'Hoping to satisfy yourself that way, are you, with your own eager fingers? Oh, no, monsieur! Hands behind your back, I said!'

She leaned her plump buttocks comfortably back against the edge of the high bed, her legs still apart, her thighs smooth and golden above the white silk stockings. The man's eyes seemed to be fastened almost helplessly on the juicy folds of flesh at the apex of that tawny triangle, on the thick ivory stem that disappeared so tantalisingly into her sweet sex-lips; Nicole heard him sigh, and she smiled wickedly to herself. Then, with one hand levelling the pistol at his chest, she reached down with her other hand for the ivory penis, gripping its base, and began to work it slowly, lasciviously up and down her aching, honeyed love-channel.

The man watched her, his hands behind his back, his dark, angular face still and impassive.

But Nicole, shivering visibly now at the onslaught of near-rapture as she pleasured herself with the delicious ivory, saw how his huge phallus jerked hungrily towards her from its cradle of dark hair, saw how his heavy balls tightened up against his body, betraying all his torment. Gasping for breath, half-closing her dreamy eyes, she tensed her hips against the hard ivory shaft, pushing harder, quicker, deeper. Nearly there, oh, nearly there . . .

'*Chérie*,' the man said softly, 'I wish you would stop. Truly, I do.'

Panting with lust, she continued to lewdly slide the slick ivory penis in and out of her swollen flesh-lips. 'Why should I?' she retorted, her voice husky and exultant with power.

'Because,' and the man Jacques hesitated, 'I dread to think what might happen to that pistol when you reach your crisis of pleasure, my fair Nicolette. Especially as you seem to have consumed the best part of a bottle of vintage wine. And also,' he smiled darkly, 'because I think you would enjoy yourself far more with me.'

Nicole laughed nastily, her hand still on the ivory. 'Arrogant fool! All men think they are incomparable!' But her next words died on her lips.

Because, lithe as a cat, Jacques sprang to his booted feet and walked purposefully across the room to her, his shirt hanging loose, his erect member jutting proudly towards her, swaying slightly, from his open breeches.

Nicole gasped, gripping the pistol with both hands

and pointing it at his chest. 'Stop! Stop, or I'll shoot! I mean it!'

'You won't shoot,' he said, still calmly advancing towards her trembling, half-naked figure. 'And shall I tell you why? Because that pistol, my little wildcat, is not even loaded.'

And, coolly knocking the pistol to the floor, Jacques scooped her up, threw her on her back on the great, high bed, and began to ease the sticky ivory shaft from between her legs.

Whether by accident or not, his palm grazed her fevered love mound and brushed her throbbing, heated clitoris so that Nicole convulsed, almost climaxing then and there as he pulled the thick ivory from her aching passage. Desperately fighting for control, she struggled to sit up; but he kneeled above her, pinioning her flailing hands on either side of her bare shoulders, and smiled kindly down at her anguished face. Still resisting him, far too aware of his massive erection that was like a dark threat in the shadows, she hissed out, *'Salaud!* Why did you give that pistol to me to defend myself, when it wasn't even loaded?'

For answer, he bent his head and slowly circled one thrusting nipple with his rasping tongue. Nicole threw her head back against the pillows and moaned in outraged delight.

'Did the pistol make you feel safer when you were alone in the house, Nicole?' Jacques asked, gently.

She gasped as his finger brushed her other yearning nipple. 'Yes! Yes, it did! Oh, stop, I beg you.'

'Well, then,' he went on calmly, his finger moving down to slide up and down her pulsing, tremulous flesh-lips with a caress that almost made her swoon. 'It served its purpose, surely? And this, *chérie*, will make you feel oh, so much better than that ivory toy, because, you see, it's the real thing.'

And reaching down to himself, he gripped his massive, iron-hard shaft and gently, very gently eased its silken head into her quivering flesh.

Nicole arched herself helplessly against him, her taut nipples caressed by his hard, naked chest, almost at the point of orgasm already. Kissing her mouth tenderly, he slid himelf relentlessly within her.

He was magnificent. Hard as bone, yet silken-gentle; powerful and strong, yet also capable of the softest, most exquisite of caresses. Nicole flung her arms round his shoulders, clutching him to her, as wave after wave of shuddering tremors began to ripple remorselessly through her; she fought them back despairingly, not wanting him to triumph so easily, but when he stopped moving she had to bite on her lip to stop herself screaming out for more.

He lifted his dark head, gazing down on her soft breasts as they spilled out above the white bodice. 'And how, then, do I compare to the comte de Polignac?' he said softly.

Nicole's small face twisted in rebellion. 'How dare you compare yourself to him? He was a great noble, not some provincial bourgeois lawyer like you!'

'Ah,' he sighed. 'So their ways are different, are they, the aristocracy? Did he not do this?'

He reached down to circle her clitoris with his thumb, careful not to touch that delicate bud itself. Nicole shuddered and clutched at his hard shaft, fighting back the onslaught of rapture.

'Or perhaps this? And this?' His other hand had slid round the back of her creamy buttocks, and was delicately probing at her tight crease, caressing that tiny, pulsing hole until she was groaning aloud.

'Oh, no – oh, yes!' she gasped, clutching desperately at his wide shoulders, feeling all the rippling strength of him beneath her fingertips, all the masculine core of him filling her body. 'Oh, yes, please . . .'

He laughed huskily in her ear. Then, biting tenderly on each of her hardened nipples in turn, drawing the turgid flesh into his mouth until her whole body was a screaming mass of desire, he withdrew his long, thick penis almost completely until she shrieked aloud with loss; then plunged himself in, again and again, with such sure, devastating strength that Nicole exploded into the most shattering climax she had ever known in her life.

On and on the savage pleasure engulfed her body, as with immense skill he pleasured her, savoured her, teased her, kissing away her sobs and cries of wonder until at last she was sated. Then he drove himself to his own harsh, convulsive climax deep within her, his teeth gritted in the darkness of his face.

Nicole lay in his arms, frightened and stunned by what she felt for this enigmatic man. The candle on the dressing table flickered uncertainly, as if about to go out; then it recovered, throwing its wan, inadequate light on the faded hangings, the sad magnificence of this abandoned room. Of all the places, in all of Paris, to find herself here, like this, with the demonic lover of her dreams.

And she didn't even know his proper name.

He smiled at her bewildered silence and said, 'Now, I wonder what's going on in that little head of yours, *chérie.*'

Badly disturbed, because the tenderness in his dark eyes made her feel so vulnerable, she drew herself away and took refuge in indignation. 'I'll tell you! I'm trying to work out why you left me here with a pistol that you knew wasn't loaded – '

'Correct.'

'And yet,' pressed on Nicole fiercely, 'and yet, at the beginning, when I made you kneel, and – and – '

'And undress?' he supplied helpfully.

'Yes! When I made you undress, you could have told me then, that it was not loaded!'

'I could.' His dark eyes danced. 'But I was rather enjoying myself. So were you, I think. And besides, my Nicolette, I was testing you.'

She moved further away, still kneeling on the bed, her small hands clenched. 'Testing me?'

'Ah, my Nicole. So very beautiful.' He reached out

33

one lean brown hand to languorously caress her breasts as they pouted ripely above her tight bodice, and she shuddered as the pleasurable afterwash of orgasm rippled anew through her sensitised body. 'Did you moan aloud like that for your Gerard?' he went on silkily. 'Did he bring you, I wonder, to such an exquisite release every time?'

'Of course! Gerard was a wonderful lover!' she lied fiercely.

'So you keep telling me. But you hate him now? You would turn him over to the tribunal if you could?'

'Yes! Because he left me, alone in Paris! Because he had no more use for me.' Her voice trembled. Damn him, this man's tenderness unnerved her strangely. As he lay back on the bed with that lithe, easy grace of his, he looked so beautiful, so self-possessed. 'What did you mean,' she went on suspiciously, 'about *testing* me?'

He drew himself up on one elbow to face her, his dark eyes suddenly intent.

'I spoke to you earlier about revenge,' he said. 'How would you like the chance, Nicole, to humiliate the very people who have brought our country to the brink of ruin; the aristocrats themselves?'

She gazed at him, then burst out laughing. 'Are you mad?'

'Far from it,' he replied calmly. 'But I want to know if you're interested in participating, Nicole. Because, from everything I've seen about you, you are eminently suitable to be my accomplice.'

His hand had abstractedly cupped her breast; his finger was toying lazily with her nipple, and Nicole suddenly found it hard to breathe. She wrenched herself away from his insidious touch and hissed out, 'Your accomplice? Oh, no, Jacques! Count me out! I'm leaving this – this mausoleum as soon as I possibly can!'

He rolled onto his back, his hands clasped behind his head. His shirt fell open; she tried hard not to look at the beautiful expanse of bare male torso, at the dark, mysterious mound of his genitals beneath his breeches.

34

With his long black hair drawn so starkly back from his tanned, finely-sculptured face, he looked like some dark angel.

'So you're leaving, are you?' he queried innocently.

'Yes! Though not right now,' she added quickly, glancing at the darkness outside pressing in on the shuttered windows and thinking of those terrifying scenes on the streets of Paris.

'A pity, that, *ma chère*, because as I said earlier, this could be your opportunity for revenge. And for pleasure. A great deal of that, because believe me, this was truly a house of pleasure for its former occupants.'

Something in the way he spoke made Nicole's mouth go dry. Her eyes were fastened helplessly to his lean, lithe figure as he yawned suddenly and drew himself up.

'However, it's your decision,' he went on calmly. 'And before you go, you must have some food. I must also light a fire in this chilly room – yes? In the meantime, I'd like you to help yourself to some clothes, my sweet, or – ' and his mouth twisted crookedly as he regarded her lusciously tempting body, 'I fear you won't be going very far at all . . .'

An hour later, Nicole lay back against the pillows with a little sigh, feeling gloriously replete. She'd wrapped herself in a beautiful loose silk robe that she'd found in a mahogany *armoire*; and when Jacques had brought up a silver tray laden with fresh crusty bread, and creamy cheese, and even some tiny crisp apples, she'd fallen on the food and eaten with such fervour that he'd sat back and watched her, amused.

Nicole said suddenly, between mouthfuls of juicy apple, 'You're not eating anything?'

He shook his head and went to lay some logs on the fire. 'I had a good meal earlier when I was out. Have as much as you want.'

Nicole put down the apple core and sat cross-legged on the bed in her silk robe, watching him suspiciously.

'How on earth did you manage to get food like this, when the ordinary people have to queue for hours for one stale rye loaf? Who *are* you?'

He turned back to her. 'I told you before. I'm just plain Jacques.'

'But how did you have the key to this wonderful house? And that man, who stopped the coach, he knew you! He seemed almost frightened of you. You're no peasant! What are you, some deputy from the south?'

Was it just her imagination, or did he hesitate before answering? 'I'm from Provence, yes.'

'So,' sneered Nicole, 'you came to Paris for a taste of power, to live out your petty bourgeois fantasies, is that it?'

He eased himself into a fragile-looking gilt chair by the fireplace and stretched out his long, booted legs. 'Aren't *you* living out your fantasies, Nicole? Weren't those people we saw tonight, in the streets?'

Nicole caught her breath as she remembered the wildness of the Paris mob, the riotous Carmagnole, the animal lust of the fervent dancers. She reached out defiantly to drink down the fresh glass of red wine he'd poured her. 'I take my pleasure as I please,' she said lightly. 'That's all there is to life!'

'Good.' He smiled crookedly, and got up to refill her glass. 'That's what I thought you'd say.'

Nicole said disparagingly, 'I'm surprised that your well-organised aristocratic fantasy doesn't include a few servants to pour out the wine for you.'

He paused as he tilted the dark bottle over the glass that stood beside her on the bedside table. 'As a matter of fact, it does, my sweet, as you'll find out.'

She reached for her replenished glass. And it was then that she saw it.

He'd rolled up his creamy shirt sleeves to light the fire, revealing his dark, sinewy forearms, thickly dusted with soft, fine hairs. And just above his inner wrist, where the skin was smooth and paler in colour, was a mark. A number, tattooed into his skin, branding him forever.

Nicole felt the blood drain from her face. She blurted out, in instinctive horror, 'You're a prisoner! A – a convict!'

He put the wine bottle down carefully, his eyes narrowed. 'I was branded as one, yes.'

But already Nicole had slipped off the bed and was backing away from him, her eyes wide with terror. 'You – you didn't tell me!'

'You didn't ask me, Nicole.'

'So you can't deny it?'

His face went hard and cold as he watched her revulsion. 'How can I possibly deny it,' he said flatly, 'when this brand will be with me for the rest of my life? Yes, I admit it. I spent two years in the Toulon *bagne*.'

Nicole didn't wait to hear any more. With a horrified cry, she ran for the door, and hurtled down the long, dark gallery, abandoning the little pool of light that issued from the chamber's doorway. She heard him shouting after her:

'Nicole! Come back, damn you!' but, her heart beating sickly in her breast, she ran on blindly. Another, narrower flight of steps led upwards; gasping and stumbling in the dark, she pulled herself up it. Here, on the next floor, the air was stale and musty; dust rose in clouds, and giant cobwebs brushed her cheeks.

She flew along another long passage, with unwelcoming doors locked against her. She thought she could hear his slow, measured footsteps following her steadily up the stairs; panting with fear she flung herself up yet another twisting staircase, almost on her knees. The staircase led to a single room and nothing else; with a pang of despair she realised that there was no turning back now. Thinking she could see the faint glow of his candle in the distance, she hurtled into the room and slammed the door shut, gasping painfully for breath.

No sound from outside. Nothing. Perhaps she'd thrown him off.

Feeling sick with fear, she turned round quickly to assess her plight. It was so dark in here, with the windows so tightly shuttered that not even the light of the moon could steal through, that she could see almost nothing. But it seemed cold and disused, and there was a faint, unfamiliar smell of faded upholstery and leather. Breathing in the almost sinister air, Nicole shivered in her thin silk robe and stepped tentatively forward, blindly searching for a possible hiding place.

The walls seemed rough and bare, with hardly any furnishings. Then her hand brushed against a kind of rack fixed to the wall, and she realised that it was filled with strange objects of leather, cold and sinister: whips! It was a rack full of whips, with long, coiled thongs and sturdy handles! But why? If it was on the ground floor, this room could be for storage, some kind of tack room. But up here? Her fingers trembled as she ran her hands over the the array of implements. What was the purpose of this horrible, frightening room?

She stumbled on and found, in the corner, a small wooden bed. It seemed hard and austere, with faded, moth-eaten hangings and a rough horse-hair blanket covering the mattress. She breathed in the musty smell, feeling dizzy. And then, she heard the slow, muffled footsteps coming up the stairs towards her. Jacques. He knew where she was; he was coming after her.

And he was a convict, perhaps even a murderer.

Whirling round, stifling her cry of fear, she blindly tugged a whip from the rack. Then she leaped onto the bed and crouched behind the faded curtains. She heard the door opening very slowly, and stifled her scream with her own clenched fist. Perhaps he didn't really know she was in here! Perhaps he would turn round and go out again!

There was a long, petrifying silence while the flickering glow of his candle penetrated the dark shadows of the bedcurtains. Then she heard his slow, measured tread, pacing the room; heard him pause for a moment.

She didn't dare to breathe as he came closer, closer, towards the bed. She buried her face in her hands.

When she felt his hand on her shoulder, she whirled round, the whip tense in her hand, and lashed out blindly at his face with all the strength she possessed.

She heard the hiss of his indrawn breath as the lash caught his cheek, and then he chuckled softly. 'You shouldn't have done that, my Nicole. Fortunately, I suspected something of the kind and was well protected.'

She fell back against the bed and stared up at his powerful figure, white with fear. By the wan light of the candle he'd brought, she could see that he was wearing a mask, a soft black leather mask, that clung to his features, with slits for eyes and a hole for his mouth. She shuddered openly, seeing also that all around this little secret room were racks of whips, and masks, and leather harnesses, and other sinister toys that she could not begin to name. Truly, a room of terror!

With a wild cry, she leaped to her feet and made for the door. But with a soft, menacing laugh, he caught her and quickly tipped her back onto the small, hard bed; and when she still struggled, he threw himself on top of her, his powerful frame knocking all the breath from her body, his eyes glittering strangely behind the clinging leather mask. Nicole fought frantically to recover, feeling him doing something deftly with his fingers to her outstretched wrists; then he was at her feet, doing the same to her ankles. Too late, she realised that she was tied up, fastened with leather straps to the four corners of the bed.

She struggled wildly, trying to kick out, but all that happened was that her flimsy silk wrap fell apart, revealing the tempting combination of her smooth golden skin and the white bodice and stockings.

Jacques stood back, regarding his handiwork contemplatively. 'Steady, my little wildcat,' he murmured silkily. 'Welcome to the former residents' unique room of pleasure. I was going to show it to you myself later, but as if by instinct, you've found it yourself.'

'Pleasure?' shrieked Nicole, gazing up at his masked face. 'You perverted, devilish fiend!'

'I advise you to wait and see before you form an opinion.'

'I have no choice, damn you!'

'Exactly,' he said kindly. 'And that, *ma chère*, is all part of the fun, as you will find out.'

As he stood above her, lithe and muscular in his open-necked shirt and breeches, his face inscrutable behind that devilish mask, she felt a terrible stab of longing. Even as she struggled helplessly in her bonds, she felt her belly churning with need, felt the soft, secret flesh melting with sweet moisture. And the way she was pinioned added to her shameful arousal. Because of the way her silk robe had slipped aside, her trembling breasts lay fully exposed above the tight white bodice, their crests already dark and stiff; and her stockinged legs were pulled helplessly apart by her bonds, so he could see the plump, honeyed folds of flesh at the apex of her thighs. Her breasts heaved in her distress, and she gazed up helplessly into that faceless mask of this frightening, powerfully masculine man.

A convict . . .

Jacques had picked up the whip she'd struck him with, and was fingering it thoughtfully. Moving closer to her, so that she flinched instinctively, he reached out to trail the tip of the lash across her soft breasts, letting it linger on the engorged crests. Nicole shut her eyes briefly as the wild excitement coursed through her and her nipples stood out, quivering for more. He reached out and squeezed them, hard; she leaped in her bonds with the fierce pain-pleasure that invaded her body.

Then he drew the whip carefully down her soft abdomen and used both his hands to loop the lash behind the crease of her buttocks, pulling it up taut so that it was touching her all along her wet, slippery cleft. He started to pull it gently to and fro, so that the taut leather gently caressed her pulsing clitoris, her engorged vulva, even the dark little bottom-hole that quivered, too, in dark, shameful need. Closing her eyes again, Nicole cried out, and arched her hips convulsively, feeling the bonds tighten warningly at her wrists and ankles. She wanted him. She wanted all the dark, forbidden pleasure her silent tormentor was promising, as he stood over her, silently, skilfully manipulating that menacing leather strap against all her most secret places.

Her head was moving slowly, convulsively from side to side; she knew that her hair and her skin must be damp with perspiration. She gasped aloud as he reversed the whip suddenly and drew the hard leather handle softly against her hot, swollen flesh. His voice, muffled by the mask, was low and calm. 'What do you want, Nicole, *chérie*? What do you really want?'

The whip handle was warm and solid against her sex-lips; she bit her lip, moaning, 'Beast. Beast.'

'So you want me to go?'

Her eyes flew wide open. 'You would leave me here, like this?'

'Perhaps, yes.' He drew the whip handle reluctantly from her wet folds, brushing it tantalisingly against her quivering pleasure bud; she sighed with the terrible disappointment of it. 'Just,' he went on soothingly, 'until you learn some gratitude.'

'Gratitude?' She almost shrieked at him. 'Gratitude to you, a convict? When you've made me your prisoner in this dreadful house?'

'You seemed to be enjoying yourself enough a short while ago. Perhaps I really had better leave for a while, and give you a chance to revise your opinion.' He shrugged his shoulders and set off towards the door.

Nicole, frantic now, called out, 'No!'

He turned. She could imagine the sardonic lift of the eyebrows beneath the mask. 'You want me to stay?' he enquired in cool surprise.

'Yes! I do!'

41

'Then try asking me nicely, *chérie.*'

'Yes, please – damn you, Jacques!'

He walked back slowly, and sat on the bed beside her captive figure. Staring at her intently, he reached out his long, wonderful fingers to lightly stroke her straining nipples. Nicole wanted to weep with frustration.

'What, exactly,' he said, 'do you want me to do?'

The clinging leather mask, so close now, was hypnotic, because it both repelled and excited her. His eyes were dark slits; his mouth a mysterious cavity, where she could see only his tongue as he talked. She shivered, filled with dreadful need. Flushed with shame, she licked her lips and whispered, 'I want you to touch me. Down there.'

'How? With my fingers, Nicole?'

'Yes,' she muttered brokenly. 'And – and . . .'

'And?'

'With your tongue . . .'

'Like this?' Slowly, his tongue protruded from the black mouth hole of the mask; strong, glistening, wickedly tempting. Nicole closed her eyes in shameful despair. 'Yes. Oh, yes.'

With a low chuckle, Jacques kneeled between her legs and bent his head.

His tongue was long and incredibly powerful. She felt the cold kiss of the soft black leather mask against her warm, pulsing vulva as his tongue, hot and wet, stroked her swollen flesh-lips with exquisite sensitivity. Nicole drew a long, shuddering breath, every muscle of her body straining at her bonds, because never before had she known such warm liquid rapture.

He moved up to her breasts and tongued her stiffened teats; she cried aloud as the sensual shafts of pleasure arrowed down to her melting loins. She gazed into his face, hypnotised by those dark eyes glittering in the slits of the mask, by the long nose covered in soft leather, the long, fleshy tongue protruding from the mouth hole, thinking that he must be the devil himself, to use her like this. She recalled the way his long, pulsing penis had pleasured her earlier, and the exquisite rapture lifted her; she writhed her hips beneath him, moaning his name longingly.

'Patience, my Nicolette.'

His head moved down again and he lapped at her slowly, thoroughly, his long tongue rasping her sensitised flesh so lasciviously that she threw herself around the bed as far as her bonds allowed her, crying out for fulfilment. Gripping her hips with his hands to steady her, he began to thrust and delve deliciously into her quivering love-channel with his hard-pointed tongue while his hawk-like leatherclad nose rubbed steadily against her pubic region, pulling at her throbbing pleasure bud until it burned with excitement. His tongue pushed and twisted, deep and hot and snakelike within her; with a wild cry of abandon Nicole lifted her hips to meet him, grinding her clitoris against his hard-boned face, clutching at his wriggling tongue, shrieking out her shattering climax as with exquisite skill he continued to draw every last drop of excruciating pleasure from her quivering flesh.

She fell back limply on the bed, the last throbs of orgasm washing deliciously through her exhausted body. Never had she known such wildly sensual delight.

He stood above her, his hands on his hips, his eyes dark slits behind the leather mask. 'Now you know, *chérie*,' he purred, 'why the former inhabitants of our secret abode called this the room of pleasure. How very cunning of you to flee to it so unerringly.'

Nicole was silent in her bonds as she gazed up at him; she was filled with a desperate shame at what she'd let him do to her, and yet her half-naked body was still shivering with hot excitement at the memory of it all. Jacques' leather mask was wet and slick with her juices; he took it off slowly, and smiled.

'Are you going to untie me now, you brute?' she said in a low voice.

He put his dark head mockingly on one side. 'Perhaps. Perhaps not. I'm not sure that you've learned to trust me yet, *chérie.*'

'Trust you?' Her voice was icy with scorn. She let her gaze rest on that small, branded mark, the mark of the *forçat*, so sinister and chilling against the smooth flesh of his inner forearm. 'An escaped convict? Why on earth should I trust you?'

'Because, he said quietly, 'I didn't do what they said I did.' He untied her carefully and she crouched on the bed, wrapping her silk robe around her body. She shivered at his words.

'How can I believe you?'

'You can't.' He walked across to the sinister racks of equipment, to put back the whip she'd snatched for her own defence. Then he turned back to face her. 'No-one believed me then, even though I was stubborn enough to keep protesting my innocence. I also kept trying to escape – and I've got this to show for it.'

In one swift move, he shrugged off his white shirt. Nicole's heart thudded, because he was like some sleek, beautiful animal in this candle-lit room, with his wide, bronzed shoulders and thickly muscled chest. Then he deliberately turned his back to her; and she bit back a cry of horror. For the symmetrical beauty of his shoulders was cruelly marred by ridge after ridge of scar tissue; it was long healed now, but there was no mistaking the mark of the whip. Used not in fun, not in some sweet, tormenting pleasure, but in the harsh penal floggings that she had heard could kill a man.

Her heart turned over; she swallowed hard, moistening her dry throat. 'You were on the galleys?'

'No.' His mouth twisted grimly as he eased his shirt on again. 'Fortunately, that particular form of punishment exists only on the statute books. I doubt I would have survived that. No, my sweet Nicole, I was breaking stone, for the roads. In between escape attempts, of course.'

Nicole nodded slowly. So that explained his steely muscles, his immense, sinewy strength beneath that graceful exterior. A man had to be strong, to survive all that. 'And what did they accuse you of, Jacques?' she breathed softly.

Carefully he fastened the buttons of his silk shirt. 'They accused me of raping someone,' he said simply. 'I was denounced by *lettre de cachet* and imprisoned without trial, as the law of our fair country used to permit.'

Nicole leaned forward on the bed, her face pale and anguished. 'And was it true, Jacques? Did you rape her?'

He looked at her, assessing her. 'When I first met her,' he said at last, 'she was the mistress of a great nobleman, who lived near Marseilles. She had grown tired of her rich protector, and decided that she wanted me. But she had a dilemma, you see; she very much enjoyed the status, the wealth and power that accrued to her as a rich nobleman's companion.' He paused, and Nicole's heart wrenched somehow at the stark impassivity with which he told his story.

' She was persuasive, however. We became lovers, in secret,' he went on. 'She was very beautiful, you see; very skilled in her art. But then, things went wrong. Her rich protector had his spies; someone reported us, and she defended herself by telling him that I'd raped her, and then blackmailed her into continuing the affair.'

'And they all believed her?'

He frowned at that, just a little. 'Of course. Wouldn't you have believed her, Nicole? Her word against mine? She was very clever, remember. Very clever and beautiful, and her tears would have melted anyone's heart as she denounced me. Would you have taken my word against hers?'

She gazed up at him, and was stunned by what she felt. Yes. She would have believed him. This man had no need to force himself on any woman. Just the sound of his voice made her shiver with need; already, she realised, she was melting again for his dark, lean figure. 'I believe you were innocent,' she said quietly.

His eyes gleamed; he let out a short, sharp exclamation of surprise. 'Well, my Nicole. Perhaps we have more in common than we thought. It seems that both of us are united in our desire for revenge against the great nobles who have used us so badly.' He walked slowly round the little chamber, fingering the array of whips, of straps and masks. He pulled out a great bullwhip and ran his long fingers gently up and down its hard leather handle, as if he were fondling his own rigid penis; Nicole felt herself tingle all over.

'You keep talking of revenge,' she breathed. 'What are your plans?'

He turned towards her and smiled, still holding the whip. 'No blood. No killing. There's been enough of that. But think, Nicole. What is the best, the most thorough way to humiliate people? Why, through sexual gratification, of course. To expose their innermost desires, their private fantasies, and then mercilessly exploit them ... You look bewildered, *chérie*. Tomorrow, you'll find out more.'

'If I'm still here tomorrow!' she spat back. 'I've told you, I want to leave! As soon as it's daylight! Why should I submit to any of your crazy plans?'

'Because you're fascinated,' he replied calmly. 'You want to know more, much more. And also, you rather suspect that you might enjoy yourself.'

Nicole clenched her fists, suddenly overwrought. 'Has anyone ever told you you've got an overweening sense of your own importance, citizen Jacques? Why, you're nothing but a provincial, bourgeois nobody, with a criminal record!'

He jerked his thumb meaningfully towards the rack of whips, his eyes suddenly alight with laughter. 'You want to punish me, Nicolette?'

'Yes!' she hissed. 'But I expect you'd enjoy it too much!'

'You're right, *chérie*, I would.' He grinned at her openly. 'Sometime soon, perhaps, if you can bear to wait. Well. It's getting late. I take it you're going to

46

condescend to spend the night in this . . . mausoleum, as you call it?'

'Only because it's too late to go anywhere else!'

He nodded and turned towards the door; picking up the guttering candle on his way; Nicole said, uncertainly, 'You're – you're going?'

'Only to my own room. I have certain things to attend to, but I won't be far away. Disappointed?'

'Of course not!'

But she was. Wildly disappointed. He must have been strongly aroused by the pleasure he'd given her, by the sight of her own frantic passion, he must! And yet he was going off, coldly leaving her. She slipped hurriedly from the bed and stumbled after him as he led the way downstairs. He stopped outside her room, and turned to go.

Unable to restrain herself, Nicole said in a low voice, not daring to meet his mocking eyes, 'Jacques. Are you sure you don't want anything else from me tonight?'

He threw his head back and laughed. 'A kind thought, *chérie*, but no. You see, after two years in prison, I've developed something called self-control. A good wine is better for the keeping, hadn't you heard? You really must try not to let your passion for me become so obvious, *chérie* . . .'

She lashed out to slap him; he caught her easily, clasping both her wrists in his strong hands.

'Sleep tight, my little wildcat. Try to keep your hands away from that little box of ivory treasures, won't you? Sweet dreams!'

She hurled a string of unladylike obscenities after his retreating back. The man was utterly crazy, with all his talk of humiliating aristocrats. Crazy, and fiendish!

She went over to the window of her room and, pushing back the dusty lattice blinds, saw the red fires that still glowed dully in the dark Paris skies, outlining the twin towers of Notre Dame. She shivered, remembering the mob, and the distant, smothered screams.

Then, suddenly, she realised that the food had been

47

cleared away, and the bed had been smoothed into its former pristine condition. Jacques? No, it couldn't be him. He'd followed her immediately, pursuing her relentlessly as she fled up the stairs to the turret room. Who had been in to tidy her chamber? The big house had seemed quite deserted; but in that, as in so many things tonight, she seemed to have got it totally wrong.

She undressed and wrapped herself in a white, freshly-laundered cotton nightgown that she found laid on the pillow. Then she climbed into the big, high bed, between the crisp linen sheets, and lay there with her arms wrapped round herself, unable to sleep, thinking of Jacques.

When at last sleep did come, it brought dreams in its wake; dark and shadowy dreams, filled with the whirling, frenzied figures of the Carmagnole. Nicole was lost in their midst, drowning in their clutches; the redjacketed soldiers had caught her and were scrabbling at her clothes, grasping her breasts with their dirty hands, fondling their own blatantly swelling erections beneath their rough trousers and licking their lips in anticipation of this tasty female morsel.

Twisting and turning in sweat-drenched sleep, Nicole heard herself screaming, calling out for Jacques to help her; but he wasn't there, and she was conscious of an overwhelming despair. There was only one face she knew in the crowd, and it was that of Gerard de Polignac, who was watching her torment from the safety of the shadows, just as Jacques had done. The difference was that Gerard was laughing, openly enjoying the obscene spectacle of the Paris mob indulging in its drunken orgy on the streets. Just as he'd laughed at her that last night before he left Paris, when she'd begged him to take her with him to Austria, begged him on her knees not to leave her all alone.

Even as Nicole screamed at him in her dream to help her escape from her crude tormentors, even as they ripped the clothes from her and gloated over her high, naked breasts, he was pulling a willing, pretty street-girl into the alley and was pushing her to her knees in front of him. Then he thrust his pale, rigid penis with lascivious relish into her eager mouth, and even as he watched Nicole's distress with narrowed, gloating eyes, he pumped himself to swift, spurting ejaculation down the girl's moist throat . . .

Nicole woke up with a cry of despair still on her lips, the perspiration damp on her heated brow. It was still dark, still the middle of the night; she was trembling with fear in the oppressive silence of the big house.

Then she remembered that Jacques was somewhere nearby, and the knowledge soothed her. You're crazy, she told herself scornfully. Almost as crazy as he is, to think you can trust a scarred, sex-obsessed ex-convict! Even so, she felt safer, thinking of him, and she slept heavily till dawn.

Chapter Three

Nicole woke the next morning to see the sunlight streaming through the shutters. Climbing sleepily out of her high bed, she yawned and stretched. The cotton nightgown she'd worn scratched her soft, sleep-warm flesh; she pulled it off and wrapped herself instead in the long silk dressing robe she'd worn last night.

Then she went across the room to push back the blinds, throwing the windows wide open.

The fresh, heady scents from the luxuriously over-grown garden, still wet from yesterday's rain, flooded into her room. She breathed in deeply. In the daylight, this great, walled mansion was even more magnificent than she remembered. So it was all true, then, and not some dark dream. Last night, the house, the man Jacques. Especially the man Jacques.

She shivered, remembering her own abandoned wantonness in his strong arms, the incredible, sensual pleasure he'd aroused in her.

Then, suddenly, an unexpected sound assaulted her ears in the silence, the chilling sound of a woman's scream. Her blood ran cold as she remembered the dreadful scenes on the streets of Paris last night. Her heart thudding, she leaned out of the window and saw a dark-haired girl running along the gravel paths towards the house, with a big, roughly-dressed man in pursuit. Nicole gasped, then relaxed as she realised that the girl *wanted* to be caught! Near the wall of the house, almost below Nicole's window, she paused by a great stone urn full of rampant scarlet geraniums, and turned, panting and laughing, to face her pursuer, her hands on her plump hips.

Nicole realised suddenly that this was the ghost-girl she'd seen peeping out from between the shadowy carriages last night. No ghost this, no pale aristocrat, but a beautiful, real young woman with pink cheeks and tousled black hair, in a fresh cotton dress and a maid's white apron.

Then, Nicole gasped again. The big man had caught the girl in his arms, and was kissing her roughly, demandingly; at first the girl pushed him off, giggling, but only so she could unlace her bodice and use her cupped hands to lift up her own full, rosy breasts, greedy for his lascivious embrace.

With a shout of gruff laughter, the man bent to guzzle at her dark nipples, while Nicole watched, transfixed, the colour rushing to her cheeks. He was a big, heavily muscular man, with a dark beard; he wore trousers and wooden *sabots*, and looked like some kind of manservant. The blood was pounding in Nicole's veins as she watched the big man's mouth pull and suckle at the girl's ripe teats while he pushed her breasts together with his rough hands. The girl had thrown her head back, her eyes glazed with ecstasy; Nicole felt her own inexorably rising excitement, the melting between her thighs, and gripped the window ledge hard with her fingers, wishing the bearded man's frenzied mouth was licking and pulling at her own aching breasts in that lewd, abandoned way.

Then she had to bite on her lip to stop herself crying out.

Because, below her, the man had sunk to his knees beside the stone urn and was fumbling with his trousers, eventually pulling out an enormous, gnarled penis that thrust quivering into the empty air. The dark-haired girl squealed in delight and knelt down eagerly to face him, clutching her bare breasts and rubbing her hardened nipples against the swollen, purple glans of the man's exposed member in a frenzy of sexual excitement.

The man groaned aloud as her breasts caressed his great phallus; clutching her long, tousled hair, he pulled her flushed face down over his loins, forcing her to take the extremity of that huge knob into his mouth; then he proceeded to finger and squeeze at her thrusting nip-ples as the girl rapturously began to pleasure him, sliding her soft, moist lips up and down that great, thick stem.

Nicole shut her eyes. Her hand brushed her own swollen, aching breasts beneath her silken robe. Then, relentlessly, her fingers slipped down across her taut belly to find the soft, melting folds of flesh at the apex of her thighs, to lightly caress her little bud of pleasure. Already it was pulsing hotly, hungrily; with a little groan of need she slid her finger along her honeyed crease, longing with all her being for that huge, primi-tive organ that the girl was kissing so hungrily to be rammed up inside her.

Too late, she heard the door open quietly behind her. She whirled round to see Jacques leaning against the doorframe, his mouth twisting crookedly.

Nicole pulled her robe across her flushed breasts and hissed furiously, 'Were you never taught to knock at a lady's bedroom door?'

'I see no lady.' He smiled and walked towards her. Nicole saw that already he was shaved and dressed, damn him, as immaculately as ever, in an exquisitely tailored beige coat with dark brown breeches and tan jockey boots. 'I see,' he went on imperturbably, 'a delicious little Parisienne strumpet, waiting, indeed longing, for attention. What was it, my little Nicole, that excited you so? You're certainly finding plenty of entertainment in this house, aren't you?'

She darted swiftly away from the open window, violently ashamed of her own voyeurism. But Jacques calmly seized her wrist, and dragged her back to his side, and looked out into the garden himself.

A slow, fiendish smile lit his face, and his arm encircled Nicole's slender waist, drawing her even closer to him.

'Ah, I see,' he murmured. 'You were watching those two sturdy peasants pleasuring one another. A charming scene, is it not? So refreshingly honest and simple.'

Nicole, hot and sticky and ashamed, looked out again; and again was unable to drag her wide eyes away from what she beheld. The man, hugely engorged, was still on his knees, his trousers down around his muscular, hairy thighs; the young maid was taking as much as she could of his massive appendage between her soft lips, bobbing her head up and down energetically; but so long was his penis that several inches of thick shaft remained unattended, and so she was gripping and stroking the base with one eager hand until his bulky testicles jerked and danced at her busy attentions.

The bearded man's rapt face suddenly began to darken with the onslaught of approaching climax. Even as Nicole watched, breathless, he threw back his shaggy head and gave a great roar. The girl lifted her head quickly, while her busy hand continued its labours more frantically than ever; the man's swollen, glistening knob began to quiver and shake as his milky semen gouted forth in jet after luxuriant jet, spurting across the girl's ripe breasts. With little guttural moans, the girl bent to rub her nipples against his huge, empurpled glans, writhing in ecstasy at the touch of the firm, velvety flesh on her sensitive buds.

Nicole shuddered and shut her eyes. The man Jacques let his hand slide softly under her silken robe. At the merest touch of his cool palm on her hips, she

53

thought she would faint. Then his fingers slipped down without warning to her hot, honeyed crease; quickly his forefinger found the wet, delicious moistness that dripped from her swollen flesh-folds, and she cried out in stark need. A slow, devilish smile flooded his handsome features.

'Time, I think, Nicole, for your first lesson. A lesson in self-control.'

And before she could even begin to compose herself, he drew his hand away from her quivering vulva, leaving her cold and bereft, and called out through the window, 'Hey, Marianne! And you, Armand! Get yourselves up here, to my lady's chamber, this instant, you hear me?'

He turned casually back to the horrified Nicole. 'Friends of mine,' he explained lightly. 'Armand is quite splendidly endowed, is he not?'

Nicole blushed wildly; Jacques grinned.

'As I thought. He'll be perfect for our first lesson. Because you, my sweet, as I told you last night, have much to learn in the matter of self-control, and there's no time like the present, is there?'

Nicole dived frenziedly towards the big chest of drawers, rifling through the garments there. 'You insufferable beast. You've told those people to come up here, and I'm not even dressed!'

'No. And you look quite exquisite as you are.'

'Fiend!' she hissed, pulling the silk robe angrily across her breasts. What the hell was this madman talking about? *First lesson? Self control?* He was utterly crazy! But already the dark sweetness of arousal was enflaming her heated blood; her stiffened nipples stood out proudly against the flimsy silk, and she felt wildly, incredibly excited at what might be in store.

They came in together, bowing and scraping; the big man Armand's gaze glittered hotly as he took in Nicole's tantalising figure, then he dropped his eyes swiftly to the ground as Jacques went on easily, 'Citizeness Nicole is the new mistress of the chateau; you understand, Armand and Marianne? You are to obey her, my friends, in every single thing she commands!'

Marianne, plump and pretty in her now laced-up cotton gown, moistened her lips, her blue eyes dancing eagerly. Nicole realised suddenly that the girl had not taken her eyes off Jacques once since she came in the room. The plump little maid was obviously besotted with him. More fool her!

'Yes, monsieur Jacques,' Marianne was saying softly. 'Whatever you say, monsieur Jacques.'

'Not what I say,' corrected Jacques, 'but what Nicole says, Marianne.'

The girl nodded eagerly. She'd agree to anything Jacques said, even if he asked her to throw herself out of that window here and now, thought Nicole sourly.

Jacques, meanwhile, had pulled a chair from the wall and turned it round so he could sit astride it with his arms resting on its back. 'Then it's time to proceed, Nicole.'

She stared at him, bewildered.

'Proceed,' he repeated kindly. 'Give them their orders. They'll do whatever you ask them to, believe me. Now's your chance to practise being my accomplice, chérie.'

'I've told you – don't want to be your damned accomplice!'

'Ah.' He frowned thoughtfully. 'I forgot. You're leaving, aren't you? Never mind, just humour me, this last time. Punish them, my Nicolette. They offended you, didn't they, with their lewd behaviour in the garden below your window just now? Well then, make them do penance. Anything you like.' His dark eyes glinted. 'I assure you; the more wicked your commands, the more they'll like it.'

Nicole swallowed hard. This was absurd, unreal!

Yet wasn't this what she wanted? Power, of the kind that men had. Satisfaction, in whatever way she wanted. Her stomach churned with excitement. Already, the room seemed to be vibrant with arousal, with the sexual heat of these beautiful, expectant people, waiting for her command.

Nicole took a deep, steadying breath. Very well, then – she would humour him! And she would give him something to remember her by before she left!

Drawing herself up proudly, she started to walk slowly across the room, her silk gown swishing against her long, slender legs, and her glorious tawny hair cascading round her shoulders. She noticed with secret delight that Armand couldn't keep his eyes off her. She knew he'd recently climaxed – her legs quaked suddenly at the memory of that magnificent, primitive explosion as his seed jetted across the girl's ripe breasts – so she needed now to build up his arousal anew.

She turned to the watching Jacques with a sweetly innocent smile on her lips.

'Am I to take it,' she purred, 'that you too are to obey my orders?'

His eyes glinted in approval as he gazed up at her from his chair; he bowed his dark head in acknowledgement. 'Absolutely, citizeness.'

'Then I must tell you that I intend to punish this brutal man Armand for his shameful indulgence just now. Fetch me some suitable implements, please, Jacques, from the tower room. I'm sure I can leave the choice to you!'

He bowed again. 'But of course!' Then he rose and left the room.

Nicole turned back to Armand, who was watching her again with that hot, hungry look in his eyes. She was really beginning to enjoy this. This was better than being on the stage at the *Comédie Française!*

'Kneel, Armand,' she said coldly, imitating Jacques' dispassionate manner. 'Kneel, before Marianne and myself.' As she spoke, she moved next to the pretty little servant, who looked breathless with excitement.

'Now,' she went on, 'you must prepare to accept your punishment, Armand. You deserve to be punished, for pursuing Marianne through the garden, for exposing your huge, obscene male member to her as you did, for seizing her roughly by the hair, and forcing her to place her hot little lips round your swollen cock, when you know it's far too big for such pleasures. Isn't it?'

'Yes,' he groaned. 'Truly I deserve to be punished, my lady . . .'

'And then,' went on Nicole severely, 'you are to be punished for spurting your lascivious seed all over her juicy breasts, for anointing her pretty nipples until they were wet and glistening with that lewd substance.'

'I'm sorry.' His voice was a whimper now. 'Oh, I'm sorry.'

'Then show us, Armand. Show us how repentant you are, by abasing yourself before Marianne and myself!'

The man moaned and grovelled on the floor, just as Jacques came into the room. He was carrying a whip, and some leather belts; without a word to him, Nicole, her head held high and proud, took the implements from him. She passed them on to Marianne, whose eyes were shining.

'Do what you will with Armand, Marianne. He is yours to punish.'

Marianne moistened her lips eagerly. 'By your leave, mistress, anything?'

Nicole drew a deep breath. 'Anything at all.'

Eagerly Marianne turned on Armand, taking up the big whip in her small, plump hands, assuming a superbly haughty expression. 'Up on your knees, dog! Unfasten yourself and show us your shameful nakedness!'

Fumbling with his trousers, Armand pulled them down round his muscular hips. Already, even though he'd climaxed scarcely ten minutes ago, his huge organ, lying heavily against his hairy thighs, was bulging and stiffening. Marianne raised the whip threateningly. 'Kneel, dog, before me!'

Armand grovelled abjectly, his hairy bottom protruding

obscenely from beneath his shirt tails. Jacques, Nicole saw, was watching carefully, leaning with his back against the closed door, his arms folded across his chest and that infuriating secret smile on his face.

Gently, Marianne drew the lash of the whip across Armand's tight buttocks. He groaned aloud. Then Marianne raised the whip, and struck. He shuddered with excitement; Nicole saw his penis thicken and swell, jerking massively up against his belly in his excitement.

'Again!' said Nicole sharply. 'Again!'

And Marianne went on, kissing him softly with the leather lash, stinging him, tantalising him, until his bottom-cheeks were red and shiny. Nicole, her throat dry with excitement, saw the exquisite pulsing of his huge penis at each stroke of the lash, saw how his massive balls jerked and tightened against his groin in his extremity.

Marianne stepped back at last, her cheeks flushed with excitement. 'More?' she whispered to Nicole.

Nicole considered thoughtfully. Then, with an exquisite sense of daring, she bent down to investigate his arousal, and put her own trembling fingers round that huge, hot shaft. The heat of his excitement scorched her palm; she felt the great rod quiver and twitch in her small hand, and was overwhelmed with longing to feel it driving deep, deep inside her. Swallowing hard, she forced herself to let go and stood up again. 'I don't know, Marianne,' she said, frowning. 'He certainly hasn't suffered enough yet. What do you think we should do?'

Jacques, straightening himself, broke in coldly. 'Nicole. Do I have to remind you that you are the one in charge? You are the mistress of this room. It's up to you to devise some devilish torment for Armand, not Marianne. I thought I made that plain earlier.'

Nicole flashed him a look of wild resentment. How dare he speak to her like that, as if she were some stupid child? Putting her hands on her hips defiantly, she said, 'Do I assume, citizen Jacques, that you too are under my command?'

'Absolutely.'

Nicole's amber eyes danced with pure mischief. 'Then I command you to bring out the walnut box of treasures that you saw last night.'

His eyes widened; then he gave a slow grin of approval and went to the drawers to do as she said, bringing out the box of ivory love-aids and placing them meaningfully on the dressing table. Nicole turned back to Marianne.

'Marianne, I command you to tie the wicked Armand's hands behind his back so that he is unable to relieve himself, however great his extremity.' Then she tossed back her hair and glared at Jacques defiantly. 'And you, Jacques, are to pleasure Marianne with the biggest of the ivory penises, while Armand is to watch!'

Armand shuddered in despair, his hands pinioned behind his back as he kneeled on the floor, his huge phallus rearing upwards darkly. Marianne's face was rapt with delight when she heard Nicole's words. 'On the bed? Shall I lie on the bed for monsieur Jacques?'

'On the bed,' commanded Nicole, picking up the big leather whip herself and deliberately letting her robe fall open to display her own ripe breasts and glistening crotch. She was amazed at how much she was enjoying herself. 'On the bed, slut! Lie back, and raise your knees; pull up your skirt to your waist, so Jacques can see that you are ready and ripe for him.'

Armand groaned aloud, and Nicole too was almost unbearably excited at the sight of the girl's plump white thighs, the folds of moist, crinkled flesh that peeped from beneath her bush of dark hair. She felt the sudden urge to pay homage herself to the girl's eager sex, to taste, to lick that lascivious, wanton flesh. With an effort, she pulled her gaze away and turned to Jacques.

'Now,' she said with a sweet smile, 'I'm quite sure that *you* need no further instruction on what to do!'

Jacques smiled back equally sweetly, and drew a

slender ivory phallus from the box of treasures. Then he walked slowly, purposefully towards the bed, and Marianne gasped, her eyes already glazed with desire as the tall, dark man hovered over her with the weapon of delight grasped in his strong hand.

Nicole frowned. She suddenly realised that she'd made a big mistake. She'd totally forgotten her earlier observation that the serving girl was quite besotted with the handsome Jacques. And now, waiting for his devastating attentions, it looked as if Marianne was on the brink of extremity already.

Jacques looked back at Nicole. 'You're quite sure about this?' He knew, too, that one caress from his lean, sunbrowned fingers would send the luscious little Marianne crashing into orgasm.

But Nicole wasn't going to retreat now. 'Of course I'm sure! Go ahead!' she snapped crossly.

And she watched, biting her lip as Jacques gently inserted the long, smooth piece of ivory between the girl's honeyed flesh lips. Behind her, she heard the crouching Armand's despairing groan as he gazed avidly at the scene.

Nicole wished it was her on the bed. She wished Jacques was pleasuring her with that long, cool ivory shaft, because by now her own loins were churning with exquisite need. Armand was making little guttural noises in his throat, his eyes wide and dark, his rampant penis twitching uncontrollably into the air. The thought of that huge, empurpled phallus, ridged with veins, jerking inside her own yearning love passage made Nicole feel faint with the pain of desire.

She forced her eyes back to the bed, where Jacques was slowly pleasuring Marianne with the ivory penis. Nicole tried to look on, impassive and cool, as she knew Jacques would do. To be fair to him, she thought grudgingly, he was doing his very best to draw out the girl's pleasure. But already, Marianne's plump thighs were trembling, her hips arching; and as Jacques slid the sweet ivory softly into her flesh, she threw herself against it with a wild scream, bucking and thrashing in contorted pleasure; while Jacques, a grim smile on his face, did his very best to hold the phallus deep within her, to pleasure her fully, to give her all the exquisite satisfaction she so craved.

Marianne fell back at last against the pillows, her face flushed with rapture, her secret flesh still pulsing sweetly around the stem of the ivory penis. Armand had closed his eyes in despair.

Nicole swallowed hard, trying desperately to conceal her own treacherous excitement. She picked up the whip, and trailed the lash across Armand's bulging, muscle-corded thighs. 'Open your eyes, Armand,' she chided him. 'You enjoyed that, did you? You wished it was you, giving such exquisite pleasure to Marianne? Driving your big penis hard inside her sweet flesh, feeling her clutching you deep inside her, hearing her soft moans of delight . . .'

'Yes!' groaned the pinioned Armand, his shaft throbbing unbearably into empty air. 'Oh, yes.'

Then Nicole turned abruptly back to the bed, alerted by a sudden sound. Behind her back, Marianne had pulled Jacques impatiently down to the bed beside her, and with busy, frantic little fingers she was pulling open his shirt, fumbling at his breeches. As Nicole watched, burning with anger, Marianne eased out his strong, fine shaft; fully erect already, it leaped eagerly into her cool palm as she crooned tenderly over it. Jacques, sprawled back on the bed, was shaking his head helplessly as she assaulted him, his dark eyes glinting with laughter. He caught Nicole's furious expression and choked out, 'Wait, my little Marianne, for Nicole's orders.'

But Nicole by now was full of a wild, seething rage. She found it intolerable that Jacques should have let himself become so hugely aroused by this slut of a serving girl, pretty though she was, when he'd rejected her, Nicole, only last night. It was obvious what type of woman *he* was happiest with.

'Please yourself, Jacques,' she said, her voice icy with fury. 'Obviously I'm not the only person in this room who needs a lesson in self-control.'

'Nicole!' he pleaded despairingly, though his eyes were still full of amusement. 'I – oh, Marianne, *chérie* – you know that drives me wild – '

He'd broken off abruptly, because Marianne's little pink tongue was dancing along his beautiful, silken penis, licking teasingly at the swollen glans, and as Nicole watched in cold disdain, Marianne was already opening her eager pink mouth to encircle his hardened flesh, muttering hot little words of endearment as her dark hair spread enticingly over his loins and belly.

Jacques threw himself helplessly back onto the bed, his hands clasped behind his head, his eyes closed with rapture; and Marianne wriggled to crouch right over him, her moist mouth working adoringly on his stiffened penis, her fingers caressing the taut, velvety pouch of his exposed testicles, her lips sliding with cataclysmic effect up and down his long, pulsing shaft.

Nicole gritted her teeth. It was quite obviously not the first time that Marianne had attended to him in this way. Self-control, indeed!

She swung round towards Armand, who was almost faint with need. Nicole, her own juices stirring hot and sweet within her aching love channel, muttered to him, 'I think, friend Armand, that you and I deserve our pleasure now. Don't you?'

The man's eyes widened ecstatically. 'My lady.' He gazed hotly at her parted gown, her high, ripe breasts, at the softly curling tawny triangle through which the swollen flesh lips could be glimpsed, moist and ripe. 'For you, anything. Command me, I am yours!'

Almost faint with desire herself at the sight of that huge, obscene rod jerking from his loins, so ready and willing, Nicole bent to unfasten his hands from behind his back.

Then, throwing off her robe, she crouched in front of him on all fours, knowing that the sight of her plump bottom cheeks with the pink, glistening flesh peeping between them would drive him to a wild, animal frenzy.

She was right. With a harsh groan, Armand gripped her bottom with one big hand and used the other to grasp and guide his great penis carefully between her tender lips. She gasped aloud at the feel of him, huge and hot and urgent, forcing her wide open. His big hands reached for her dangling breasts, stroking them, teasing her hard nipples. Then he began to thrust his huge shaft hard into her, sliding his full length against her juicy passage; and Nicole, feeling the great, solid penis ravishing her so exquisitely, filling her to delicious extremity, felt the rapturous heat of orgasm begain to envelop her at last.

He clutched fiercely at her nipples with his fingers, squeezing them hard, and Nicole threw her head back, hearing her own little animal moans of ecstasy as his long, bone-hard shaft pumped into her. With a great shout, Armand, sensing her release, pounded to his own climax, jerking deep within her; and Nicole convulsed wildly as the intense waves of pleasure engulfed her entire body, leaving her dazed and exhausted.

With a last, shuddering sigh, Armand was finished, though she could still feel him pulsing deeply within her own sated flesh. Slowly, she pulled herself away from him and rolled onto the floor; he bent over her in silent adoration, and contentedly she let him nuzzle at her breasts, revelling in the sweet rasp of his black, bristling beard against her soft flesh as the melting afterglow spread through her body. 'Well done, my fine Armand,' she whispered.

Smiling softly, she drew herself up and started to pull her robe around herself.

Then she looked at the bed, and all her pleasure died. Because Jacques was still lying there, his shirt and breeches still open, with the little servant wench lying snugly in his arms. They'd been watching it all with evident pleasure; the girl's hand was still cupped lovingly at his groin, and Jacques was whispering and chuckling into Marianne's ear, his hand fondling her breasts.

Nicole felt a white, seething shaft of fury shoot through her. Jealousy? No, impossible!

Carefully fastening her robe around her waist, she glared at Jacques and said icily, 'When you've restored yourself to some sort of order, monsieur, perhaps you, the great expert, can give me your considered opinion as to how this first lesson of mine went. Though it might be a little difficult for you to appraise it successfully, seeing as you were so anxious for your own pleasure!'

Slowly, with a secret word in Marianne's ear that made Nicole shake with fury at the intimacy of it, Jacques drew himself up and swung his long legs over the side of the bed. Because his white shirt was still unfastened, she could see the soft, smooth gleam of his suntanned flesh, the flat contours of his belly, the tantalising pelt of silky black hair that swept down to his groin.

She knew, with a sudden, despairing realisation, that it had been *him*, not Armand, that she'd wanted. Him that she'd fantasised about, even as she reached her glorious climax with Armand's shaft pulsing deep inside her.

Jacques was saying lazily as he began to button up his shirt, 'You seemed to achieve a fine level of pleasure yourself, *ma chérie*. Thanks to Armand.'

Nicole struggled for words, but she was speechlessly indignant. Jacques, watching her, stood up with a low laugh.

'You've done well, my Nicolette,' he said. 'Now, I have some business to attend to, and I might be gone for several hours. But I'll be back tonight, never fear. Meanwhile Marianne and Armand will look after you, Nicole, and answer any questions you may have; trust them in everything.'

He pulled on his beige coat and turned to leave the room. Marianne watched him wistfully from the bed;

Armand, still busy dressing, nodded his farewell. But Nicole flew after Jacques, catching up with him on the corridor outside, her fists clenched and her small face white with fury. 'I sincerely hope you don't expect me to submit to any more of your games.'

His eyebrows lifted in surprise. 'Submit? But, my Nicolette, you weren't submitting to anything. You were in charge!'

She hissed furiously, 'It didn't feel like it. It certainly didn't take long for you to let pretty little Marianne get her hands on you, did it?'

'Why, my Nicole, I do believe you're jealous. You could have ordered us to stop, you know. But I assumed you were eager to try out friend Armand. I thought I'd give you the chance to enjoy him, which you evidently did.'

She gazed speechlessly up at him. Of course she'd enjoyed being pleasured by the stalwart Armand. It had been a superb experience. But she'd wanted Jacques. He obsessed her, this dark, elusive stranger; tantalised her, drove her mad even now with wanting him. If he knew of her infatuation, how he would laugh at her.

Tossing back her long, tawny hair, she smiled up at him complacently. 'You were right about Armand,' she said in a casual voice. 'He was quite, quite magnificent. In fact, I've never experienced anything like it.'

He threw back his head and laughed, his teeth gleaming. 'You are superb, my little Nicole. A wonderful actress, and I love you.'

To her utter consternation, he bent to kiss her tenderly on the lips.

'Remember, *chérie*. Stay here with us a little longer and soon, I promise you, you will have your chance for revenge.'

'On you?' she muttered, still flustered by his kiss.

He laughed again. 'On whoever you like. Revenge, and much, much pleasure. You did well just now, *chérie*. That little encounter will stand you in good stead for practising on some real live aristocrats tonight. I'll give you your instructions later.' And with that, he turned on his heel and headed off down the corridor towards the great staircase.

'I've told you – I won't be here tonight! I'm leaving!' she screamed after his retreating back.

If he heard her, he made no acknowledgement. She heard his booted feet, light on the stairs; heard his echoing steps in the great hall below, and the final slam of the big front door. She stood there, already missing him. 'I *am* leaving!' she repeated stubbornly to herself, and wondered just who she was trying to convince.

Armand and Marianne went out soon afterwards, to buy food in the streetmarkets of Paris. Nicole asked quickly if she could come with them, seeing this as her chance to slip quietly away; but Marianne told her that no, monsieur Jacques had said that it would be far better if she stayed here in the house, for her own safety, of course.

Nicole nodded, feigning agreement; but the minute the servants had gone, she ran anxiously up to her room, pulling on her old clothes and her shabby cloak. All the time, her thoughts kept returning to Jacques. The memory of last night, his devastating prowess as a lover, the piercing sweetness of sensuality he'd aroused her to, made her blood run hot with mingled shame and desire.

She fastened up her cloak with trembling fingers, feeling his strong pull on her even now, even in the act of leaving. Who was he? All she knew about him was that he was a dangerous, whip-scarred convict, full of twisted plans for some kind of sexual revenge in order to get his own back on those who'd so wronged him. Well, she wanted no part in it. The sooner she was away from this haunted mansion the better, even if she did run the risk of being caught once more by the mob. Defiantly closing the bedroom door behind her, she flew down the stairs and hurried across the vast hallway towards the big front doors.

They were locked.

Chapter Four

*B*y the time Armand and Marianne had returned three hours later, Nicole had explored every ground-floor room in the house in an effort to get away, and had found every door, every window, securely fastened. It was for her own safety that they'd locked her in, she told herself shakily again and again, not daring to contemplate any other reason. Of course she wasn't a prisoner – that was too ridiculous! She'd just have to alter her plans slightly, and leave that evening, under cover of darkness.

She succeeded in being quite calm and composed when Armand and Marianne eventually returned. Marianne chattered to her companionably as she unpacked her purchases, telling her proudly how she'd managed to find fresh bread at eight *sous* a loaf, together with a tasty knuckle of veal and some vegetables that had been brought in fresh from the suburbs that very morning. Nicole helped her to make a delicious casserole, and the three of them ate supper together at the big scrubbed oak table in the stone-flagged kitchen. It was already dark, and the rain was pouring down outside; but it didn't seem to matter in here, where the numerous tallow candles were cheerfully reflected in the gleaming copper pots and pans that were arrayed around the walls.

Nobody had made any mention of the strange sexual tableau that they had all enacted only that morning. Nicole, feeling the good food warming her stomach, wondered with a sudden sinking feeling if it was because they were so used to such goings-on that they didn't even merit a conversation. Pushing the unsettling thought to the back of her mind, she found herself enjoying their undemanding company, feeling relaxed and warm and almost happy as they drank mellow red wine with the veal casserole and the stove crackled warmly in the corner. No-one mentioned Jacques at all, and she was glad, because she didn't want to think about him. She went to bed early, pleading tiredness, and lay awake on her bed, still fully dressed, meaning to make her escape in a little while, when they would think her asleep. It was still pouring down outside, and she had to stiffen her resolve. Just another half hour, and the rain might have stopped. Just a little while longer . . .

She must have dozed off, because she found herself waking with a sudden start. By the light of the dimly glowing fire, she could just make out the time on the ormolu clock that sat on the marble mantel; midnight. She dragged herself up with a cry of horror. Dear God, she should have made her escape hours ago! Praying that somewhere there would be a door unlocked, a window unlatched, she grabbed a dark cloak, slipped on her shoes, and hurried for the door.

Then she heard it. In the heavy stillness of midnight, far away, like something in a dream, she heard voices: the distant musical tinkle of women's laughter, the husky murmur of men talking. Bewildered and confused, she edged her way along the shadowy landing, losing her bearings completely in the darkness of this vast house.

Again, the sound of light laughter, tantalising, like a dream. She turned down a first-floor corridor she didn't remember; then she opened a panelled door, and caught her breath.

She was standing on a balustraded musicians' gallery, looking down into an ornate, candlelit room that glittered with chandeliers and gilt mirrors. As she gazed, she was convinced now that she must be dreaming, because what met her astonished eyes was a scene from a vanished age, like a glimpse of the opulent magnificence of the court at the doomed palace of Versailles. As she shrank back instictively into the shadows, she could still see that people were drifting below her in ever-changing patterns on the black and white tiled floor; men and women, dressed exquisitely in fine peacock-coloured silks and satins that no-one dared to wear nowadays. The women's hair was piled high *à la* Pompadour; their white rice-powdered complexions were adorned with beauty patches and they waved their fans delicately as they simpered up at the men, who were equally exquisitely attired in satin frock coats with their hair frizzed and powdered.

Nicole leaned back, shaken, against the wall. The scent of their rich perfumes wafted up towards her. Ghosts, she thought dizzily, her heart pounding. Spirits of the former occupants of this marvellous house, gathered here at midnight . . .

But they weren't all ghosts. Her heart thumped even louder as she saw that one of them was only too real, in his sombre yet distinguished grey coat and breeches, with his starkly unpowdered hair drawn back in a black velvet ribbon.

Jacques was back. What had he said to her earlier? 'This little encounter will stand you in good stead for practising on some real live aristocrats tonight.' Nicole gasped, and leaned forward over the balcony, unable to believe her eyes.

And then she saw no more; because suddenly two men clothed all in black had sprung out from the shadows behind her, and were grasping her wrists fiercely, hurting her. 'Got a little spy, have we?' one of them muttered. 'Let's see what citizen Jacques makes of this.' She tried to cry out, but one of them thrust a black velvet gag across her mouth; she fought even more fiercely then, so that her cloak slipped to the floor, but it was hopeless. Then she heard more footsteps, and a familiar low voice, and she gave up, sagging in despair in her captors' grip.

Jacques walked round slowly to face her, pulling the gag from her mouth; she gasped for breath, for words, as his minions gripped her arms.

'Well, my Nicole,' said Jacques softly. 'What are you up to this time?'

'Running away from this hell-hole!' she spat out, renewing her struggle to get free. 'What else?'

'Really?' He looked amused. 'And I thought you were spying! I'd have invited you properly, *chérie*, only little Marianne said that you needed your beauty sleep.'

She struggled again, desperately aware that as he towered so casually above her he exuded sexual magnetism from every pore of his body, and already she felt that familiar sweet ache of longing at the very pit of her stomach. 'Let me go!' she whispered.

'Let you go? Oh, I'm afraid not, *ma chère*. That's impossible. I'm afraid you've seen far too much.'

'You can't keep me here! You can't!'

He nodded to the two silent men. 'Tie her up.'

Nicole was really frightened then as the men took her wrists and pulled them apart, and fastened them with silken cords to the carved pillars that were interspaced along the gallery. The black-coated minions melted away; she twisted her head violently round to find Jacques, and her face was white. 'Please, let me go. I won't say anything about all this, I promise! I wasn't even looking!'

'Ah.' Jacques smiled slowly and his voice was silky as he said, 'Then you ought to be looking, Nicole. Look at the marquise, for example. Isn't she beautiful?'

Nicole whispered, 'I don't believe this. I don't believe you.' But almost against her will, she found herself looking again down into the opulent room.

Most of the candles had been extinguished so that

there was only a soft glow, and the figures were shifting again, like dancers in a dream. In the midst of it all, the focal point of all their attention as she stood in the soft candlelight by the low satin couch, was a beautiful woman in an *eau-de-nil* silk gown, the one Jacques called the marquise. And moving in on her steadily, purposefully, were four more silent men in the black garb of servants – Jacques' servants. Nicole saw with a gasp of shock that their penises were exposed; even as they surrounded the marquise they were pulling on their members, rubbing at them menacingly until they were fully erect, and the marquise's white, bejewelled hand was at her mouth, her eyes wide with fear as she looked round desperately for escape.

Then suddenly the men lunged towards her and tipped her up on the couch, holding her down, tugging at her clothing so that her beautiful silk skirts were rumpled high round her waist, pulling her stockinged legs wide apart so that her glistening secret flesh was exposed. Two men held her legs; two more her arms, and one of them had ripped her bodice, and was rubbing his long, stiff penis enticingly against her exposed white breasts.

Nicole gave a soft moan of despair, tugging uselessly at the bonds that held her arms high and taut. She felt sick and revolted by the spectacle; yet at the same time she felt her blood race with dark, shameful excitement as she saw how one of the men was crouching between the marquise's slender legs and rubbing the swollen head of his erect member up and down the woman's juicy cleft, anointing it lasciviously with her secret moisture before thrusting it deep, deep within her.

Nicole cried out in despair to Jacques; 'No! You must stop them!' But at the same time, she was aware of Jacques moving up closer behind her, his wine-scented breath warm on the top of her head as his cool hands slipped inside her tight bodice and began to play tantalisingly with her nipples. They jutted out instantly, the darkened flesh shamefully responsive to his wicked touch; Nicole shuddered in despair as Jacques whispered in her ear, 'Why should I stop them, *chérie*, when they're all enjoying themselves so much?'

'No!' Yet somehow Nicole couldn't drag her eyes from the lewd sight of the big, black-coated man so vigorously pleasuring the beautiful marquise with his fine, thick shaft, thrusting it deep within her quivering flesh until she writhed helplessly beneath him, muttering out her delight. Another man was masturbating himself openly against her pouting breasts, jerking strongly until his milky seed creamed over her nipples; a third man rubbed his obscene purple shaft lasciviously against her ripe mouth and started to slide himself slowly between her lips; she arched back to welcome him, sucking and tonguing enthusiastically. All around them, in the shadowy recesses of the big room, other couples were watching and fondling one another, or slipping away into the shadows to copulate urgently.

Suddenly she remembered what he'd said last night, in that sinister turret room.

'What's the best way to humiliate people? Why, through sexual gratification, of course. To expose their innermost desires, their private fantasies, and then mercilessly exploit them . . .

Jacques' cool hands cupped Nicole's throbbing breasts. 'They're all enjoying themselves, Nicole. Just as you are.'

She wrenched desperately at her bonds. 'You're fiendish! Why are you doing this?'

'This is the marquise's punishment. She used to beat her servants, and make them perform sexually for her and her friends, at exotic parties. Now, the tables are turned. The only trouble is, I think she's rather enjoying it.' His fingers tightened on Nicole's stiffened nipples; she caught her lip between her teeth as the fierce spasm of pleasure shot down to her belly, and squeezed her thighs together, unable to drag her eyes away from the sight of the debased marquise, whose hips were grind-

72

ing frantically now against the man's solid, glistening pillar of flesh as she moaned her way to noisy orgasm.

Nicole was burning as she felt Jacques' taut, muscular body pressing against her own captive one. The secret folds of flesh between her thighs were plump and swollen with need, her honeyed juices flowing freely. How she longed to feel a man's hard, hot penis deep within her, assuaging that terrible sweet ache that all but consumed her!

Then she writhed helplessly in her bonds as Jacques' hand slipped low beneath her skirt, pulling it up to rove between her thighs, caressing the soft, moist flesh at the top of her stockings. 'So,' he was murmuring, 'you were trying to escape tonight, my Nicole, my little accomplice?'

'Yes!'

'Why?'

'Because you're crazy, and dangerous, and – oh . . .

His fingers had found her soaking bud of pleasure, and Nicole ground down hungrily on his hand, unable to restrain herself as she despairingly watched the men below, one pumping into the marquise's willing mouth, the other plunging with strong, powerful strokes deep into the marquise's moist, sated loins. Nicole could see his glistening penis each time he withdrew, could hear his hoarse gasps as he ravished his willing victim, and Nicole felt herself thrusting her hips helplessly back against Jacques' muscular loins, grinding against him. Coolly, deliberately, Jacques pulled up her skirts around her waist so she could feel the cool air on her buttocks; and then Nicole, almost shaking with need, felt his hot, hard member slipping wonderfully between her honeyed thighs.

'Oh,' she whispered, 'please. Please.'

She felt his massively erect shaft nudging between her swollen sex lips, the tip brushing her clitoris. The need, the urgent longing gathered in the pit of her belly. As soon as his hardened flesh slipped into her

73

wet opening, she thrust wildly back against him, impaling herself.

'Steady, my little wildcat,' he murmured from behind her. There was a hint of mockery in his voice, but she heard the huskiness of desire too, and thrust back harder, until the silken cords bit into her wrists.

But just when she thought she must shudder into delicious climax, he slipped out and kept her there, trembling with need; just caressing the outer rim of her soaking, quivering vulva with the deliciously velvety tip of his penis, while his hands continued to stroke and squeeze at her throbbing breasts. The hunger in her was like a flame, licking at her flesh, consuming her; she tore frantically at her bonds, groaning aloud at the empty ache, the sense of loss; and when she looked down into the hall again, the tableau had changed.

In the dim candlelight, a man, young and handsome with long dark hair, had been forced to his knees by the black-coated servants. His breeches had been gently pulled from his hips, exposing his tight, small buttocks, and Nicole quivered in anguish as she saw that Jacques' men were gathering around him, fondling him, stroking him. Already his penis was lifting and jerking helplessly in response to their skilled caresses. Then one of the men, the only one who hadn't pleasured himself with the marquise, was kneeling behind the man's buttocks, and Nicole suddenly realised, with a jolt of horror, that his long, glistening penis was poised at the man's dark bottom cleft, prodding and thrusting at that puckered, forbidden entrance as he clutched and stroked at the smooth bottom cheeks so brazenly presented for his attention. Nicole stopped breathing, the blood rushing to her cheeks as the man's shaft suddenly slipped in, and she saw the rapt ecstasy on both men's faces as that lengthy penis penetrated deep within the kneeling man's tight, dark hole.

Nicole shook her head slowly, disbelievingly, as the terrible excitement coursed through her and heightened the hungry longing in her own loins. 'Oh, God. You're evil, depraved . . . Is he being punished too? Is this all part of your scheme?'

Jacques' velvety penis nudged between her soaking sex lips; she bit back her cry of need as he said softly in her ear, 'Yes. That's Gaston, a nobly born priest. He confessed to us earlier about his wicked ways, how he prefers young men to women. We thought we'd make a spectacle of him, but again he looks as though he's rather enjoying it. Are you enjoying it, Nicole? Are you glad now, *ma chère* that you didn't escape?'

His fingers tightened lovingly on her nipples, sending shocking waves of pleasure rippling to her core, and she almost orgasmed there and then. 'No. Yes oh, please don't stop!'

His hands pulled gently at her swollen crests, soothing her nipples again, assuaging the terrible ache there only to exacerbate the other one, the burning need in her loins to feel him driving into her, thrusting his silken, bone-hard flesh deep, deep against her hungry womb. She glimpsed the men below her, frantically driving to their own climax, and she sobbed aloud, pulling at her cords, her whole body exquisitely exposed and helpless. 'Jacques. I need you.'

And then he was there, the head of his thick phallus slipping between her swollen sex lips, ravishing her with long, slow strokes, while his hands soothed her breasts, pulled at her nipples, and she felt the pleasure gather and surge relentlessly until she exploded with little sobs, clutching desperately at the wonderful length of his penis as it filled her, delighted her, and finally drove her into mindless, exquisite rapture.

Her flesh continued to pulse sweetly long after the moment of orgasm, long after he'd driven himself to his own harsh, powerful climax. Then he withdrew himself from her and she was cold without him, suddenly realising that the people in the room below had disappeared as swiftly as if they really were ghosts. Her head sagged between her bound wrists, and she closed her eyes in despair, because she'd never known such sweet, hard, relentless pleasure, and she couldn't bear to think that she'd never have it again.

Silently he untied her, and because she nearly fell, he picked her up and carried her back to her room, where he laid her almost gently on her bed and lit two candles from the embers of the fire. She lay there, silent and shaking; he placed the candles carefully in their holders and turned to her. 'What's the matter, my Nicole?' he said almost tenderly as he drew up a chair beside her bed. 'Didn't you enjoy our little entertainment?'

She shuddered. 'No! It was degrading, sickening!'

'I see. And that's why you welcomed my attentions so avidly?'

She turned her face to the wall, white with shame. He said quietly, 'Nicole. You're being perverse and stupid, and failing to understand your own needs. Listen, while I explain.'

'I really don't think I want to know!'

'Well, I'm going to tell you anyway,' he said calmly. 'Since this house came into my possession, I've had a succession of guests. They are all people in danger of their lives; aristocrats, priests, rich bourgeoisie, anyone with royal connections. And they've all been brought to me, Nicole, from the heart of Paris's prisons. Those people you saw down there tonight know very well that if they hadn't been brought here by my men, they would most likely have been butchered on the streets.'

He was too near for her to think straight as he leaned over her, holding her with his eyes. She could still remember the feel of his hands on her breasts, could remember the feel of his strong, wonderful penis, spasming deep inside her . . . Her voice trembled as she attempted to sneer, 'How very benevolent of you. Citizen Jacques – rescuer of doomed *aristos*.'

She saw his eyes glimmer slightly in amusement. 'True, my Nicole, I set my guests free. But first I teach them a lesson, a lesson they'll never forget.'

'So you call what was happening down there a *lesson*? You amaze me!'

His eyes burned into her. 'Yes. A lesson. I want those people to realise what it's like to be totally humiliated, totally degraded in front of other people.'

Something in his harsh tone made Nicole catch her breath. 'As you were? In that prison in Toulon?'

His face suddenly tightened in the darkness; she saw how his fingers of his left hand had moved to the cruel brand on his inner wrist, stroking it as if it hurt him still. His eyes filled with a bleak emptiness that somehow chilled her to the bone. 'Perhaps.' There was absolute silence; then he turned to her again, and said, 'Tomorrow, Nicole, I want you to help me.'

She recoiled with a gasp. 'Oh, no! I'm leaving! Didn't I make that quite clear?'

He was shaking his head, smiling gently now. 'I'm afraid you can't leave, Nicole. You see, as I've told you before, you're going to be my accomplice.'

She caught her breath. 'You're crazy,' she whispered. 'I want nothing to do with it.' But already her blood was racing with shameful excitement.

His hand touched her forearm; his fingers brushed the soft golden skin and she trembled. 'Nicole,' he said softly, 'you'll be perfect. My guests will love you, Nicole, men and women alike. You're so beautiful, so sensual that they'll do anything you want.'

She sank back against her pillow, dazed. Beautiful, he had called her. Sensual. Did he really mean it? Or was he just laughing at her again? 'Anything?' she stammered.

'Oh, yes. Anything. Remember,' he was saying, 'that these people are proscribed aristocrats, under virtual sentence of death in this grim city of ours. They've already been rescued from prison, thanks to my helpers.'

The men in black. The sinister men who'd tied her up and serviced his guests; his silent henchmen.

'My men bring me suitable candidates,' he went on, 'and as with previous guests, if they promise to serve us loyally and show true signs of repentance, then I see

77

that they are provided with all the necessary papers for them to escape from Paris. In other words, I save their arrogant necks for them. Those people you saw down there will be well past the barriers and on their way to freedom by dawn tomorrow.'

He spoke with such calm certainty of rescuing these people from prison, of providing them with the papers that normally only the highest revolutionary authorities had access to, that he took Nicole's breath away. 'Who are you, Jacques?' she breathed. 'How do you manage all this?'

He turned those dark, inscrutable eyes on her anguished face. 'I have certain friends, as I've just told you. And certain resources of my own.'

Nicole clenched her fists, suddenly overwrought. 'As far as I can see, all you've got is a totally exaggerated sense of your own importance!' she snapped back. 'I want nothing to do with your crazy schemes. I told you before – I'm leaving!'

He stood up, towering above the bed, and again she felt the shiver of fear.

'You still don't quite understand,' he said very softly. 'I'm afraid you can't leave – not now. You see, you know too much.'

She sprang to her feet, her face white as she confronted him. 'You're keeping me a prisoner?'

'Let me put it this way. Before you waste your time, and mine, perhaps I'd better inform you that all the doors, all the gates, are kept securely locked, at all times.' He gave her a slow, knowing smile that made her blood run riot with mingled shame and desire. 'So you might as well enjoy yourself, Nicole. As you did earlier tonight. And get your revenge.'

His eyes glinted wickedly; his meaning was explicit. He turned to go; and as he left her, shutting the door firmly behind him, Nicole sank back against the bed, realising with a sudden blinding clarity that she didn't want to leave at all. In fact she had the feeling that she was just on the edge of an incredible adventure. Oh,

God. He was so wildly, devastatingly attractive; the warm arousal trickled through her just at the sound of his voice.

Her mouth was dry with excitement at the thought of what tomorrow might bring.

Four kilometres to the north of the big house in the Faubourg St Germain, the female prisoners of St Lazare were settling down for another long night of captivity. The only light, apart from a brazier, came from the single tallow candle held by one of the three guards who'd brought the women their meagre rations for the night. As well as being dark, it stank, this huge common cell into which they'd all been herded; there was only one high, barred grill for air, the straw on the floor had not been changed for weeks, and the cold, green-stained walls ran with damp.

The guards had stripped the women when they'd arrived two days ago, in a pretence of searching them for weapons, laughing and gloating over their prize: a fine bunch of *filles* from the Palais Royal. They'd soon discovered the more accommodating of them, those who'd willingly do anything for a jug of wine, or an extra loaf of dry bread, or just for pleasure. Some of the women, of course, hoped to become pregnant in an effort to stave off execution when they faced the grim tribunals that were being set up all over Paris, and the guards were only too willing to assist them in their efforts.

Certainly the guards appreciated their fair prisoners. On this cold, damp September night, when the entire city hummed with horrible rumours of the massacres taking place in other prisons, the guards had taken pity on their feminine charges and brought them the iron brazier, which glowed dully in the corner and gave out a pretence of warmth in this high, chilly cell.

Louise de Lamartine had drawn closer to it along with the other women, though she didn't care to get too close to them. After two days in this disgusting

79

place, she knew them only too well, from Madame Dupont and her fine friends, who boasted that they used to charge their aristocratic clients twenty-five livres a time, to the less exotic Françoise, who charged only six, and used to be a favourite with the rustic conscripts from the provinces until the red-capped soldiers decided to throw her into St Lazare along with all the other women of pleasure.

She, Louise, had never charged for her services. At least, not in money. But when her quest seemed to have failed, and they caught her at the West Barricade trying to escape from Paris without the proper papers, she'd pretended to be one of the ladies of pleasure, deciding that her chances of survival were better that way than if they knew the real truth about her.

Even now, even in her shabby, prison-stained clothes, Louise was beautiful enough to make the other women eye her narrowly, with her cascades of silvery-blonde hair, her wide-set, haunting violet eyes, and her exquisite figure. Secretly she scorned all these *poules*, especially those who stupidly gave their favours for nothing to the crude guards, hugging to herself the knowledge that she herself had once been the prized possession of a rich, powerful marquis. But even though she scorned them she knew that she needed to keep her place here, because so far St Lazare had escaped the dreadful massacres that had engulfed the other prisons. The guards in this place knew they were on to a good thing.

Louise moved imperceptibly closer to Françoise, because she was talking again about a subject that interested Louise very much. 'Of course,' Françoise was sighing to her friends, 'we all know that there is only one man in Paris who can get any of us out of here.'

There were nods, and avid murmurs of agreement. Louise, her eyes wide and innocent, said, 'So you've said before, my dear friend. Who is this mysterious man?'

Françoise leaned forward, her eyes shining with

excitement. 'They call him Jacques. But no-one seems to know anything else about him; he's very careful, you see, to keep his identity a complete secret. To get to where he lives, you have to be blindfolded, and once there, you have to undergo a kind of interrogation. If you pass, he'll give you the papers to leave Paris – '

She broke off hastily as the door rattled and the guards came in to collect up the remnants of the food and the jugs of water. Then Françoise moistened her lips, and they all leaned instinctively closer as she whispered, 'But from what I've heard, most people don't *want* to leave, because, you see, citizen Jacques is reputed to be a fascinating man, and a wonderful lover.'

The women chuckled noisily among themselves, and Louise, on the edge of their circle, could hear no more. Smothering her disappointment, she found her eyes being drawn over to a dark corner, where one of the guards was avidly kissing a girl and drawing her down onto the straw-covered floor. Louise gazed at them with disdain, but inwardly her love-starved blood was heated by the sight of the guard's thick, sturdy penis as the girl parted his breeches and took his erect member eagerly into her mouth, running her full lips around it in lascivious pleasure.

Jacques, she pondered. How strange.

Once, she, Louise, had had a wonderful lover. Oh, she'd had many since then; but none to compare with him. She'd never, ever been able to forget him, and she'd come to Paris to find him, but without success. He'd been called Jacques too, but it was a common enough name, and this citizen Jacques that these stupid women babbled about couldn't, surely, be as magnificent as him. But she would like the chance to find out. Especially if it meant an escape from this hellhole.

In the corner, the guard had tipped the giggling girl to the floor so that her skirts were rucked up, and was plunging his hot fleshy shaft deep inside her. The girl was gasping and moaning her pleasure, her legs clasped round his jerking hips as they both reached their noisy climax; and Louise felt her own urgent, suppressed need rising inexorably, that burning, familiar hunger at the very core of her being that tormented her so, and had done ever since she had grown into womanhood. The need had been driven away, just for a while, by fear; but now it was licking at her soft flesh like a flame.

She moved back into the group and said casually to Françoise, 'How does one get in touch with him, this citizen Jacques?'

'You don't. *He* gets in touch with you, if he wants to. He has friends everywhere, but they work in secret, and their loyalty to him is unbounded.'

Just then the big heavy door opened again and a guard bearing a flickering tallow candle called out to the man on the floor, 'Hey, friend Pierre! You want to be locked in here all night? These wenches will milk you dry!'

'Yes. But what a way to go, eh?' And, reluctantly dragging himself up, the man Pierre hauled himself reluctantly to his feet, buttoning up his coarse breeches as he staggered somewhat unsteadily towards the door.

Louise watched him go, her lovely violet eyes thoughtful. How she despised them all; the rough guards, the indiscriminate *poules*. But Françoise's last words were still burning in her mind: 'He'll get in touch with you. If he wants to.'

He'll want to, whoever he is, vowed Louise de Lamartine. I'll *make* him want to.

Chapter Five

'What do you think, madame Nicole? Like this? Or perhaps like this?'

It was evening. Outside the rain fell relentlessly, hammering against the windows; but in Nicole's spacious bedchamber everywhere was glittering opulence, with the shutters drawn against the night, and the candles lit in their gilt holders, and a big log fire glowing in the grate. Nicole herself was sitting on a low stool before the mahogany dressing table, while Marianne was lovingly dressing her thick hair.

Nicole gazed at her reflection in the mirror, her heart pounding with suppressed excitement. The transformation was astonishing. In the last two days, she'd been metamorphosed from a shabby, penniless cast-off, living on the run in one of the worst quarters of Paris, to a great lady who would not have disgraced Versailles itself. She wasn't thinking of escaping any more. In fact she was tingling with anticipation, especially when she thought of Jacques.

Earlier this evening she had bathed luxuriously in the big wooden tub, filled to the brim with hot water that the valiant Armand had hauled bucket by bucket up the stairs from the stove in the kitchen. She'd washed and brushed her hair so that it gleamed like burnished copper, and lavishly anointed herself with some of the exquisite perfumes and potions that sat in silver-topped bottles on the dressing table, so that every inch of her skin was scented deliciously with jasmine and almond oil. Then she'd dressed herself with great care, in a gown of heavy cream silk with long sleeves and a tight-fitting, low-cut bodice, twirling round in delight to enjoy the movement of the full, hooped skirt.

And now Marianne was attending to the finishing touch, her hair. Marianne's merry, dimpled face was for once solemn with concentration as she piled up the gleaming, tawny tresses in the elaborate manner of the ladies who used to adorn the court, letting just a few tantalising tendrils stray down the slender column of Nicole's white neck.

'Marianne,' said Nicole fervently as she gazed at her new self in the looking glass, 'I think you are a true *artiste!* Where on earth did you learn such skills?'

Marianne blushed, her big blue eyes filled with shy pleasure. 'I used to be a lady's maid, madame.'

'Please, won't you call me Nicole? And have some more wine, do!' As if to seal their friendship, Nicole refilled the two crystal glasses from the cool, refreshing bottle of white wine that Armand had fetched up from the cellar below the kitchen. 'Monsieur Jacques left me the key,' the burly manservant had explained. 'He said you were to have whatever you wanted.'

Again, as Nicole sipped at the delicious, pale liquor, she found her thoughts returning to Jacques. Who was he? How did he come to have possession of this magnificent, mysterious house? Who were his friends, who brought the prisoners to him?

She realised that she wanted Jacques now. Her body felt ripe and luscious, like a juicy peach, what with the effect of the sensuous warm bath, and the sweet-scented oils she'd caressed herself with.

She drank down her wine to cool herself, and tried to push Jacques from her mind. She must be crazy to stay in this strange place, where people came and went like ghosts from the past, all of them dominated by the mysterious figure of the whip-scarred ex-convict who went by the name of citizen Jacques. Crazy she might be, but she knew that she didn't want to leave.

Now, as she sat before the looking glass, she decided to question Marianne a little more. 'You were telling me,' she said lightly, 'that you used to be a maid, Marianne. Was your mistress a very great lady?'

Marianne hesitated, just a fraction. 'Oh, yes, madame Nicole! At least, her husband was of the old nobility; but his family had become impoverished through extravagant spending, so he had to marry for money. Madame's father was a wealthy banker, a member of the bourgeoisie, so Madame was not really of noble blood.'

Nicole nodded. In the last few years, members of some of the proudest, most ancient families in France had found themselves on the verge of bankruptcy, and had been forced to marry into families well beneath them in status. Proud nobles like Gerard had utterly despised these alliances with the lower classes, refusing even to acknowledge the 'money-wives,' as he called them, at receptions.

'But was she kind to you, Marianne?'

Marianne's face was suddenly shadowed. 'She conducted herself in many ways like the great lady she pretended to be. But she was haughty, and so, so cruel!' A blush stained her cheeks. 'Sometimes, madame, she used to make me do things I didn't want to do.'

Something in her voice made Nicole catch her breath. 'What do you mean, Marianne?'

Marianne blushed again. 'Her husband, the Seigneur, was not interested in her, madame Nicole. He was more interested in young men. You understand? Madame had failed to give him heirs, so he lost any interest in her. She was lonely, and hungry for love, and revenge.'

Nicole said quietly, 'Sit down, Marianne. Here, next to me, by the fire. And tell me everything.'

The candles flickered brightly in the big, opulent room, their light reflected a hundredfold in the big gilt mirrors that adorned the walls. A sudden flurry of rain beat on the windows outside as Marianne moistened her lips and began her story.

'Madame d'Argency was beautiful; older than you and I, of course, but still very striking. She was tall, and stately, and proud, proud as only those raised to unexpected heights can be! She had as few menservants as possible in the great chateau near Beauvais, because of the way that the Seigneur looked at them. There was an old, shrivelled-up butler, and a scrawny coachman for her own carriage, and that was all. But she appointed plenty of fresh young country girls like me, who were naive, and innocent, and truly flattered to be chosen to work at the great chateau.

'Of course, we heard rumours; strange, whispered warnings of her ladyship's ways. But,' and Marianne shrugged, 'times were hard. I was from a respectable family, you understand, and was educated by the nuns; but I had many brothers and sisters, and when times grew hard, I had to work. At least it meant a few extra *sous* a week to send back to my poor family, so I was deaf to any warnings.

'When I first entered Madame's service, there was another girl there, Jeanette, whose bedroom I was ordered to share.' She blushed and looked up at Nicole. 'We were fond of each other, Jeanette and I. We played games, as girls will when there are no men around; kissing and caressing one another as we lay in our snug bed on the cold winter nights, toying with one another's nipples to experience those delicious tingling sensations that melted our blood; tangling our fingers in our silky triangles of hair; and touching our most secret places, very lightly, you understand, so that we shivered deliciously. We sighed, and murmured, and whispered tales about men, because we had heard frightening stories about their massive appendages, and half-feared, half-longed to try them out for ourselves.

86

'One evening, Madame came suddenly into the darkness of our room. She looked strange, and her eyes were glittering. She carried a riding crop in her hand, and I think that she had been drinking.'

Marianne lowered her eyes. 'Oh, Nicole, she made us remove our heavy cotton nightgowns and pleasure one another, while she watched! I remember it all, so well. I remember Jeanette's sweet little pink tongue on my hardened nipples, her gentle fingers stroking my secret flesh until it was moist and plump. Madame watched us sternly, and told us to carry on, or we would be punished.

'By then, we couldn't have stopped ourselves anyway. We kissed, our tongues entwining sweetly; Jeanette caressed my pouting little breasts with her knowing fingers, while her slender thigh slid between my legs and rubbed hard against my glistening inner flesh. I was flushed and gasping, as if I was in a fever; but then I began to realise that I was on the verge of the sweetest, the most exquisite pleasure.

'Jeanette, who was also in a frenzy by now, grabbed my hand urgently and made me stroke her. I was astonished, at first, by the feel of her warm, swollen feminine flesh, thrusting so wantonly against me; but wildly aroused as well. As I rubbed and stroked, her nether lips parted lasciviously, soaking with secret moisture; my fingertips brushed her hot, throbbing kernel of pleasure, and Jeanette exploded in my arms, her delicious kisses covering my cheeks. Then Jeanette licked her forefinger, and stroked me so exquisitely, Nicole, that I thought I would swoon! Her wicked finger slid down my parted lips, and wriggled its way into my tight, virginal hole, and thrust steadily while her thumb caressed my hot bud, leading me to explode in delicious ecstasy.'

There was a silence. A log slipped and crackled in the fireplace.

'And what did Madame do then?' asked Nicole softly.

'She watched us, her eyes glittering, her face

strangely flushed, as if she was in a trance. Then she snapped that if we ever, ever told anyone what had just occurred, she would beat our plump bottoms with her riding crop until they were red. As soon as she left, Jeanette and I fell sighing into each other's arms. It was the first of many of such nights of pleasure.

'Then I met Armand.' Marianne's sweet face dimpled. 'It was the time of the spring ploughing, when Madame's husband took on extra men from the village to help with the heavy work, and it was my job to take refreshment out to them at noon. I noticed Armand straight away; his fine eyes seemed to burn for me, Nicole, and I was so excited! When Jeanette caressed me that night, I thought only of him, pretended it was his hands, his mouth touching me. He was only a peasant, but he had a good, strong build and a quiet masculine dignity that somehow fascinated me.

'The first time he kissed me, behind the barn, I forgot all about Jeanette. His strong, hot tongue thrusting deep within my tremulous mouth seemed to promise all kinds of dark delights; and Jeanette's girlish embraces suddenly seemed nothing to me. I realised I was falling in love with Armand. And then, I lay with him for the first time.' She blushed hotly. 'Madame Nicole, you too have enjoyed my Armand. He is truly magnificent, is he not? As a man, and as a lover.'

'Yes, he is,' said Nicole quietly, her own blood on fire at Marianne's poignant story.

'We were in the stables one warm April night,' went on Marianne, 'after I'd managed to steal away from Madame's gimlet eye. We'd been kissing passionately; Armand was tasting my pouting breasts, sucking and pulling at my engorged nipples until I wanted to cry out with pleasure. And when he moaned softly and asked me to put my hand inside his breeches to assuage the terrible torment he was in, I felt sorry for him, and did as I was told.

'Oh, madame Nicole, I thought I would faint with shock when my unsuspecting fingers brushed against his huge, hot pillar of flesh. It quivered and leaped eagerly at my touch, as if it had some fierce life of its own; and when my Armand unfastened his breeches to reveal this great, purple-headed monster, I nearly swooned away. I'd never seen, never dreamed of such a thing. Of course I'd seen the beasts in the fields, crudely mating; but to see, to feel a man's fine weapon in my fingers brought the blood rushing to my face.'

She gave a happy little laugh, and Nicole smiled softly as she poured Marianne more wine, her own face soft and shadowy in the candlelight. 'Go on, Marianne,' she said huskily, her own excitement rising inexorably.

'Well, Armand groaned aloud when I touched him with my trembling fingers. He seemed in such agony, his hot shaft so engorged, so rampant, that I took pity on him. And besides, by now, my own blood was racing with exquisite need, as if I was in a fever.

'Gently, my sturdy Armand laid me back on the sweet-smelling straw, and lifted up my skirts around my waist. Then he parted my thighs, and bent his head, and started to lick my luscious, glistening folds with his fine long tongue. I thrust towards him, moaning, as he gripped his huge penis in his manly fist. I hardly dared look at it, because I knew it would scare me so, the thought of that lengthy, massive shaft somehow fitting into my tiny, unused woman's place, But he was gentle, my Armand, strong yet gentle. As I felt that wonderful velvety knob stroking between my honeyed lips, pushing very gently to gain entrance to my secret chamber of delight, I quivered and longed for more. He eased himelf into me with infinite care, an inch at a time, stretching me, filling me. And oh, to feel all of that thick, solid shaft caressing my tenderest parts was such heavenly bliss that I lay whimpering and moaning in delirious pleasure.

'But my Armand had hardly begun. Thrusting himself in up to the hilt, he lifted my hips with his hands and rode me like a magnificent stallion, impaling me again and again with his massive penis, lapping eagerly at my breasts, reaching to caress my throbbing bud of pleasure with his calloused thumb, until I toppled over the edge, writhing deliciously beneath his strong body, my inner flesh spasming in ecstasy as he drove himself deep, deep within me and exploded with passion.'

Her eyes were bright, her lips full as she recounted the tale. Nicole felt the need churning in her own loins as she imagined Marianne's horrified wonder on beholding Armand's astounding virility and pictured the lewd, passionate coupling in the haybarn.

'And were you able to see each other often?' she pressed gently in enquiry, as the other girl, her blue eyes rapt, became lost in her dreams.

'Oh, often! We met most nights in the barn, or the stables, or even out under the stars. We planned to marry. But then, things went wrong.

'Jeanette was jealous, you see, because I was no longer interested in her tender little embraces. She followed me, and found out about Armand, and told Madame. And one warm, sultry spring night, when we were in the haybarn pleasuring one another, Madame burst in upon us.'

Marianne swallowed, the memory of that hateful night still obviously painful.

'Madame screamed aloud in horror, as if we were doing something terribly wicked, instead of giving one another the sweetest, most natural love. She had poor Armand dragged away, his big body half-naked, and had him bound in the stableyard, to be humiliated by her husband's minions in their own perverted, obscene way. And oh, Nicole, I was forced to watch!'

She trembled, her eyes bright with tears, and went on, 'They trussed him to the stout wooden fence that bordered the yard, so that he was forced onto his knees, and they ripped off the rest of his clothes, so that his naked buttocks were thrust high to meet their greedy gaze. It was a warm, still night, and the full moon shone brightly, so I could see every detail of his fine bollocks, his thick penis, hanging heavy and helpless between his thighs.

'The men laughed at him, those silk-clad, mincing fops who were the Seigneur's minions. One of them reached out to fondle poor Armand's manhood, laughing nastily, and saying, "By God! I didn't realise our filthy peasants were hung like stallions!" Then, he drew back the tender foreskin, exposing the glistening purple plum, gliding it back and forth relentlessly until my Armand's proud shaft trembled and jerked into life. Poor Armand groaned aloud and shut his eyes, as they all admired him and took it in turns to handle his fine big prick, which by now was throbbing against his taut belly, hot with need.

'Then, Nicole, they rubbed oil on his muscular buttocks, laughing and whispering all the while, and pulled them apart, exposing that dark, secret cleft. And one of them, their leader, pulled out his slender white penis, which was but a boy's, compared to my Armand's, and pumped it to fulness. Then, to the laughing cheers of his companions, he thrust it to the hilt into Armand's tight, secret hole.'

Marianne clenched her fists, her cheeks pale at the memory. 'I wanted to run at him, to pound the animal brute with my fists as he gasped and grunted his way to his perverted pleasure, clutching at my Armand's fine buttocks as he slid his slim prick in and out of that forbidden entrance.

'But then, I realised, to my shock, that Armand was *enjoying* it! His own mighty shaft leaped into even more magnificent life as he felt that slender penis pierce and pleasure his tight bottom-hole. I could see it pulsing angrily, beating against his flat, hairy belly; could see his balls tighten lustily against the base of his shaft, could see how the purple tip wept clear tears of pure desire.

'The other men had seen it too. One of them stood by his shoulders and reached underneath to grip him, squeeze him, luxuriating in the throbbing heat of his great rod of pleasure. The scented young fop who made free with Armand's body was nearly at his extremity now; drawing out his prick almost to its tip, so that I could see its pale, glistening length, he drove it back into that tightly collared hole and writhed in ecstasy, uttering hoarse cries of delight as his release overwhelmed him. My Armand too gave a great groan of agonised rapture as the other man continued to pump his hot penis up and down; I saw his magnificent weapon twitch and leap in its extremity before his semen spurted in milky jets across the soft earth.

'All the spectators cheered and clapped, many of them openly aroused by the spectacle they'd just enjoyed; as I was. Oh, how I wished that my fine Armand had been spending himself within my hungry flesh, ravishing my moist love-channel with his beautiful stout weapon! But it was not to be. Poor Armand was dragged away, still bound, and Madame, whose eyes glittered dangerously at what she had just seen, called me inside and told me that I, too, was to be punished.'

Nicole was frowning. 'Poor Marianne. How did she punish you?'

Marianne bowed her head. 'It was dreadful,' she whispered. 'She took me into her private chamber, which was all dark and oppressive, and and heavy with the scent of the sandalwood perfume she favoured. She told me that unless I did exactly as she said, poor Armand would be beaten. She put me across her knees and spanked my plump bottom with her hard palm, then she forced me to kneel before her, and pushed my head between her parted legs, so I could see the white flesh of her thighs abover her stockings. She made me lick her, Nicole; made me lap and nuzzle at her secret folds, while she gripped my hair and writhed her hips against me until my whole face was rubbing at her hairy mound. I hated it, yet in a way I found it exciting, I suppose, to have her in my power; to hear her moan and whimper as I ran my tongue lasciviously up her juicy cleft and circled her quivering pleasure bud until she cried out in rapture. I could sense that her crisis was close, and licked all the harder, rubbing her with my nose, pushing my little fingers deep into her pulsing wet hole as she gasped and clutched at my breasts, her heavy silks rustling around her waist as she bucked and spasmed to her release, her hot juices smearing my face. I was aroused myself, and felt shafts of excitement as her thin fingers kneaded my thrusting nipples; but I hated her, too, because of what she'd done to Armand.

'Afterwards, she pulled her fine skirts and petticoats down over her still trembling legs as if nothing had happened, though her face was flushed and damp with perspiration. Then she told me that Armand would die if I ever told anyone what had just happened.

'That night, I escaped from the chateau. Armand was waiting for me in the yard; we fled to Paris, and took what jobs we could, until one day Armand met monsieur Jacques, and told him our story. Monsieur Jacques told Armand that he needed two trustworthy servants who despised the *aristos* as much as he did. We have been here ever since.'

Nicole said carefully, not wanting to betray too much interest, 'So that's how you met Jacques. Tell me, Marianne, how on earth did he come to be in possession of such a magnificent house?'

'Why, madame Nicole, it had been declared forfeit, of course! It had been empty for months, I believe, because the owner, a fine marquis, had fled to Austria; and you will remember that in February this year, the property of all *émigrés* was declared to be the property of the nation. So in effect it belongs to nobody. Monsieur Jacques says he is looking after it for the people of France!'

'Generous of him,' frowned Nicole. 'But however did he get hold of the keys? And why had it not been looted and ransacked, like so many of the great houses?'

Marianne's face puckered up as she thought. 'Of course, it is secluded, behind these high walls, in this

93

quiet quarter of Paris. Not many people know it exists. And, though he will not talk about it, citizen Jacques has a wide network of friends in useful places.'

'So I gather,' said Nicole, shivering as she remembered the black-coated, silent men. 'Marianne, who exactly is he?'

Marianne shrugged. 'I don't know. And does it matter? Monsieur Jacques has his secrets, it is true; but all that matters to me is that he gave Armand and me a home when we needed it. Madame d'Argency had tried to ruin us, to separate us for ever; Jacques has ensured that we will always be together. And he too wants his revenge on the *aristos*, for what they did to him, throwing him into that foul prison for a crime he didn't commit. Oh, Nicole, enough of this solemn talk! Stand up and let me see how you look!'

Nicole jumped to her feet, pirouetting round the room in her new finery; Marianne dimpled with pleasure and clapped her hands. 'Madame Nicole, you look truly beautiful, just like one of the great ladies of court. But you need a sash for your waist; I will fetch you one from my room!' And she hurried eagerly on her errand.

Nicole went still suddenly and gazed thoughtfully at herself in a full-length mirror. She looked almost ethereal in the cream silk gown, adorned with tiny seed pearls. The tight-cut bodice cradled her breasts and emphasised her tiny waist. Her face was a perfect oval within its frame of carefully arranged chestnut curls; her lips were full and tremulous, her thick-lashed amber eyes heavy-lidded with forbidden desire. She felt weak when she wondered about her tormentor's plans for tonight.

Jacques, she thought suddenly, her hands cupping her breasts in their tight bodice, trying to ease their aching fulness. Oh, Jacques. You're playing games with all of us. You've captured us all within your dark, hypnotic web.

Then the door opened, sending a draught of fresh air

94

through the overheated room. Nicole turned round smiling, expecting Marianne. But it wasn't Marianne. It was Jacques.

He wore a long, many-caped riding coat that emphasised his formidable yet graceful build. His long hair, drawn back in its usual ribbon, was quite black from the rain; the glistening moisture on his face served only to accentuate his hard, clearly-defined features.

Nicole, her breath caught in her throat at the shock of his arrival, felt the colour rise slowly in her cheeks. She saw how his glance swept round the disordered room, then came to rest on her gown, her hair, her upthrust breasts.

'Well?' she said at last, unable to bear the silence any longer. 'I'm waiting.'

He watched her kindly, leaning with one hand against the door frame. 'Whatever for, *chérie*?'

Nicole lifted her chin. 'For your caustic comment about my transformation.'

He laughed and moved towards her at last, throwing the high-crowned hat he was carrying onto the bed. 'You look superb,' he said. 'Dressed for the guillotine, *ma chère*.'

Nicole snapped hotly, 'Whatever do you mean?'

'Just what I say. You have the appearance of a true aristocrat. Whether your costume will serve for tonight's little entertainment is another question.'

Tonight's entertainment. At his casually uttered words, Nicole's heart began to beat painfully. Just being in the same room as him brought back all the heated memories of last night, when she'd moaned and shuddered in his strong arms to the sweetest, most glorious release she'd ever known. Dazed with suppressed longing, she watched in silence as he eased off his long, heavy coat with perfect grace and draped it over the back of a chair. Then, from deep within its capacious pockets, he drew a small, worn leather box.

'Here, my Nicolette. For you.'

She gazed up at him suspiciously, but his shadowy

face was unreadable. Swiftly she tugged open the lid and gasped, her pretence at composure shattered into pieces.

Diamonds. A truly exquisite diamond necklace, lying like cold, captured moonlight in the black velvet caress of the leather case. It had a beautiful gold clasp, engraved with a tiny rose; dazed, she fingered the perfect gems and gazed up at him with wide, vulnerable eyes, not understanding the meaning of this gift. 'They – they're beautiful, Jacques. Wherever did you get them?'

He shrugged, his face still inscrutable. 'You could say they came with the house.'

So they weren't his to give. She snapped the lid shut, feeling confused and uncertain, taking refuge in her own anger. 'You're just a thief, aren't you, Jacques? A common, despicable thief. Just as bad as any of the looters who roam the streets of Paris, only worse, because you're trying to pretend that you're different!'

For a moment, his face tightened in sudden, bleak anger, and Nicole felt a spasm of fear, remembering his formidable strength. Then he laughed coldly and said, 'If I were truly a thief, I'd have sold them off long ago instead of giving them to you.'

She stammered out, 'By giving them to me, you're just trying to make me your accomplice, aren't you?'

'That's right,' he agreed, his voice quite calm now. 'And what an accomplice! Come along, my little wildcat. We have a guest waiting below for you to interview.' Calmly he took the box from her and lifted out the necklace. With well-practised fingers, he fastened the jewelled clasp with its delicate rose emblem at the nape of her neck; and as his cool fingertips brushed her skin, she felt herself burn with sudden, violent longing.

Fighting it back, she faltered, 'A guest?'

'Of course,' he replied calmly. 'You remember our little arrangement, don't you? Down below is a young nobleman who is only too eager to confess to all his heinous crimes, especially if it means he can get those

96

precious papers that will enable him to leave Paris. It's up to you, my Nicole, to elicit his shameful confession and punish him accordingly.' He stood back, regarding her quizzically. 'Unless you feel that you're not up to the challenge after all?'

She turned on him angrily. 'Of course I am! Isn't that why I'm here? For revenge?'

He gazed down at her, his dark eyes glinting with amusement. 'For pleasure too, *chérie*. Always remember that.' His gaze swept her low *décolletage*; she blushed, longing to feel his cool hands there instead of his impassive gaze, and equally desperate that he shouldn't know of her longing.

'Who is this guest?' she asked lightly.

There was a pause; then he said, 'Better, I think, that you should know as little as possible about him. Marianne will be with you. She will know what to do.'

'And what will *you* be doing during all this?'

He grinned. 'I'll find something to entertain myself. Playing backgammon with Armand, perhaps?'

Nicole hissed in anger, and lunged towards him. But he caught her clenched hands easily and said in a soothing voice, 'Of course I won't actually be visible, Nicole. But I'll be very close at hand at all times, I promise you. Though I expect you, *ma chère*, to stay in charge at all times, you understand? Oh, and one other thing. I meant it when I said you were overdressed. Take off that gown.'

'What?'

'Take it off.' Already, he was rummaging through drawers and cupboards, sifting through the heaps of garments already piled on the floor. Burning with rage, more at his cool indifference than anything else, Nicole unlaced her beautiful gown with trembling fingers and let it slither to the floor in a rich, opulent pile of silk and lace. She stood there in her chemise and stockings, her cheeks warm with shame.

Hardly glancing at her, he turned round, holding out a single black garment. 'Here. This will do.'

Slowly, she took it in her hands. It was an old-fashioned pair of leather stays, of the kind worn by country ladies earlier in the century; boned to give it added stiffness, with eyelets and laces at back and front. On its own, it looked flat and uninteresting; but she suddenly imagined it fastened round her ribcage, thrusting up her breasts, contrasting enticingly with the pale golden flesh of her loins. She felt the secret excitement stirring deep inside her.

But it was his choice, not hers! And somehow the black leather was ominous and threatening, just like that mysterious turret room.

She envisaged rebellion, followed by the inevitable failure, and gave in. She said in a low voice, 'Are you going to leave the room while I change?'

He grinned, folding his arms across the ruffled front of his shirt. 'Frightened I might leap on you? I'm here as a dispassionate observer, *chérie*; helping you to organise a further stage in our revenge, our little masquerade.'

Her amber eyes stormy with rage, she marched into the adjourning dressing room, pulled off her chemise, and laced the stiff leather corset tightly round her ribcage. It was cunningly shaped to push up her high, proud breasts; they spilled enticingly over the restriction of the corset, her rosy nipples already enlarged and hard. The garment came down in a v-shape as far as her navel; her hips, her buttocks and her lower belly were completely exposed. Desperately she pulled her silk stockings higher up her thighs, re-fastening the silk garters; but that did nothing to hide her shame, for the whole of her private parts were revealed, from her plump bottom-cheeks to the tawny triangle of her silken fleece. In sheer defiance, she lifted her hands to pull down her pinned-up hair so that it cascaded in a glorious tawny mass around her shoulders. Then she stormed back into the room to face him. She was uncomfortably aware as she walked that her labia were slick and swollen; they chafed together as she moved, and she tried desperately to fight down the tormenting pulse of need at the very core of her being.

She stood in front of him defiantly, her hands on her hips, the diamonds glinting coldly at her throat. 'There. Is that better?'

He smiled crookedly, leaning with his back against the wall, his arms folded. Nicole thought she glimpsed a telltale bulge where his skintight black breeches skimmed his groin, and felt a vicious stab of triumph.

'It certainly is,' he agreed levelly. He walked slowly across the room to her, his boots echoing softly on the carpeted floor, and her mouth went dry at the cool, arrogant masculinity of him. He reached out his hand and fondled one exposed nipple thoughtfully; it stiffened anew, and seemed to thrust itself against his cool palm. Nicole gave a little gasp and closed her eyes at the sweet spasm of desire that arrowed down to her belly, flooding it with warmth. Then Jacques' hand dropped, and his palm enclosed her hot, pulsing mound of femininity. Casually, his face impassive, he let his long, lean finger slide down her moist, pouting flesh-folds; the heat seared through her, and she trembled visibly, knowing that he could feel all her exquisite need.

'I'm a little worried, though, my Nicole,' he went on softly, still toying with her excruciatingly as he gazed into her eyes, 'that you seem to be almost on the verge already. How can you hope to sit in cool judgement, ordering another person's sexual humiliation, when you seem to be almost at the point of no return yourself?'

She drew herself away from his tormenting hand with a great, shuddering effort. Oh, how she wanted this man. How she wanted him to grasp her in his arms, to ravish her where she stood with his delicious manhood, to thrust into her lascivious flesh again and again until she spasmed in exquisite release.

'*Salaud!*' she hissed. 'You torment me like this, and yet you still expect me to stay cool and calm?'

He shrugged infuriatingly. 'I'm cool and calm. Even though I have such a magnificently wanton *poule* standing just in front of me, displaying herself so enticingly.'

Nicole shook with rage. 'You're inhuman, Jacques; that's the only reason for your indifference! Either that, or – ' and her full mouth curled nastily as she tossed back her tawny hair – 'or could it be that you have somewhat unorthodox tastes?'

'Careful, my Nicole.'

But she was beyond care. Wild with anger and frustration, she pressed on scathingly, 'How, I wonder, did you take your pleasure during those years of captivity in the Toulon *bagne*? Did you acquire a taste for the other convicts, citizen Jacques? Did you perhaps enjoy being impaled by some big, burly *forçat*? I bet you were a favourite with them all, with your fine manners and your elegant figure!'

For a second his eyes narrowed dangerously in cold, bleak rage and she thought, with a spasm of fear, that he was going to hit her. She saw how he fingered the brand on his wrist, as if the hot iron was still hissing against his skin. Then, slowly, deliberately, he went over to the *armoire* beside her bed and drew out a long silken cord; he walked back towards her and she shivered, knowing that her nipples were tautening deliciously, her moist flesh lips pouting obscenely from beneath her moist pubic curls.

'A lesson for you, my little wildcat,' he said quietly. 'A lesson to cool your heated blood, before you go downstairs to take part in our little masquerade.' And, before she could move, before she could even guess what he intended, he gripped both her wrists and pulled them behind her back; then he roped them tightly to the carved mahogany post of the big bed. She struggled and pulled, shivering helplessly with need as the thick wooden column pressed into her shoulder blades and smoothly caressed the dark cleft of her bottom cheeks. The slick moisture glistened anew on her inner thighs, and she moaned her frustration. Oh, but he was fiendish! And she wanted him, so much.

He was holding her, leaning over her, so that her mouth went dry. 'Do you want me, *ma chère*? Do you want to feel my cock sliding up inside your pretty, quivering flesh? Do you want me to ravish you until you sigh with pleasure?'

Something in his male arrogance, his cool assumption of her acute need for him, made her see red. Struggling for self-control, she drew a deep breath and snapped out, 'If you like. Though, believe me, one man is very much like another!'

'Is that so?'

'Oh, yes! Believe me, citizen Jacques,' she said lightly, '*you* have nothing special to offer!'

He smiled at her, almost pleasantly. Then he sauntered slowly over to the door and opened it wide, leaning against it with his arms folded casually across his chest. 'Armand!' he called out.

Nicole froze with shock. What devilish game was this?

She didn't have to wait long to find out. When the burly manservant came into the candlelit room, his eyes lit up at the sight of the helpless Nicole bound to the bed; and when Jacques, still leaning against the door, said casually, 'Take her; she's yours,' he could hardly contain his excitement.

Neither could Nicole. She'd wanted Jacques. She still wanted Jacques, and he knew it, the fiend! But she was in a state of acute need, and when Armand released his own gnarled, already erect penis and advanced towards her with a threatening swagger, she squirmed in helpless delight, her stomach churning with excitement. And Armand knew exactly what she needed, because he gripped her breasts hard, teasing her thrusting nipples between his calloused fingers, and growled, 'So. You need to be punished, do you? Need to be shown how to behave for a man.' She gasped aloud as he gripped his veined, throbbing penis purposefully in his fist, bent his knees to position himself, and thrust it up into her moist, juicy opening, almost lifting her off her feet.

Nicole shuddered with rapture, her eyes softly closed, her mouth parted. It was exquisite, after such long torment, to finally feel that thick, fleshy shaft gliding slickly within her, ravishing her again and again, with no pretence at finesse or politeness; just a man, a hungry, virile man, impaling her magnificently with his iron-hard rod, growling obscenities into her ear before bending his head to rasp roughly at her engorged nipples with his bearded mouth. Then Armand's big hand slid down her belly to finger her soaking clitoris; she writhed on his wonderfully strong penis, thrusting herself as far onto it as she could, and spasmed instantly into wonderful, rapturous orgasm, shuddering and crying out her delight as he drove himself to his own climax deep within her.

For a brief moment he held her tenderly in his arms, kissing the top of her head. Then he detached himself, and re-ordered his clothes, and turned to Jacques for further instruction.

Jacques, who had been watching with inhuman impassivity from the doorway, moved forward at last. 'Thank you, Armand,' was all he said. 'That will be all.'

It was then that she realised the full extent of his frightening self-control, his innate coldness. Was there anyone, anywhere, who could break through that barrier? Or was his heart scarred for life too, just like his body?

Carefully he unfastened the trembling Nicole, who was still flushed from her glorious orgasm. 'You should now,' he said, 'be able to participate in our little spectacle downstairs with at least a certain amount of composure, my Nicolette.' He moved across the room to the heap of clothes that lay by the bed and picked up a silk dressing robe. 'Here, put this on. And remember to stay in charge.'

She felt like hurling obscenities at him, and throwing

102

the clothes and the diamonds in his face, and stalking out into the cold, wet Paris night. If only she could get her own back on him, make him shudder with despairing need; make him grovel at her knees, begging her for sexual release, while she chastised him scornfully.

But she couldn't think of anything to say. As she struggled for words, he was disdainfully nudging the piles of clothes on the floor with his booted foot, and saying, 'I suppose I'd better send Marianne to tidy all this up. Domesticity isn't exactly one of your virtues, is it, my Nicole?'

Then he left the room, leaving her speechless with rage.

Chapter Six

*T*wenty-one year old Jules d'Amar, once heir to one of the richest estates in France and now informed that he was just a citizen of the new Republic like everyone else, paced the small ante-room and shivered with fear. He wished he was strong enough, brave enough to make a dash for freedom from this strange house to which he'd been brought blindfolded. But he was feeling neither strong nor brave, and anyway, the chains that fettered his wrists and ankles would stop him getting far.

The dark, lush opulence of the ante-room they'd left him in oppressed his already low spirits. He hated the heavy red hangings, the great Chinese vases on the inlaid tables, the dark laquer work of the cabinets. There were only a few candles lit, as well, which did little to relieve the gloom; but he was quite glad of the lack of light, because then they might not see how frightened he was. The silent, anonymous men who had brought him here had left him some food and wine, but he was unable to eat because his teeth were chattering so much.

He thought he would never forget last night, that terrible night when the mob came for the prisoners. Numb with fear, he'd been hauled from his damp, dark cell to face the so-called Tribunal, that gang of filthy, rough men who imposed their authority on the prison; some were drunk, some were almost asleep, but all wore the ominous red cap and tricolour. They sat round their winestained wooden table and scarcely glanced at the prisoners who were dragged before them one by one. Some they sent back to their cells; some, for no apparent reason that Jules could discern, they set free. Others were ordered to confess their crimes against the citizens of France, and were then thrown to the mob.

Jules tried to be brave when they questioned him, but when the man who was their leader banged his dirty, blackened pipe on the table and pronounced him guilty, his legs gave way. He felt waves of dizzy nausea sweeping over him as they dragged him outside to meet his death and he heard the Paris mob baying for blood.

Then, suddenly, he felt himself being pulled aside into a dark alleyway by several dark-coated men whom he didn't recognise. He struggled and fought at first, calling for help, and despising himself even more because his voice was so shrill. They gagged him, and tied his arms behind his back; and then the tall, softly-voiced man whom they all called citizen Jacques looked at him and nodded, saying simply, 'Yes. Bring him.'

He'd been bundled into a filthy farm cart, and blind-folded. He expected death any minute. But instead of killing him, they brought him to this vast, empty house, and bathed him, and dressed him in simple but clean clothes.

He still expected death, any minute, and he hoped very much that he'd be brave, because a lot of the people that he'd seen die last night hadn't been. He wished he was strong and powerful and brave, like the tall man that they called Jacques.

He jumped as the wide doors that led through to the salon opened almost silently, and a soft feminine voice said, 'Come in, Jules. We are ready for you now.'

Dazzled by the sudden blaze of candelabra, he stumbled forward blinking, his chains rattling at his ankles;

then he stopped and gaped, because, reclining before him, nestling together on a spacious day-bed, were two of the most beautiful women he had ever seen in his life.

Jules stared openly. One of the women was small and plump, with clouds of curly dark hair framing her sweetly pretty face. But it was the other who took his breath away, because she was simply stunning. Slender and graceful, with glorious tawny hair that cascaded around her shoulders, she reclined on the couch like a sleek wild cat, clad in a cream silk dressing robe that clung to her figure in entrancing folds. And her face, he saw, was exquisite; both haughty and serene, with high cheekbones and a full, pouting mouth; and sultry amber eyes that gazed on him with a silent contempt that turned his limbs to water.

'Kneel,' said the plump dark-haired one warningly. 'Prostrate yourself, citizen Jules, before your betters!'

He wasn't going to argue with them. He stumbled to his knees, clumsy because of his chains, and his blood ran hot and cold as the glorious, tawny-haired goddess stared at him openly, then whispered behind her hand into her friend's ear. Then he heard her say clearly, thoughtfully, 'He has potential, I suppose, Marianne. He has a pleasant enough face, and I like his silky, corn-coloured hair. But he's ever so skinny and pale, and he's so young. He's bound to be terribly inexperienced!' She sighed, cupping her chin in her hands. 'What do you think, *chérie*? Shall we try him out? He might give us some entertainment for an hour or two, I suppose.'

'Five minutes, from the look of him,' giggled the dark-haired one. 'Worth the trouble, do you think, Nicole?'

The tawny-haired one stood up, and as she did so her robe slipped slightly to reveal a stupendous diamond necklace, and a glimpse of cleavage that made Jules feel quite faint. She walked towards him slowly, her silk gown rustling, with the dark-haired one following behind like a shadow; she was bending over him so he could breathe in the delicious, heady perfume of jasmine from her golden skin; she was unfastening his breeches with practised hands, and pulling them open.

She was laughing. 'You're right, he's not worth the trouble. He wouldn't even last five minutes.'

Jules gasped as if she'd hit him. Scrambling to his feet, his breeches slipping round his thighs, he stammered out, 'I'll have you know I'm heir to the baron d'Amar! How dare you insult me thus!' Then the words died in his throat, and he sank helplessly to the ground again, because the tawny-haired beauty had pushed him to his knees with one disdainful hand. As she did so, her robe fell apart, and Jules saw with quite dizzying clarity that beneath it she was wearing a tighly-laced black corset that revealed her glorious breasts, with their rosy, pouting nipples; other than that she wore nothing but a pair of flimsy white silk stockings, gartered at her thighs, and a pair of exquisite little red-heeled shoes. He saw the tawny triangle of curling hair at the apex of her delicious thighs, glimpsed the soft, melting pink flesh beneath, and his mouth went dry.

'I insult you,' hissed Nicole, 'because it's what you, and men like you, have done to women all your lives! You've talked about us, assessed us openly, coarsely, with your boastful friends, just as if we weren't there!' She turned to her friend. 'What shall we do with him, Marianne?'

'Whatever he deserves,' said the other casually. 'Get him to confess his crimes, and then we'll decide.'

'Confess? But – I have already confessed, to the tribunal in that filthy prison! Apart from the accident of my noble birth, I've done nothing wrong, I swear!' Then his voice trailed away as he felt his member growing hot and hard at last, and he blushed in his agony, feeling utterly helpless with his arms and legs in chains.

Marianne had noticed it too, because suddenly she was crouching down beside him, and to his shock she reached out her plump fingers to stroke and toy with his penis. 'It's quite pretty, Nicole, really! See, how it grows to an almost respectable size if I stroke it. Perhaps there is some point to him after all!'

Nicole said thoughtfully, 'He needs to be taught a lesson.' She turned to her friend. 'I suppose, Marianne, that we could educate him by showing him what a *real* man looks like.'

'Armand, you mean?' Marianne got slowly to her feet, her blue eyes sparkling. 'What an excellent idea, *chérie*.' And she ran to the door and called out, 'Armand! You may enter now!'

Jules saw the big bearded man, the one the others called Armand, walking in. 'You wanted me, Marianne?'

'I most certainly do,' breathed Marianne, licking her rosebud mouth with her little pink tongue. And she laid herself on the wide couch, drawing up her robe so that her stockinged thighs were spread invitingly open, her hands behind her head to cushion it as the burly Armand advanced purposefully towards her, already reaching to unbutton his breeches. Jules gave a little moan of despair and bowed his head. The ultimate humiliation. Or was it?

Nicole watched it all with a deep, pulsing excitement. From the moment the blond-haired youth had walked trembling towards them from the ante-room, she had felt the power sing through her blood, had felt the heady aphrodisiac of dominance that men, she reflected, must feel all the time in their dealings with women. This, at least, was some recompense for the way Jacques had humiliated her earlier!

She felt almost sorry for Jules as she draped herself on a low velvet couch just beside his kneeling, chained figure, noting how crushed and despairing he looked as he watched Armand kiss the pretty, wanton Marianne. His slender manhood still stood stiffly to attention, and his breeches were round his thighs; but with

108

his hands shackled behind his back, there was nothing he could do to conceal his degradation.

Nicole, her own blood stirring thickly with excitement, toyed with the idea of letting Jules pleasure her. No, she decided; he would climax within seconds. As Marianne said, he wasn't worth the trouble. Then she thought of something else; a final, exquisite torment for him.

Swiftly she got up and unfastened the chains that bound his wrists with the heavy iron key that Jacques had entrusted her with earlier. Jules gazed up at her pleadingly, like a bereft puppy with his big brown eyes, eyes that were full of worship and open lust. 'Please,' he croaked thickly, 'please release me from my torment! I swear I will do anything you say.'

Thoughtfully Nicole looked down at his slim, silken shaft as it rose from its thicket of soft blond curls at the base of his flat belly. She felt her ripe nipples tingle, was aware of the warm moisture trickling from her secret folds. She frowned and said sternly, 'But your punishment is not complete yet, Jules! You must watch Armand, and see how a real man pleasures his woman, tantalises her, cherishes her, drives her to a frenzy of long, exquisite pleasure. If you can watch all that, Jules, without touching yourself once, then you can do what you want with me!'

He paled with excitement. 'Anything, madame?'

'Anything. But first, you must outlast Armand. And believe me, you will not find that so easy!'

With a little sigh, the youth sat back on his haunches, his brown eyes filled with despair, his hands clenched firmly behind his back of his own accord; though Nicole guessed that he must be feeling the most desperate desire to grip his engorged shaft and jerk it until his seed spurted, thus putting a swift end to his agony. He closed his eyes. Nicole touched him gently with the toe of her red-heeled shoe. 'Oh, no. You must watch, as I will, because watching is part of the bargain, Jules.'

Frowning in despair, the boy gazed across the room

to the settee where Marianne and Armand were ardently embracing. Nicole draped herself comfortably on her own low couch, her legs curled up beneath her silk robe, and gazed likewise; and then she began to wonder if she, too, would last out.

Marianne was ready and ripe to be taken, like some luscious fruit. Her robe was rumpled up round her waist; her breasts, plump and flushed with desire, had crested, and their rosy peaks were moist from the attentions of Armand's strong, seductive tongue. Her legs were flung wide apart; Nicole could see her glistening sex lips beneath the nest of curling brown hair, could see the moist, dark pink flesh that led the way to her honeyed love channel. Armand was on his knees before her, his dark head between her spread thighs, and even as Nicole watched, he bent to cherish her petal-like flesh folds with his strong tongue, while his hands moved swiftly to unfasten his breeches.

He licked her, tasted her, savoured her, running his long, rasping tongue up and down those plumply swollen folds, nibbling at her little pearl of pleasure, until Marianne was thrashing about on her pillows, clutching at his big, muscular shoulders and crying out in her exquisite need. Nicole felt the colour warming her own cheeks, only too aware of a hot lick of desire as she imagined what it would feel like to have Armand's fine tongue sliding slowly, lasciviously up and down her moist cleft then plunging, hot and deep and wicked within her own pulsing love-channel. She clenched her fists tightly, trying to watch the lewd coupling with the kind of cool detachment that she knew Jacques would show. She found it difficult.

It became even harder for her as Armand, lifting himself for a moment from Marianne's writhing hips, released his own proud member and gripped it in his fist, revealing it to be fully engorged and rampant, like some great beast of prey swooping heavily towards its willing captive. Nicole caught her breath at the sight of his penis, remembering only too well the exquisite pleasure it had bestowed on her earlier that evening under Jacques' impassive scrutiny. Marianne, too, was overwhelmed with delight at the sight of it, wrapping her legs eagerly round his strong thighs as Armand, with a grim smile on his bearded face, pressed the swollen tip of his gnarled phallus against her soaking wet sex and slid the great shaft deep, deep within her juicy flesh.

He held himself very still for a moment as Marianne writhed beneath him, gasping out her exquisite rapture at finding him at last so solid within her. Then Armand planted his big, sunbrowned hands on the couch on either side of her, and began to ride her, slowly at first, withdrawing with cool deliberation then plunging deep inside her again, pleasuring those dark, honeyed recesses until Marianne, her head thrown back and her eyes dark with passion, looked ready to swoon with the joy of feeling his hardened flesh move so exquisitely within her.

Nicole too was almost on the brink, and she was only too aware of her dilemma. The sight of Armand's massively heavy penis, its full, glistening length almost fully exposed to her view every time he withdrew from Marianne's soft flesh, was almost more than she could bear.

It was certainly too much for Jules. With a low cry of utter despair, the fair-haired youth gripped his own slender stem in his fingers and began rubbing it fiercely, while he gaped open-mouthed at the couple on the bed. Within moments he gave a frenzied shout as his seed spurted jerkily into the air; his eyes were glazed as his fist continued to pump gently at his penis, desperate to extract every last ounce of pleasure, every last drop of semen.

Then he seemed to sag to the ground, his head in his hands, as he realised that he had failed.

Nicole watched him with burning pity, knowing only too well how he felt. Her own hands strayed to her naked breasts, stroking them and squeezing them,

111

trying to soothe her own anguish and only succeeding in heightening it as the fierce, insatiable pleasure-darts arrowed from her nipples to her loins. As Marianne and Armand exploded in a noisy convulsion of mutual delight, Nicole's fingers brushed the cold, hard diamonds at her throat; she thought of Jacques, and her own sexual need licked through her belly like a white-hot flame.

Quite unable to bear her own agonised frustration any longer, she reached across to the bowed, despairing youth and touched him on the shoulder. 'Jules,' she whispered.

He lifted his head towards her. 'I have failed,' he said miserably. 'Oh, madame, I have failed.'

'No, you haven't. Jules, did you see how Armand pleasured Marianne earlier, with his tongue, and his fingers, and his mouth? Well, I want you to do the same to me.'

His brown eyes lit up for a moment, but then his face sagged with despair again. 'I do not know how. I have no wish to fail you again.'

'You will not fail!' said Nicole urgently. 'I will tell you exactly what to do. Oh, quickly, Jules! I need you.'

As the boy lurched hungrily towards her, she leaned back on the couch, drawing up her knees and parting her stockinged legs lasciviously, and began to stroke herself in her urgent need, whispering low instructions. 'Put your head between my thighs, Jules. You see, don't you, how my flesh is swollen and moist, and longs for a man's fine touch! Oh, use your sweet tongue on me, Jules; taste me as if I were a fine wine, lick me, savour me, lap at my flowing juices, ah, yes . . .'

With a cry of muffled delight, Jules had buried his face at the apex of her thighs, breathing in the heady scent of her like a drowning man breathing air, using his tongue with tentative adoration at first but gradually increasing the vigorous pressure as Nicole encouraged him. Gripping her own knees, holding them wide apart to lay herself open to him, she writhed against his mouth in aching delight; as he found her throbbing pleasure bud, she groaned aloud her rapture and muttered, 'Yes, Jules, yes, just there. Your tongue is so fine, so hot and wet and firm. How I love to feel it, stroking me, kissing me.'

Rapturously, Jules grew in confidence, and when he first dared to thrust his tongue deep inside her yearning love channel, he burned with delight as he felt her arch beneath him and cry out his name. Emboldened, he stiffened his tongue and thrust it out as far as he could, stimulating the action of a penis as he rasped against her soft, melting flesh. With tiny sobs of pleasure, Nicole clutched gratefully at the hard, warm flesh of his juicy tongue and shuddered into a sweet, melting climax. He stayed deep within her, his tongue instinctively making little fluttering motions until her last spasm died away and she sank into sated languor. Then he drew away from her, his face sombre and serious.

'Thank you,' he said in a low voice. 'I don't mind now about going back to that prison. Now that I've known you, madame, I feel as if I can face anything.'

Nicole stretched like a cat and drew herself up, wrapping her silk robe around her voluptuous nakedness. She reached out to stroke his downy cheek. 'Jules,' she said huskily, 'you're not going anywhere for the moment. I think, my sweet little aristocrat, that you show considerable promise.'

Suddenly, the doors to the ante-room opened wide, and the startled Nicole looked up to see Jacques standing there, a silent, brooding presence. She felt herself grow hot and hostile and somehow vulnerable. Had he been watching? Did he know what had just happened?

'Nicole,' he said. 'If you can spare the time, I would like you to join me for supper in the *petit salon* in one hour's time.'

Nicole stared haughtily back at him, her amber eyes alight with defiance. 'Certainly, Jacques. It will be my pleasure.'

His eyebrows lifted slightly. 'Oh, no. The pleasure will be all mine.'

Nicole pretended to be calm and collected as she prepared herself for supper with Jacques, but her stomach was filled with nervous butterflies as she thought of being alone with him once more. She bathed herself again, noting with wry amusement that Armand had enlisted the willing Jules to help him carry the hot water upstairs; and then, in determined defiance, she dressed herself in the exquisite gown of heavy cream silk that Jacques had criticised earlier. In the same mood of defiance she decided not to wear the necklace, but placed it carefully in its velvet box on her dressing table.

Finally, she brushed her long, thick hair until it gleamed like burnished copper, then coiled the topmost tresses on the crown of her head, and let the rest of it fall in gleaming tendrils round her neck and shoulders. At last, her heart beating strangely at the thought of the approaching encounter, she glided softly down the great staircase towards the *petit salon*, enjoying the cool rustle of lace and silk. She'd done well tonight, hadn't she? She felt ready for anything, even Jacques.

When she entered the room, he had his back to her as he lit the big wax candles on the onyx fireplace, so she had a few moments in which to absorb the details of the scene. It was a beautiful room, a miniature replica of the grand salon, and she found herself struck anew by the quiet, restrained elegance of the pale silk hangings, by the exquisite delicacy of the rosewood furniture, the perfect proportions of the high, corniced ceiling.

A log fire burned in the grate, casting warm shadows, and in one corner of the room there was a small, candlelit alcove with a low settee covered in dark red velvet. The mahogany table in the centre of the room was laid already, the white damask cloth almost invisible beneath silver and crystal. Plates of delicious cold food tempted her eyes and nostrils, and she gazed longingly at the fine pates and cheeses, the dishes of golden Normandy butter, the fresh crisp baguettes and bowls of plump purple grapes. How did this man do it? Where did he get the ingredients for such a miraculous repast, in a Paris brought virtually to the edge of starvation by war and deprivation?

Then Jacques swung round to face her, and all other topics of thought were driven from the tumult of her mind.

He was wearing a dark grey coat, simply but superbly cut, and the immaculate ruffles of his cravat, edged with priceless Mechlin lace, emphasised to perfection his lean, smoothly-shaven features. His dark hair, gleaming softly in the candlelight, was drawn back in a narrow black ribbon; he wore tight-fitting breeches and black leather riding boots, and he looked, she realised with a little lurch to her stomach, absolutely exquisite. She felt her heart thud faster, felt the colour rise in her cheeks as he in turn assessed her, his thin mouth curling a little as he took in the plunging *décolletage* of her extravagant court gown.

'Nicole.' He inclined his head. 'You play the role of a fine lady quite exquisitely, *ma chère*.'

Nicole smiled sweetly up at his tall figure. 'And you, monsieur, affect the manners of a nobleman with some considerable success. For a convict, that is!' she flashed back.

He smiled in amused acknowledgement. 'You are too kind, *chérie*. You will be seated?'

As he drew back her chair for her, and poured her a glass of deliciously crisp white wine that fizzed slightly on her tongue, Nicole felt her confidence burgeoning. She knew that tonight she looked truly beautiful; his eyes told her so. She'd conducted her first interview with panache and sensuality, making a virtual slave of the young aristocrat Jules d'Amar, and she ate and drank with a good appetite.

Jacques ate rather less. She should have noticed that, and been prepared.

115

'So,' he said at last, his voice deceptively light and casual, 'You think that this boy Jules shows promise, do you?'

Nicole bit into a luscious grape and began to spread more creamy cheese onto a fresh slice of fragrant white bread. 'Oh, indeed,' she replied airily. 'He was truly repentant. In fact, Marianne and I quickly persuaded him to confess his past sins quite easily, and then we humbled him completely by making him watch Armand with Marianne. By the end, Jacques, he was totally reformed. I swear to you, we could have done whatever we wanted with him!'

Jacques nodded, toying thoughtfully with his still full glass, the candlelight glinting on the small gold signet ring on his left hand. 'So it would seem,' he said.

Nicole watched him surreptitiously. How he suited this room, this whole house, she thought suddenly. He might have been brought up to inhabit a palatial mansion such as this. No-one would guess that he was just a bourgeois provincial, with a decidedly shady past.

The soft candlelight gleamed tantalisingly on his taut, enigmatic face as he gazed at the fine crystal of his glass, and Nicole realised, with a sudden wrench at her heart, that she wanted him desperately. Jules' attentions had been sweet, but no more than an appetiser. It was this man that she needed to assuage her aching emptiness with his dark, mysterious core; this man who had somehow become, for her, the very epitome of masculinity, the expression of all her secret, unexpressed dreams. She needed the hard, sweet pleasure of his penis deep inside her; she felt her secret flesh grow moist and swollen at the thought, felt the delicious wine singing in her veins.

'So you considered that it went well tonight, did you?' he said. 'With Jules?'

She glanced at him, surprised. 'Yes. Didn't I say so?'

He leaned forward, his expression ominously cold. 'You seem to have forgotten one rather important thing,

116

Nicole. Did I, or did I not give you orders to stay completely in charge, at all times?'

Startled, she gasped out, 'But I did stay in charge! They all did exactly as I told them; Marianne, Jules, even Armand!' She clenched her fists, aware that her small hands were trembling, that her whole body was shaking with the burning disappointment at his disapproval. 'What's the matter, Jacques? Are you jealous because you didn't get the chance to take part and show off as usual?'

Jacques, ignoring her jibe, said with quiet scorn, 'Let's get one thing straight, Nicole. All right, they all did exactly as you said. But you rather seemed to forget one crucial fact. You weren't supposed to take part in any of it yourself. But you couldn't resist, could you? Couldn't resist indulging in your own utterly wanton pleasure!'

Nicole went white as his tongue lashed her. So he knew it all. Had he listened? Had he even watched, as she had squirmed so deliciously beneath the boy's eager, thrusting tongue? Fighting back her desperate tears of humiliation, she said in a low voice, 'So what were you doing, then? Spying on us all? Did you enjoy it? Did you fondle yourself, I wonder, as you watched, and bring yourself to a solitary, voyeuristic little climax as you gazed at us all? Is that your idea of enjoyment? My God, what a sordid little provincial you are!'

He said, 'I've told you before, *ma chère*. I'm the proud possessor of something you'll be a long time learning. It's called self-control.'

With a violent hiss, Nicole leaped to her feet, shoving back her delicate rosewood chair so that it fell with a crash to the ground, then in the same second she picked up her full wineglass and hurled the contents in her tormentor's face.

There was a moment's horrifying silence as the pale gold liquid dripped relentlessly down his frozen features and pooled in the creamy ruffles of his immaculate cravat. Without a word, Jacques picked up his linen napkin from the table and wiped his face dry. Still in silence, he stood up, took off his splashed coat, picked up the bottle of wine and walked slowly round the table to trickle it slowly and deliberately down the tempting *décolletage* of her beautiful gown.

'My Nicole,' he said thoughtfully as he poured. 'Undoubtedly a rose, complete with thorns.'

Nicole gasped aloud in shock as the cold liquid caressed her breasts. Her nipples tugged and stiffened, as if it were the man himself who moistened them with his sensual mouth. Unable to utter a word, she gazed, anguished, up into his lean dark face.

And then, she saw his eyes gleam and saw how his mouth twisted at one corner. Damn him, but he was laughing at her again! And what was all that nonsense about a rose complete with thorns? *'Imbécile!'* she spat at him. 'You have the manners and breeding of a pig!'

His thin, sensual mouth widened still further. 'I certainly,' he agreed lazily, 'have some novel ways of savouring fine wine, Nicole.' And, even as his dark gaze held her captive, he reached to tear her soaking bodice apart with slow, deliberate fingers and bent his head to lick the spilled wine from her breasts.

Nicole closed her eyes in despair, dizzy with the onslaught of rapture as his hands supported her full breasts and his mouth fastened onto her nipples. Oh, but he was exquisite. His strong tongue laved her aching, stiffened crests; his white teeth pulled and nibbled gently, extending the rosy teats with delicious skill until the hot shafts of sensation arrowed down to her belly, setting her blood on fire with wanting him. His hot, wet mouth was drawing the very soul from her; anguished, she thrust her aching breasts helplessly against his lips, longing for release.

Without a word, he lifted her up in his strong arms and carried her over to the velvet settee in the alcove, where he laid her down with exquisite gentleness and continued his ministrations, covering her throat, her shoulders, her breasts with light, tantalising kisses until

118

she heard low moaning sounds and realised that they were her own.

She wanted him; it was no use trying to deny it. She wanted more than anything in this world to feel his hard, magnificent body naked against her own, to take his beautiful manhood deep within her, to enfold it with her own silken flesh and feel it assuaging that terrible, yearning ache at her very centre. She shuddered helplessly in his arms at the very thought, her loins convulsing with need.

But then what?

Afterwards, Jacques would mock her, laugh at her, even as the waves of tremulous pleasure were still rippling through her body. He would tease her about her lack of self-control, her impetuous wantonness, her greed for libidinous pleasure. She felt a sudden surge of stubborn rebellion.

She sat up suddenly, her hand to her throat. 'My throat is so dry; I really must have some wine! Please Jacques, would you fetch some for me?'

He watched her questioningly, his eyebrows arched in surmise. Then he stood up from the couch and walked across to the table, returning with a full glass, which he offered her warily. 'Not in my face, I hope.'

'Oh, no.' She smiled up at him, very sweetly. 'Not in your face, Jacques.' Then she tipped the glass very carefully down the front of his breeches.

'Morbleu!' His face dark with astonishment, he leaped back and began instinctively to unfasten his buttons, struggling to relieve himself of the sodden, tight fabric that clung to his loins. 'Thank God,' he was muttering fervently, 'that there's no wine left. Nicole, I know you think me a profligate extravagant, and that I have endless supplies of such luxuries, but those bottles cost me ten livres apiece!'

'Well worth it, don't you think, considering the entertainment that it's given us?' commented Nicole with sweet acidity, resting her chin on her hands as she leaned forward to watch him. He grunted something

119

indiscernible in reply, engrossed in peeling his breeches from his hips. Nicole caught a sudden glimpse of the taut, vulnerable flesh of his flat belly, and saw the dark silky line of hair that arrowed down to his loins, and her throat went dry. Now was the moment. Standing up casually, she took a deep breath and pushed him, hard, so that he overbalanced and fell back onto the couch, landing sprawled among the cushions.

'Now, my fine citizen Jacques,' she murmured with relish, 'we shall see just how much you really know about self-control.'

Realising her intentions a moment too late, Jacques struggled to sit up, but she was already upon him, kneeling astride him to prevent his escape, and then she was lowering herself onto him so that her still-exposed breasts were stroking his groin, and she realised with a thrilling spasm of delight that he didn't actually want to escape any more.

She eased his damp breeches down around his iron-hard thighs and saw that his penis, already engorged with blood, lay thick and heavy against his belly. Shivering with delight, she reached down to cup the heavy, velvety sac of his testicles in her trembling palm, and bent her head to kiss him, lightly trailing her lips along the beautiful length of his manhood. It quivered at her touch, growing perceptibly, and as he groaned aloud she said softly, 'Now, Jacques. Self-control, remember?'

And, sticking out her small pink tongue, she softly licked him in tiny, exquisite caresses until his penis jerked hungrily towards her, magnificently erect, the moist, empurpled glans thrusting proudly into the air.

With a deep sigh of satisfaction, Nicole formed a perfect 'O' with her mouth and slid her lips over the velvety tip, her pointed tongue darting and licking as she did so, running round the rim and diving into the tiny slit which was already salty and moist. He tasted exquisitely hot and potent, a mixture of male musk and wine, the very essence of masculinity. Reaching down, she felt his balls jerk and tighten helplessly, and as she softly caressed them, taking each vulnerable globe into her fingers in turn, she felt his massive shaft grown even thicker in the dark recesses of her soft mouth. She could hear his breathing become harsh and ragged as he fought for control, and was conscious of a sudden devastating feeling of mastery as she realised that at long last she had this man in her power.

Slowly, lingering over every inch of the deliciously hardened pillar of flesh, she withdrew her mouth, though she found it much more difficult to withdraw her eyes from his magnificent phallus as it jerked so hungrily towards her, its single eye already weeping with lust.

'Perhaps,' she said sadly, 'I ought to leave you now, Jacques. And then you can demonstrate to me that wonderful self-control of which I've heard so much.'

His face was hard and tight in the shadows, his breathing still irregular as she crouched over him, pinning him down; but somehow he managed an infuriating smile. 'Feel free to go, Nicole. I'll survive.'

Damn him, thought Nicole furiously, watching him as he put his hands behind his back and leaned back on the cushions, closing his eyes in feigned indifference. She would break him, she would make him plead with her, if it was the very last thing she did!

Her amber eyes flashing in challenge, she bent quickly over his groin and her lips enfolded him again, her tongue licking, caressing, sliding down as much of that lengthy shaft as she could manage, until at last, with a secret thrill of pleasure, she felt his strong, lithe body tauten and arch beneath her. Quickly she slid her mouth away again, letting her tongue-tip swirl languorously round the swollen glans before saying, 'Shall I stop now?'

This time, his eyes were almost black, and his voice was less sure, less steady. But he still managed to say, with maddening nonchalance, 'If you like.'

With a hiss, Nicole plunged to take his hot penis once more in her mouth, swallowing as much as she could of its sturdy, silky length until she could feel him throbbing hard against the very back of her throat, while with her hand she cupped and teased his heavy balls, squeezing them gently and registering with inner delight that they were already tightening helplessly and drawing up against his groin in the inevitable preliminary to orgasm.

She lifted her head away, her eyes bright, her cheeks flushed. 'Do you want me to stop?'

He clenched his teeth this time. She could see the beads of perspiration standing out on his wide forehead, could see the lines of strain that ran from his flared nostrils to the corners of his mouth. But still he managed to grate out, 'If you can't cope with me, then stop by all means. I warn you, I'll be a long time yet, *chérie.*'

'You think so?' She licked her finger very slowly and deliberately, flickering her tongue over its tip, sliding her lips up and down its length in a lascivious gesture that forced him to close his eyes. With grim satisfaction, Nicole let her hand slide under the heavy, hair-roughened pouch of his testicles and along the tight cleft of his bottom-cheeks towards that dark, secret hole, which she realised was already quivering with yearning. Shaking with excitement herself, she stroked the puckered outer rim with one delicate fingertip, then thrust her saliva-moist forefinger deep into the hot, tight darkness, wickedly pushing past his instinctive resistance, sliding it in and out lasciviously until she heard him groan aloud. Trembling with excitement herself, her own secret flesh wet and pulsing, she saw how his huge penis jerked hungrily at this new onslaught, a tear of moisture weeping from the swollen tip. Nicole leaned forward impulsively and let her own breasts brush yearningly against the darkly swollen plum, rubbing her stiffened nipples to and fro against it in a rapturous sensation that almost brought her to her own peak of pleasure, while Jacques, lying contorted on the couch beneath her, gasped aloud at the sweet caress.

'Still in control, Jacques?' she murmured silkily, her finger once more thrusting deep into his quivering anus. 'Still going to be a long time?'

It was then that he shuddered and broke. Grating out her name, he reached up to grasp at her thick hair and pulled her face down hard against his throbbing, tormented phallus. Eagerly Nicole took him deep in her throat, sucking and licking and bestowing all the pleasure she could think of as his strong body arched helplessly beneath her; and then she heard his cry of despair and felt him thrust hard, hard within her, pumping his great penis avidly into the luscious, velvety softness of her moist mouth, so that his seed jetted into her throat in hot, salty bursts of such force that they racked his entire body.

At last he lay back sated, his eyes closed. Wordlessly he pulled the exhausted Nicole down beside him, so that her cheek was on his shoulder; she gazed silently at his face, drinking in every detail of his exquisite, pleasure-softened features.

She realised suddenly that even though she'd won this one battle, Jacques still had too much power over her. And it was the power to destroy her utterly, because she was falling helplessly in love with him.

The thought stunned her. She lay very still until at last he stirred, and moved his mouth against her hair, murmuring, 'Magnificent, my Nicole.'

The words of cool appraisal hurt her desperately. It's just a game, she reminded herself blindly. Jacques had told her, right at the beginning, that it was a game of revenge, because revenge was the only thing in life that mattered to him. And when the game was played out, the occupants of this ghostly mansion would all go their separate ways.

Suddenly Nicole felt hot tears stinging at the back of

her eyes. She scrambled quickly off the couch, pulling her torn gown together, and headed for the door.

Jacques called out to her, surprised. 'Nicole! You needn't go yet!'

She stopped and turned at the door. 'Whatever makes you think I want to stay?' she said quietly. And, head held high, she stormed from the room, her eyes burning with unshed tears.

She was on fire, burning for him. She wanted nothing more than to run back into the room, and throw herself into his arms, and beg him, plead with him to make passionate, exquisite love to her all night long.

But she couldn't go back. She couldn't ever tell him how she felt, because then she'd be in his power, and that power would destroy her.

Rubbing angrily at her stinging eyes, utterly despising herself for her weakness, she walked blindly across the vast, echoing hallway, until she felt a sudden, sweet draught of fresh air on her hot cheeks and realised that the main doors were ajar. Without hesitation, she headed towards them and glided down the broad sweep of stone steps onto the terrace outside.

The moonlit September night seemed to hold its breath; the air was fragrant and velvety soft. For a moment, the sweet scents from the riotously overgrown gardens all but overpowered Nicole, and she stood very still, holding onto the stone balustrade to steady herself as her eyes adjusted to the shadowy darkness, drinking it all in.

Every flower, every leaf, every blade of grass was outlined softly by the silvery moonlight. A nightingale sang from the gnarled branch of an old mulberry tree, its haunting, liquid notes falling like wine in the still night air. The dreadful reality of the bloodstained streets of Paris could have been a thousand miles away. As she remembered everything that had happened to her in these last few days, Nicole felt her heart suddenly wrenched by loneliness. Who was Jacques? And why, oh why had she let him cast his dark spell over her, when she'd sworn never again to be at the mercy of any man?

Taking a deep, unsteady breath, she turned her gaze from the garden to look up at the blind, shuttered facade of the great mansion that Jacques had made his own. It was magnificent, imposing enough for the greatest of French nobles. Her eyes were drawn to the great stone lintel that ran the length of the studded oak doors; at its centre was some sort of crest, worn and faded with age. She narrowed her eyes, staring up at it, trying to make it out in the darkness, because suddenly it seemed important. Gradually she made it out, realising that it was a carving of a rose, stylised and symmetrical with its five petals, each indented at the outer edge like the wild roses that grew so rampantly in the fields and hedgerows of her native Normandy. Nicole frowned. Hadn't she seen the rose emblem somewhere before, only recently?

Shaking her head slowly, unable to place it, she endeavoured to read the curling inscription carved below it.

'Saint Maury. Sans épines.'

Saint Maury. Without thorns. A rose without thorns. What had Jacques said to her, only this evening? He'd told her that she, Nicole, was a rose, but he'd pointed out that she very definitely had thorns. So Jacques, too, was aware of the motto of the family that used to live here, the aristocratic family of St Maury; again, the name struck a vague chord in Nicole's mind, but she was unable to recollect anything definite. The members of the St Maury family, with their strange taste for dark, forbidden pleasures, must have fled Paris or been killed by the mob a long time since, perhaps even at the start of these three dreadful years of turmoil, when the Bastille was stormed and it suddenly became apparent to the arrogant rulers of France that the country and its people were on the verge of irredeemable, violent chaos.

125

Nicole, reluctant to go in yet, wandered slowly on round the rambling house, her feet echoing softly on the gravel paths, until she could no longer hear the nightingale's liquid song. She came across an overgrown rose-garden where the air was sweet with scent; there was a lichened sundial at its centre, and a little summerhouse, covered enticingly with a profusion of luscious pink ramblers that glimmered palely in the moonlight. A place for lovers.

Suddenly feeling unbearably lonely, Nicole turned abruptly to go back into the house and swiftly climbed up the silent stairs to her room.

There, the candle was still lit, though it burned low in its holder. And, lying on her bed, was a long-stemmed red rose, with a scrawled note beside it.

'Roses with thorns have by far the sweeter scent. J.'

She clutched the note in her hand, transfixed. An apology! Or at least as near to an apology as she would ever get from him. He must have come up here to find her, and if she'd been here, who knew what might have happened? Her pulse was racing unevenly, and she was filled with an overwhelming desire to find him, to speak to him.

She raced downstairs towards the salon where they'd dined. A glow of candlelight emanated from behind the half-closed doors; he was still there, waiting for her! She burst into the room, her eyes soft with need, and saw Marianne clearing away the remains of their supper.

'Jacques?' Nicole stammered out. 'Where is Jacques?'

Marianne said quickly, 'Oh, madame Nicole, he's gone. One of his men came with a message, and he had to leave immediately.'

Nicole, sick with disappointment, leaned against the door. 'But he'll be back later?'

'No, madame Nicole. He said he might be away for a few days. He said to tell you that –'

But Nicole didn't hear any more, because she'd run from the room, back up the wide stairs to the sanctuary of her own bedchamber. The rose still lay there, on her bed; she scrunched it up in her hands until the thorns pierced her skin and the blood stood out in bright red drops. Then she threw it to the floor.

Chapter Seven

*L*ouise de Lamartine paced to and fro in the small, dank cell. She knew that she hadn't got much time now. Last night, before she was thrown into solitary confinement for deliberately being insolent to one of the guards, she'd felt the rippling tide of panic spread through every bleak cell and corridor of the prison as the news spread that the mob had pulled forty prostitutes from the prison of La Saltpetrière and slaughtered them openly on the streets. After that, the dark stone walls of St Lazare stank with fear.

But Louise tossed back her loose fair hair, and tilted her chin proudly, because she wasn't finished yet, not by a long way. Her clothes were torn and shabby, but she still had the power to make men weak, and she would use that power to get what she wanted, to get out of here and find the one man who could save her.

Louise shivered deliciously. Even in this foul, frightening place, her body still had its needs. Every night she fantasised about the man they called citizen Jacques. Was he really the man she was looking for? How astonishing, how wonderful if he was. She closed her eyes and imagined him sweeping through the barred doors of St Lazare, and carrying her off in his strong arms to make wild, dangerous love to her out on the dark streets of Paris. It was a long time since she'd had a man – too long. Her breasts tingled with need at the thought.

The doors opened, and two guards came in, one of them carrying a tallow candle. 'Time's up, citizeness.' He jerked his thumb towards the door. 'They want you. Out there.'

They. The prison tribunal, the rough, drunken scum who pronounced life or death on prisoners like her. Fear lapped at her mind like a grey wave, but she pushed it away resolutely and felt the seeds of her idea growing.

She drew herself up to her full height, which wasn't great, and looked at the two guards with openly scornful eyes. They were both young, both sturdily built, and good-looking, in spite of their stubbled faces and those hideous red caps that they all wore nowadays. They looked a little more intelligent, a little less half-starved than most of the mean prison guards. And as they looked at her, didn't their eyes gleam with interest, an interest they couldn't quite hide?

Louise shook her head defiantly, so that her long, silvery hair shimmered in the light of the tallow candle, and let her sultry violet eyes smoulder derisively. 'You lay a finger on me, you vermin,' she said, very slowly and deliberately, 'and I'll have you horse-whipped.'

They laughed at that, as she knew they would, but one of them also went to shut the cell door firmly, and drew the rusty bolt across. Just what she wanted. She tried to conceal her delight as the first guard swaggered towards her, rubbing his hands together.

'Well, well. Seems like we've got ourselves an arrogant little *aristo* here tonight, eh, Jean-Paul? Know what's happening to your sort out there on the streets, citizeness?'

Louise gazed up at him defiantly, even though her heart was thudding in fear. His rough homespun shirt was open to his navel; she could see the pelt of hair that covered the muscular curve of his chest, could see the faint sheen of perspiration on his forehead, and her mind raced. He was an animal, a coarse peasant animal, but a fine specimen none the less, with strong, aggressive thighs and a telltale bulge at his groin.

Knowing the risk she was taking, she said, coldly and deliberately, 'I know that people of your kind are the scum of the streets, and that you should all be destroyed like the vermin you are.'

It worked. The one called Jean-Pierre snorted in sudden anger and lurched towards her, grunting, '*Morbleu!* You heard her, Pierre? You dare to speak to us like that? My fine citizeness, I think you need teaching a lesson!'

Taking careful aim, Louise spat at him, her spittle catching him full in the face. They both grabbed at her, caught her and flung her down in the dirty straw; she lay there shivering with excitement, her breathing heavy and ragged, her eyes smoky with desire. 'Do what you want with me, then,' she whispered, 'vile brutes! I don't believe that either of you are man enough for me!'

The one called Pierre hissed between his teeth and began to slowly unbuckle his belt. 'Hold her, Jean-Paul. Hold her down, the proud little slut. I'll show her what a real man is made of.' And slowly, his stubbled face dark with concentration, he unfastened his trousers and drew out the proud, angry stem of his swollen-tipped phallus, rubbing the hot flesh lovingly in his fist as he stared down at her.

Louise shivered in delight. The man who crouched at her side, Jean-Paul, mistook her movements for fear and hissed softly in her ear, 'There, my proud beauty. Never seen a cock like that before, I'll warrant, never felt anything like that in your sweet, juicy little body. See what you've let yourself in for, eh?'

Louise did indeed. She watched with avid eyes as the man Pierre advanced on her. With grim concentration he thrust up her shabby skirts, gazing with hot eyes at her pale, slender legs, at the pale gold triangle of delicate hair at the top of her legs; and Louise felt her own excitement churn remorselessly under his lascivious gaze, felt her pleasure bud begin to quiver, her inner muscles twitching hungrily at the thought of that great purple shaft sliding relentlessly up inside her.

'Scum,' she said huskily, moistening her lips. 'Vile scum.'

With a low growl, Pierre flung himself to the ground between her legs, his heavy penis throbbing hungrily, and grasped her slim thighs, hauling them up round his waist and gripping them hard while he thrust blindly with his huge, prodding weapon. At the same time Jean-Paul, still crouching by her shoulders, kissed her mouth hotly, thrusting his tongue deep within her; she responded passionately, trembling at the delicious touch of his stubble-coarsened chin against her soft skin. Breathing hard, Jean-Paul reached to release her full breasts from within the confines of her bodice and squeezed them lovingly, rolling the stiffened nipples between his calloused fingers until Louise gave a soft cry of longing and clasped her legs more tightly around Pierre's sturdy thighs.

'A fine little *aristo!*' grunted Pierre. 'See, *mon ami,* how she longs for us!'

'I do,' breathed Louise. 'Please, monsieur, I beg you; let me feel your fine prick, all of it, deep inside me.'

He didn't disappoint her. Already, his heavy animal thrusts had found their target, and his engorged penis was sliding hungrily, lasciviously inside her juicy passage. Louise's inner muscles clutched eagerly at the hot, delicious male flesh as it jerked deep within her, moaning aloud her delight as the other man licked at her naked breasts, flicking at her taut nipples with his rough tongue until her hips writhed in exquisite delight.

Jean-Paul growled, 'Keep up the good work, *mon ami.* I do believe the fine lady's enjoying it. Must be a long time since she's had a real man.'

Nodding his agreement, panting in sheer lust, Pierre was trying as hard as he could to control himself, but it was difficult, with this tantalising, juicy little *aristo* moaning so rapturously beneath him. Slowly, he pulled his lengthy shaft out of her hot cavern, and slid it back in, feeling her glistening flesh engulf him entirely; she quivered with delight, and he did it again, and again, seeing how her incredible violet eyes were glazed over with delight as she breathed, 'Oh, yes, my fine, handsome lover – drive it into me again – oh, yes . . .'

And at last, she spasmed beneath the two big men, savouring every lewd caress they could offer her, clutching with her pulsing vagina at that wonderful, sturdy penis as it drove so deeply within her and the warm waves of orgasm washed through her yearning flesh. With a harsh cry of triumph Pierre jerked quickly to his own release within her, while Jean-Paul continued to suck her breasts tenderly, enjoying her soft little cries of pleasure as his own aroused phallus pressed urgently against the belt of his trousers.

Louise opened her eyes lazily, and they glittered with sated lust. 'Well, my good citizens,' she purred, 'doesn't your fine tribunal await you?'

'Like hell it does,' grated Jean-Paul, and pulled her round roughly to kiss her once more. 'My turn next, my fine lady. I want you to suck my cock.'

Louise pulled away from him jerkily, and the tears glittered suddenly in her beautiful eyes. 'Oh, monsieur,' she faltered. 'How I would love to give you such pleasure. But I fear I have not the strength, monsieur. The thought of what awaits me outside fills me with such trepidation that I can hardly breathe, for once the tribunal has finished with me, I face certain death from the Paris mob.'

Jean-Paul and Pierre looked at one another, frowning darkly. 'Damn that,' said Pierre emphatically. 'We'll not let a lovely wench like you get into their filthy hands, will we, Jean-Paul? I promise you, my pretty, that we'll get you safely out of here!'

'Out of the prison?' Louise tried hard not to sound too desperate.

'If it weren't for the fact that you need special papers, we'd get you out of Paris itself! But we'll get you out of here, don't worry. And in the meantime,' said Jean-Paul gruffly, crouching at her side and fumbling with his trousers, 'I've got something here for you.' His penis was already rampantly erect as it stood out from his thick bush of black hair, not as long as Pierre's, but still thick and strong. 'See to this fine beast,' he declared, 'and Pierre and I will keep to our side of the bargain.'

Louise glanced at his empurpled, quivering phallus as it jutted up from his groin and moistened her lips.

'With pleasure, monsieur,' she said meekly, though inwardly she was crowing with triumph. Her plan was working. Happily she leaned forward to take the stubby, engorged stem between her lips, working her mouth up and down and sucking hard, while tenderly squeezing his heavy, hairy balls with her soft white hands. Her tongue circled and drew on the glans, licking away the salty moisture that wept from its swollen tip, and she heard him groan his pleasure. They were so refreshingly basic, so uncomplicated, so male, these common men. How she enjoyed bestowing pleasure, especially when her own needs had been so exquisitely sated. For the moment, anyway.

Louise de Lamartine knew herself to be a sensual animal, with stronger, more voracious appetites than most women. She enjoyed variety, and found herself deliciously aroused by this dark, sinister cell, by these two roughly-clothed, unknown men who pleasured her so vigorously. So much better than the feeble, effete ways of so many of the nobility, who treated women like Louise as if she were made of fine porcelain, and were correspondingly useless lovers. Except for one of them; the one man in her shadowy past that she could not forget.

She felt Jean-Paul gasp and grow taut beneath her, his phallus jerking against the roof of her mouth. Swiftly she gripped the base of his thick stem in her

133

hand and swallowed and sucked as hard as she could, taking the swollen knob down to the velvety recesses of her throat; he shouted out in wild triumph, and spurted hotly into her mouth, his hips thrusting frantically in his extremity of pleasure.

Louise felt a warm rush of delight herself as she experienced his spasming liquid release. Kindly she swallowed and licked, milking him dry, until his penis grew soft and unchallenging in her mouth.

She released him at last, her face softly flushed, and gazed at the two speechless men. 'Now, my fine citizens. Your side of the bargain?'

They grinned at her in open admiration, and Pierre said longingly, 'If only we could keep you here in the prison, hidden away safely somewhere, just for us.'

Louise's heart missed a beat and she felt the familiar sick fear rising within her. That would be a disaster. But she forced herself to sound cool and calm as she said, 'Oh, *messieurs*. If only I could stay with you. The prospect of such endless pleasure with two such stalwart, virile men makes me feel quite faint. But I fear I would never be safe within the confines of this place, because someone would be sure to be jealous of your good fortune, and make trouble for you. No, I feel my only chance is to get away from here, and then, I swear, when my danger is past, I will come and find you both again.'

They still looked hesitant, understandably reluctant to let their fine prize go. With desperate inspiration, Louise wrenched the sharp dagger from Pierre's belt, and before they realised what she was doing, she'd grabbed one of her own soft ringlets as it lay on her shoulder and sliced through it. 'Here,' she breathed, handing the silvery strands to Pierre. Tears of emotion glimmered in her eyes. 'Keep this, to remind you both of me. I fear that I have nothing of real value to give you, but you can think of this as a promise, that we'll meet again.'

Pierre flushed with pleasure at the gift, and he

fondled the gleaming lock of hair as if it were some rare jewel. 'Come on, then,' he said sharply to Jean-Paul. 'What are we waiting for? Let's get this fine lady out of here!'

They were as good as their word. With the help of the big bunch of keys at Pierre's waist, they led her out secretly through a winding warren of dark, twisting passages until they came out at last into a narrow alleyway at the back of the prison.

Jean-Paul had found an old cloak which he proffered shyly to her, and he also gave her a handful of loose change. 'It isn't much,' he said humbly. 'But it's all I've got, and it will help you feed yourself for a day or two.'

Louise took it with tears misting her eyes. 'Oh, thank you! I will never, ever forget your kindness to me!'

'Better go now,' said Pierre gruffly, embarrassed by her apparent emotion, 'while the streets are quiet. Come on, Jean-Paul. Back inside, before we're missed.'

Louise watched them go, waiting till she was alone. Suddenly her wonderful violet eyes were hard and brilliant, and the tears had vanished. 'Scum,' she muttered under her breath contemptuously. 'Filthy, hopeless scum.' Then she stood there at the corner of the dark, dirty street, and breathed in deeply, revelling in the fresh night air and the sensation of freedom.

Her next task was to find the man they called citizen Jacques.

Just over a week after Jacques' abrupt departure from the St Maury mansion, Nicole awoke to a fresh, sunny morning. Pushing back the wooden shutters, she drank in the wide expanse of clear blue sky, noticing as she stood there in her thin cotton shift that already there was a crisp chill in the air. Soon it would be October; already the luxuriant foliage of the beautiful walled garden was beginning to flame with colour, with glorious reds and golds and bronzes, reminding her that soon the autumn frosts would put an end to the lingering glory of late summer.

Running her hands sleepily through her long, tousled hair, Nicole saw that Armand was working in the fruit garden that nestled against the south wall, pruning back a wilderness of spent raspberry canes with slow deliberation. And besides him was Jules d'Amar, former heir to one of the richest estates in France, eagerly helping the big manservant to carry away the spent canes to a smouldering bonfire. Nicole saw with affectionate amusement that his soft, corn-coloured hair had been cropped like a peasant's; his skin was brown from the late September sun, and his loose cotton shirt and breeches were dirty and snagged with briars. Yet in spite of his disarray, he looked supremely happy.

Nicole smiled, remembering how avidly he'd pleaded to stay at the mansion even when offered the chance to leave Paris, and how happily he'd joined their strange little household, offering to do any of the heaviest and most menial tasks there were. Nicole knew from the way he looked at her that he was desperate to give her pleasure once more, to abase his young, stalwart body and do anything she wished. Normally, Nicole would have found his devotion flattering, and Jules was far from unattractive. But she had somehow lost her appetite for sexual pleasures since Jacques had left them all so unexpectedly.

Jacques. She sighed at the thought of him, drawing back from the window and closing her eyes briefly. What a fool she was to wait so longingly for his return, to yearn to hear his voice, to see his smile. What a fool to allow herself to be used in his decadent plans, just as he used everyone else. And yet something about Jacques had reached down to the darkest part of her soul, had taken possession of her secret inner core in a way that no other man ever had, and no other man ever would again. She also knew, with a kind of quiet despair, that he was totally indifferent to her; she was nothing, absolutely nothing to him.

She washed herself in the ewer of tepid water that had been left outside her door by Marianne, then dressed herself in a simple, high-necked gown of striped cotton, and went slowly downstairs.

Marianne greeted her warmly in the spacious kitchen, and they sat by the stove and feasted happily together as they usually did on coffee and crusty bread. Nicole mentioned that she'd seen Jules working out in the garden with Armand, and they giggled softly together about Jules' transformation.

'Poor Jules. He was asking where you were a little while ago, Nicole!' laughed Marianne, licking the butter from her fingers. 'He absolutely adores you, and so does my Armand. You have them all in the palm of your hand, *chérie*.'

All except one, thought Nicole painfully. She said as lightly as she could, 'Do you think that Jacques will be back today?'

Marianne's sweet, heart-shaped face clouded over. 'How should I know?' she replied quickly. 'I told you, Nicole, that he has an errand in Paris that could take him some time.'

'But what kind of errand? He's been gone for a week, Marianne!'

Marianne hesitated. 'It's better that you don't know, really it is. I'm not sure that I understand it myself.'

'But – '

Marianne jumped to her feet. 'No more questions, dear Nicole! Mainly because I can't possibly answer them. After all, what could I possibly know about monsieur Jacques' private thoughts? Come – Armand is going out to buy food, and Jules is in the garden, and we have the whole house to ourselves. Let's explore! Have you seen the *grand salon*? Isn't it wonderful? How I'd love to open it up, and see it in use once more, just as it used to be.'

Nicole said suddenly, 'Let's.'

'Let's what?'

'Open up the *salon*. Let in the sunlight, the fresh air. Why shouldn't we use it, you and I? Why shouldn't we enjoy everything the fine ladies of the nobility used to enjoy? Things like this beautiful house, the clothes, the food and the wine!'

Marianne gazed at her raptly. 'And the men!'

'Of course,' said Nicole lightly, 'we mustn't forget the men. The men of our dreams, Marianne.'

They spent the rest of the morning in the *grand salon*, forcing open the wooden jalousie blinds to let the sun stream in, dusting the exquisite gilt furniture, sweeping the honey-coloured parquet floor and bringing the vast room to life. Gazing up at the high ceiling as the dustmotes danced in the sunlight, they saw for the first time how the gold-leafed mouldings enclosed lavishly-painted scenes from classical mythology; they gasped, the colour flushing their cheeks as they absorbed every detail of the erotically entwined, almost naked figures. 'What a waste to have such delicious paintings on the ceiling,' sighed Marianne, drinking deeply at the wine that they'd brought in to refresh themselves in their labours.

'Unless you were lying down,' pointed out Nicole mischievously.

'Oh, yes!' breathed Marianne. 'Lying down on one of these lovely satin couches, with the man of your choice. Nicole, do you think they had wicked parties in here? Can't you just imagine them all? The marquis de St Maury must have been very inventive. I wonder if he was young and handsome, as well as rich? Wouldn't it be fun if we could live in the same way? Dress up as great lords and ladies, I mean, and feast, and drink, and pleasure one another in this beautiful room.' Her voice trailed away wistfully.

Nicole said lightly, 'I should think it's already on Jacques' agenda.'

Marianne gazed at her, her blue eyes shining. 'Oh, I do hope so! Monsieur Jacques is such a wonderful lover, is he not? So handsome, so powerful, so imaginative!

'So conceited,' put in Nicole with feeling.

'Who can blame him, *chérie*?' And Marianne was on

her feet, pirouetting round the room and humming to herself, pausing only to gaze at the graphically sensual picture of the strong-thighed Mars pleasuring voluptuous Venus as the helpless Vulcan, god of fire, looked on in impotent fury.

The paintings were lascivious and explicit, yet done with exquisite skill by some master craftsman. Nicole wondered yet again about the former inhabitants, the family of St Maury. What were they really like? Rich, and decadent, and inventive, without a doubt, with a streak of malicious sadism that permeated every room in the house. Strange that Jacques suited this place so well. She remembered with a flood of shame the hidden box of ivory love-toys in her own room, remembered the secret chamber upstairs where Jacques had imprisoned her so deliciously on her very first night here. She sipped at her wine to cool her heated thoughts and said thoughtfully, 'Marianne. Do you know what happened to the people who used to live here? I'd almost forgotten, but the other night I saw a crest carved in the lintel over the main door, and a name, St Maury. Who were they?'

Marianne went still suddenly. 'I believe they were not well-known in Paris. They were a family from the south, and this was their town house. They say that the Marquis used it occasionally to entertain his friends, and then he too disappeared.'

'So there is no-one left? No-one to claim this beautiful house?'

Marianne shrugged sadly. 'Who knows? What has happened to most of the great families of France, Nicole? If the St Maurys were wise, they fled the country long ago, before our poor king and queen were imprisoned. This house is no good to them now; it would be like a sentence of death on its owner. Why should any of them trouble to claim it?'

They were both silent, and for a few moments it seemed as if the ghosts of the long-gone St Maury family were with them in that haunted room.

Marianne drank more of her wine and draped herself contentedly on a low, curved settee, looking sweetly pretty with her clouds of soft dark hair and her blue eyes sparkling happily as she gazed round the room. 'I'm glad they left the house empty,' she pronounced. 'Otherwise we wouldn't be here, enjoying all this finery! All we need now is a man; a beautiful, strongly-made man, who is ready to fulfil our every whim, to caress us until we faint with pleasure!'

Nicole smiled softly, realising that Marianne must have drunk more wine than she'd realised. 'Armand should be back soon.'

'Oh, Armand!' Marianne shrugged dismissively, spreading out the full skirts of her sprigged muslin gown. 'He's a dear, but I know him so well, and there's no excitement any more. Though, of course, I love him very much and wouldn't hurt him for the world!'

Nicole sank down onto a low stool near her friend and said carefully, 'Perhaps Jacques will be back soon. Would he do for you?'

Marianne sighed. 'Of course. But monsieur Jacques is too unpredictable, too dangerous. He does what he pleases all the time, without consulting anyone.'

'So you have no desire for him, then?'

'No desire for monsieur Jacques? *Chérie*, does the woman exist who does not want him?' Marianne laughed a little sadly. 'The first time I met him, I fell in love with him, and I don't suppose that will ever change.'

Some dark compulsion drove Nicole on to find out more, even though she didn't really want to know. 'Doesn't Armand mind that you feel like this?'

'Oh, no. You see, Armand is utterly devoted to monsieur Jacques as well. I think he knew all about it, the first time it happened, but he never questioned me, and I never told him.'

'The first time?'

'I'll tell you if you like, Nicole. Would you like me to?'

Nicole swallowed and nodded, her heart beating with

140

painful intensity as Marianne gazed into her eyes and began her story.

'It was a chilly night in spring, soon after we moved into this house. Monsieur Jacques was bathing in his chamber, with the curtains drawn and the fire lit. Armand had helped him to carry up the hot water. Armand was busy elsewhere, so I sneaked upstairs and gazed through a crack in the door, which he'd left slightly ajar. Jacques was drawing himself out of the tub, his wet hair glistening blackly, and I saw immediately how exquisitely his body was made, with those wide, muscled shoulders, his lean hips and strong legs that were dark with soft, silky hair. His skin was all bronzed and smooth in the flickering candlelight, as though he'd been kissed by fire; I longed to touch him with my fingers and lips, to see if he was real. And his secret man's parts; oh, Nicole, even then, in the half-darkness as I peeped trembling through the doorway, I could see that he was magnificent! His heavy balls seemed to bulge with the promise of endless pleasure; his member hung thick and long down his hard thigh, and I longed to take his flesh in my lips, to kiss him and feel him grow with my caresses, to see his dark face tighten in delicious torment as I pleasured him!'

Nicole felt her own excitement rise inexorably. Pouring herself more wine, she said as calmly as she could, 'What happened next?'

Marianne said breathlessly, 'I should have hurried back downstairs, but I couldn't tear myself away. Instead, I went in and curtsied before his naked figure, and I said, "Is there anything else monsieur requires?" And I licked my lips, while gazing at his beautiful prick. Nicole, it stirred and trembled into life even as I gazed at it, and I burned with longing, burned to feel it stroking me, filling me!

'But monsieur Jacques, ignoring the water dripping from his magnificent body onto the floor, gazed at me severely with his hands on his hips and said, "Marianne. Have you been spying on me?"

'"Yes, m'sieur," I whispered, blushing a fiery red. "I'm so sorry, m'sieur."

'"Then you are a wicked girl, and I must punish you," he said coldly, and I quaked.

'He sat down on a cane chair in the corner of his room, still dripping wet, and told me to take off my dress. I did so with trembling fingers, and stood before him clothed only in my black worsted stockings. He must have seen the glistening pink flesh that peeped out of the dark curls at the top of my thighs, must have noticed how my hungry nipples jutted towards him with longing, because his proud cock was lifting and swelling into delicious hardness; but he coolly ignored my wanton invitation and commanded me to lie across his lap, so that my belly was taut against his iron-hard thighs and my breasts dangled hotly into thin air, longing for his caress. I could feel his magnificent cock rubbing against the soft swell of my hip where I leaned against it, and I longed to turn and caress it, but when I twisted my face to get a glimpse at it, he brought his big hand down hard on my plump bottom.

'"Marianne," he said sternly, "you are a wicked girl to spy on your master. Aren't you?"

'"Oh, yes!" I moaned breathlessly, my hair falling in disarray around my burning face, my bottom cheeks glowing. "You must punish me, master."

'And punish me he did. Again and again he brought his strong, cool palm down on my bottom cheeks, paddling me until my skin tingled and glowed, and my private parts glistened with shameful moisture. I wriggled helplessly, trying to rub my burning pleasure-bud against his steely thigh, and then I parted my black-stockinged legs, knowing that he'd be able to see the pink folds of flesh that pulsed within my secret cleft, hoping that he'd take pity on me and touch me there with his long, powerful fingers. He must have heard me moaning out my desire, because in the end he ran his forefinger slowly, maddeningly down my juicy cleft and thrust it with startling swiftness up my quivering

142

hole. I nearly fainted with pleasure as I felt him plunge within me, and I clamped down hard upon him, wriggling around, engulfing his whole hand with my wet folds of flesh as I struggled to find satisfaction.

'Then he withdrew his hand, and I moaned aloud with disappointment. "On your knees, slut!" said Jacques, with a final slap to my rump, and as he pushed me off his thighs to the ground I caught a glimpse of his beautiful, strong prick, thrusting upwards eagerly from the cradle of silky dark hair at the base of his belly.

'I sobbed with longing, but I knew that I had to do exactly what he said. Grovelling on my knees, I lifted my reddened bottom to his face, and then to my delight I realised that he was kneeling, poised behind me. My heart pounding, I felt him grip my buttocks, felt his prick rub between my cheeks, slipping in my moisture down the silky folds that parted so eagerly for that solid shaft of delicious male flesh; I felt its swollen head gliding to and fro along my cleft until it was slick with my moisture and I was almost fainting with exquisite longing. Then, at last, just when I thought I could stand it no more, he rammed himself hard within me, right up to the hilt, and ravished me with such sweet, long strokes that I trembled with ecstasy and had difficulty in restraining my emotion. I savoured him for as long as I could, Nicole, trying to prolong every moment of feeling that deliciously long, hard penis plunging into the very depths of my hot, yearning flesh, feeling his heavy balls caressing my buttocks; but when he reached beneath me to fondle my heavy breasts and squeeze my throbbing nipples, I was utterly lost and writhed about upon his exquisite instrument of pleasure, crying out his name again and again as the sweetest of sensations engulfed my shuddering body.'

Marianne's face was flushed, her eyes glowing even now as she remembered that moment of supreme pleasure. Then she looked up at Nicole and said, almost sadly, 'From then on, I was his slave, you see.'

Nicole, silently watching her as she told her passionate

143

tale, felt unbearably aroused herself. She could picture the scene only too well; the firelit, shadowy chamber, with Marianne, naked except for her black stockings, crouched on all fours on the floor, sighing out her pleasure as Jacques drove himself into her from behind with those long, powerful strokes that Nicole knew only too well would send any woman to the brink of rapture and beyond. She squirmed in silent longing, and whispered, 'Is he really worth it, Marianne?'

Marianne stirred herself as if awakening from a dream, and gave a little sigh. 'No, I don't suppose he is. You see, Nicole, women like you and me mean nothing to him, nothing at all. We're just a convenient part of his quest, and that's all that he cares about.'

Nicole felt a new, inexplicable shiver of unease. 'His quest? You mean his revenge on the people who wronged him so?'

Marianne shook her head swiftly. 'There's more to it than that, much more. But, oh, Nicole, I won't tell you any more, because there's no point! As long as you remember that monsieur Jacques is not for you, and not for any of us. Oh!' She jumped to her feet suddenly. 'I thought I heard the front door. Perhaps Armand is back. Armand, we're in here!'

There was the sound of heavy footsteps down the main hall, and Armand came to stand in the doorway, a little hesitant.

Marianne flew across the room to him and reached up to give him a light kiss. 'Why have you taken so long, you great *imbécile*? Anyone would think you'd been with one of the ladies of pleasure from the Palais Royal!'

And Nicole saw how Armand, instead of responding with some brusque but loving response as he usually did, was silent and blushed a deep, dark red beneath his beard.

Chapter Eight

*L*ouise, desperate to avoid recapture, had spent the last few nights huddled deep in the dark crypt of a deserted church, where the silent marble effigies made chilly companions. The air down there was sharp and cold, but even so, it was so much better than the fetid, fear-filled atmosphere of St Lazare. She awoke still wrapped in the shabby cloak which Jean-Paul had given her; she'd run out of money now, and she was cold and hungry, but she was still exhilarated, because she was free to continue with her search.

That morning, she waited till she knew that the streets of Paris would be crowded and bustling, then she headed for the market, pulling the hood of her worn cloak securely over her glorious fair hair. Even so, she ran the danger of being recognised, but how else would she find him? She had to make contact somehow with the mysterious citizen Jacques.

She had one gold louis, which she'd sewn into the hem of her chemise before her capture, and that was all she had left in the world. It might make her conspicuous, she knew, amongst the poor folk of Paris, but she had to risk it or starve. Heading briskly towards the street market of the Rue Ste Marguerite, she remembered to keep her hood pulled over her hair, to keep her head bowed and keep the natural arrogance from her bearing, so that she would look humble and mix with these common people. Even so, she had to wrinkle her delicate nose, shuddering at the stink of the Paris rabble: the fishwives, the market women, the noisy *fédérés* who pretended to be soldiers, the bawling hawkers and common prostitutes. How she despised them all as she pushed her way fastidiously through the teeming throng.

There was a long, sullen queue outside the bread shop, and Louig hesitated, before joining it uncertainly. A big, bearded man with dark eyes joined the queue just behind her, and he seemed to be watching her. Louise glared at him defiantly, and dismissed him as nothing but peasant scum, in his coarse jacket and trousers and his vile red cap. Then she dropped her eyes suddenly, because she had realised that his gaze was somehow different from that of the other men who thronged the streets, more intent, more purposeful. And beneath that beard and the common peasant clothes, he looked well-made, strong and handsome.

A frisson of interest ran through her, and as she fluttered her long thick eyelashes at him, she saw the burning spark light up in his eyes.

Her turn to be served. The rye loaf was stale and hard, at least two days old and almost inedible. Louise was about to protest indignantly, then bit her lip, remembering just in time that no-one dared to complain about anything in Paris these days.

She proffered her *louis d'or*, and at the sight of the valuable golden coin all hell broke loose.

'Gold! She has gold!' shrieked the old dame behind the counter, snatching back her loaf. 'She's either a thief or a cursed *aristo!* Call the guard, seize her!'

It was the big bearded man who'd been watching her who got to her first in the general *mêlée*. Grabbing her arms, he forced them behind her back, clamped his huge, hairy hand over her mouth, and dragged her away from the shop. 'I'll take her to the authorities, never fear!' he called out above the general hubbub. Then, half-dragging, half-carrying her struggling figure, he plunged across the crowded street, weaving his way skilfully between a solid band of *fédérés* marching down the road so that her pursuers were lost from view. But the Paris mob did not let go of its prey so easily, and within moments Louise heard the triumphant shout of 'There she goes! Follow her!' and she and the man were pounding down the narrow cobbled alleys once more, Louise's heart thudding painfully.

Suddenly, she realised where she was. Down this back street was the deserted church, the dark crypt which had been her refuge for the last two nights. Tugging breathlessly at the man's hand, she panted out, 'Quickly, this way. I know where we can hide.' Nodding grimly, the big man followed her, and they flew down the street beneath the overhanging tenements to plunge down the narrow stone steps to the door beneath the church. It creaked as Louise pushed it open; the big man slammed it shut and leaned against it, and in the sudden, overpowering darkness of the crypt Louise sank to her knees and sobbed for breath.

The man watched her patiently, waiting for her to recover. 'It is not a good idea,' he said, 'to proffer gold on the streets of Ste Marguerite. The ordinary people, you see, do not have much money.'

Louise looked up slowly from where she was kneeling. He sounded solid, and slow, and kind. She would have to tread carefully with this one. Fighting down her natural, burning impatience, she fluttered her thick eyelashes again, so he could see how the tears sparkled in her violet eyes. 'I know,' she said humbly. 'But it is all the money I have in the world, you see. Oh, kind m'sieur, what is your name?'

'My name is Armand.'

'Armand. A beautiful name.' Her eyes were growing accustomed now to the darkness; a high grating let in some light from the street above, and she recognised the big chests full of mouldering vestments, the dusty candlesticks, the shadowy marble effigies that had kept her company during the hours of darkness. She didn't want to spend another night in here. It was time once more to take a risk, to gamble everything on her feminine intuition. 'Oh, Armand,' she went on, 'my life is in dreadful danger. There is only one man who can help me, and that is the man called citizen Jacques. But I do not know how to reach him, so I am in despair.'

A look of sheer amazement crossed the man's face, and Louise's heart leaped. She tried hard to conceal her joy as he rubbed thoughtfully at his beard and said slowly, 'I don't believe it. You are looking for citizen Jacques?'

'Oh, yes, indeed! He is an old friend of mine. You know him?'

He was shaking his head, saying slowly, 'Yes, but I cannot take you to him. His guests come to him by invitation only, you see. He wants no-one to find out where he lives.'

Louise, burning with impatience, let her cloak slip away from her head and shoulders, revealing her glorious silver-blonde hair and luscious figure. She choked back a little sob, and swayed slightly, as if she were about to fall to the ground. 'Oh, I feel faint! Hold me, please, Armand; you look so strong and kind.'

He came across the stoneflagged floor to her almost shyly and knelt to support her in his arms, his face suffused with colour. Louise saw him watching her out of the corner of her half-closed eyes, saw that dark, burning light in his sombre eyes that she recognised so well.

'Please monsieur,' she whispered, lying back in his arms and gazing forlornly up at him, wriggling her shoulders imperceptibly so that her shabby gown slipped a little and revealed the beginnings of her glorious cleavage. 'For you, I would do anything, because you rescued me from the mob. Your very touch sets me alight with flames of desire; I know it is very wicked of me, dear Armand, but I burn for you to take me, here, to pleasure me with your beautiful body. Do what you want with me, my hero; feel my aching breasts, and let me explore you fully. I knew from the moment I set eyes on you that your prick would be fine and strong, and I long to take it in my mouth, to savour all its glory . . .'

Armand groaned as she nestled in his arms. She was truly the most luscious, the most appetising woman he'd ever seen in his life, and her murmured crudities inflamed his blood in a way he wouldn't have believed possible, making his cock rear up fiercely against his belly. She wasn't as beautiful as the lady Nicole, of course, because nobody could be. But she was wanton and enticing, with her silvery-blonde hair and glowing witch's eyes, and already she was pulling her gown from her ripe, high breasts and thrusting them up towards his agonised face with slow deliberation. He turned his head away, his eyes clenched shut. No. He mustn't give way to temptation . . .

Then she stood up, and he gazed at her helplessly. She was undressing for him slowly, in this dark stone crypt beneath the church. Already her eyes were hazy with desire, her lips full and tremulous as she moistened them meaningfully. Her gown had fallen to the floor in a crumpled heap; now she was slipping off her chemise, so that she stood before him clad only in her white silk stockings that were gartered with silken bands around her slender thighs. Her breasts were firm and full, crested with rosy nipples that he longed to take into his mouth; her waist was so tiny that he knew his big hands would span it, and her hips flared out in luscious firmness, the base of her softly rounded belly kissed by a triangle of soft golden down that he couldn't take his eyes off. He wanted to sink his rearing hardness deep, deep within her, to ride her until she moaned out her delight and wrapped herself round every inch of him.

He shut his eyes in despair. What had monsieur

149

Jacques said before he left, the last time? Armand struggled desperately to remember, because all he could think of was his own massive hardness gathering relentlessly at his loins. 'You must never, ever tell anyone about me, or about this house. I must be the only one to select our special guests, Armand. Be wary at all times of spies; women can be just as dangerous as men.'

Louise was running her fingers over her breasts, drawing out the rosebud teats and gazing down at them with blatant longing. 'Please, monsieur Armand,' she was whispering as she fingered herself, 'can you not see how I yearn for you? I need a strong, good man to make me feel better, or I will die of need.'

'No!' Armand moaned. 'Sweet lady, I must not! I will give you some money, and then I must leave you.'

Louise pouted her disbelief and mocked him with her eyes. Then she leaned back against the cold wooden chest behind her, resting her pert buttocks on its solidly carved edge, parting her stockinged thighs slightly so that Armand could glimpse her wanton, luscious folds of flesh as they peeped from beneath the silky blonde hair that adorned her swollen mound.

She started to play with herself, licking one finger and sliding it down her cleft to part her pouting flesh lips. With careful concentration she pushed it up inside her warm, tight hole and sighed softly; then she lifted her finger once more to her lips and sucked the sweet moisture from it, sliding her lips lasciviously up and down the slender length of it. 'Oh, see, Armand! See how I long for you, burn for you! Would you condemn me to the solitary pleasure of my own tiny finger, when I long to be filled by you? If you won't let me feel your fine big shaft inside my hot flesh, then at least, I beg of you, let me see it, let me gaze on its magnificence while I soothe myself with whatever I can find!'

And before Armand could even register what she intended, she'd picked up one of the unused wax candles that lay in a heap behind the chest, and as her eyes closed in rapture, she squatted slightly and drove it lewdly between her swollen flesh lips. Her face flushed with pleasure as she slowly edged the thick, long candle deep within her clutching vulva; she pulled it out again with a little shudder, and the hypnotised Armand was unable to take his eyes from the wet moistness that engulfed the smooth wax. He felt a throbbing urgency in his testicles, felt the gathering force within his own quivering member. That was where he should be, thrusting up into her warm, juicy haven . . .

'Please, please,' she was whimpering, 'let me at least see your fine manhood, dear Armand! Show me your beautiful sturdy prick, and then I can at least imagine it thrusting hot and hard within me! Oh, take pity on me, Armand, I beg you.'

With a muffled groan, Armand unfastened himself and let his huge, rampant phallus leap forth, the great purple tip glistening angrily with lust. The beautiful blonde girl gazed at it transfixed, moaning and muttering her excitement at the sight of his penis as she drove the candle with increasing vigour in and out of her plump flesh.

'Oh, Armand,' she breathed. 'I knew you would be a fine, stalwart man – but such a weapon! Never, ever have I seen anything like it. Please, let me taste it.'

And, pulling the candle out and tossing it impatiently to the floor, she swayed gracefully towards him, her high, full breasts trembling with need. Armand stood very still, unable to move as she bent her head to take the luscious velvety head of his penis deep within her hot mouth, wrapping her tongue lasciviously round it and sucking hard while she cradled the heavy pouch of his testicles in her small hands.

Armand could stand no more. Lifting her up round her tiny waist so that she was supported effortlessly in his massive arms, he covered her face with hot kisses and lowered her onto his massive penis.

Louise nearly fainted with delight. Her hands clutched tightly round the back of his neck and her legs wrapped around his waist as she felt that hard, solid shaft slowly impale her, slipping inch by inch between her moist, hungry lips; she felt her own wanton flesh suck it in greedily, clutching at it with exquisite need, until she was sure she could take no more; and yet still there was more! She hissed aloud with delight as his hot penis thrust still deeper into her yearning cavern, and drummed her heels against his taut, hair-roughened buttocks in her excitement. 'Oh, Armand, my fine stallion,' she whispered.

And Armand was holding her tightly round her waist, lifting her up and down so that her body slid the whole length of his rampant member, pleasuring her into oblivion, bearing her aloft on that great, gnarled pillar of flesh, filling her, stretching her, while he bent his shaggy head to guzzle at her breasts until she drove her nails into his massive shoulders and bounced up and down in glazed delirium on his quivering penis. 'Oh, yes, Armand. Fill me with your fine, fat prick – oh yes, oh yes . . .'

And she shuddered into glorious release, feeling the pleasure wash relentlessly over her as he drove himself to his own jerking climax deep, deep within her exquisitely sated loins.

Afterwards he held her protectively in his arms, stroking her wonderful moon-silver hair, touching her soft silken skin with a kind of shy reverence, as if afraid that his big body would break her, hurt her. Armand felt as if he had just found himself the most precious treasure in the world.

Louise, her hands still wrapped round his neck, lifted her face to his, her full lips still parted tremulously, her violet eyes brilliant with tears of emotion. 'Oh, Armand,' she breathed, 'that was so wonderful.'

Armand reached out anxiously to brush the tears from her thick lashes with his calloused fingertips. 'Did I hurt you?'

'Oh no! Far from it.' Louise smiled tremulously up at him and fluttered her thick lashes over her incredible violet eyes. 'And now, my fine Armand, will you take me to citizen Jacques?'

Armand hesitated only a second, then said, 'He's away at the moment. But as soon as he returns, I'll take you to him, I promise.'

Louise lowered her eyes quickly so he wouldn't see the flash of triumph that shot through them.

Two nights later, Nicole was all alone in the *petit salon*, trying to concentrate on some embroidery she'd started to pass the time. Darkness seemed to have fallen early that night; the wind had been building up all day, and now it was rattling at every window, every crevice of the big house, making the candles by which she was working flicker and spurt uncertainly.

At first, she didn't hear the heavy knocking at the front door because of the noise of the wind. When at last the ominous sound penetrated her senses, she got quickly to her feet, her embroidery silks falling to the floor. Jacques. Perhaps Jacques was back at last!

But of course, he would have a key. Fighting down the numbing disappointment, she smoothed down her hair and hurried out into the hall, her heart thumping with new anxiety. Who could it be, at this hour? Marianne had gone to bed early, with a headache; Armand was out, as he so often was these days. Nicole struggled with the big key in the lock, tearing her fingernails, and when she finally pulled the door ajar a gust of wind whipped it wide open, sending a flurry of crackling brown leaves into the hallway.

A man stood there, a man in a black coat hunched up against the wind. One of Jacques' helpers, thought Nicole quickly, a fresh spasm of anxiety running through her. He was breathing hard, as if he'd been running, and his expression seemed distraught as the wind whipped his loose hair around his lined face.

153

Before she could speak, he blurted out, 'St Maury – where is he?'

Nicole was stunned by his strange words. She shook her head, her eyes shadowed with bewilderment. 'But – the St Maury family left, long ago! There's no-one here of that name!'

The man's face tightened; he drew his hand tiredly across his forehead. 'Of course, madame. How stupid of me. Tell me, is citizen Jacques at home? I really must see him.'

'He's been away for several days now. We don't know when he'll be back.'

The man's brow furrowed anew. 'Then will you give him a message as soon as he does return? Tell him – tell him that there's someone, a woman, looking for him. We'd tracked her down to the prison of St Lazare, but she's not there any more. Give him this, will you? He'll understand.'

He thrust something at her, something wrapped in a slip of silk; the wind almost seized it, and as Nicole clutched anxiously at the tiny parcel, he gave a curt bow and hurried off into the night. She pressed the great door shut against the gusts that battered the front of the house, and unfolded the silken square.

In it was a lock of beautiful, silvery-blonde hair, tied up in a slender scrap of red ribbon. *'Give him this, will you? He'll understand.'*

Understand what? Who was looking for Jacques, and why was this lock of hair so important?

Filled with nameless anxiety, she made her way up to bed and put the lock of hair in a drawer beneath her bedside table. It was probably nothing, she told herself. The sinister, distraught messenger was just another nameless figure in the ghostly masquerade that had begun when she first set foot inside this strange, obsessive house.

The wind rattled at the shutters; her candle spluttered suddenly and died. Shivering, longing hopelessly for

Jacques as always, she blew out her candle and lapsed into uneasy dreams.

She wasn't quite sure what had woken her. Footsteps on the gravel at the front of the house, perhaps, or the murmur of low voices down in the echoing hall. Whatever it was, she knew beyond a shadow of doubt that Jacques was back.

Her heart thudding madly, conscious only of her longing to see him, to tell him about the mysterious caller and the enigmatic message that had disturbed her so, she pulled on her night robe and ran down the stairs. All seemed still and quiet. Perhaps there was no-one there after all – perhaps she'd been mistaken.

Then, suddenly, she heard low voices from the little ante-room where poor Jules had cowered in nervous anticipation on her second night here. Holding her breath, she gently opened the door, and realised that the voices were coming from beyond the heavy curtains that divided off the main part of the salon. She drew nearer, straining to recognise the voices, hearing the familiar tones of Marianne and Armand, and someone else, a woman. Nicole caught her breath in dismay. Perhaps this new visitor was the blonde-haired woman that the messenger had warned her about, the one that she intuitively felt posed some mysterious threat to Jacques. She had to warn him, before it was too late . . .

She parted the curtains just the tiniest crack, and peeped through, and gasped.

In the centre of the room, crouched on all fours on the smooth parquet floor, was a woman. Her hair wasn't blonde, but chestnut-red, and it cascaded round her plump shoulders in startling contrast to her white skin, because she was almost naked, except for a strange black leather harness that fitted tightly round her upper torso. Standing round her in the dim candle-light were Marianne and Armand, as she had surmised; and the blond-haired Jules, his face pale with excitement. And she'd been right; Jacques was there too. He

155

was standing just a little behind them in the shadows, his arms folded across his chest, his face impassive as he watched Marianne. Marianne, who had supposedly gone to bed early with a headache, was standing over the crouching woman with a leather whip in her hand, a whip from that sinister little room up in the turret. Nicole felt her mouth go dry.

'So this is how you used to treat your servants, is it, Madame de Sarblay?' Marianne was saying softly, at the same time raising the whip menacingly. 'Did you beat them cruelly, while they bowed naked in front of you?'

The plump woman squirmed, her face alight with excitement. 'Yes, oh yes!' As she shifted her knees on the floor, the stunned Nicole saw how the dark cleft between her bottom cheeks was juicy and luscious with her excitement; Nicole's agonised fingers clenched on the heavy velvet of the curtains, while her eyes were drawn relentlessly to the silent figure of citizen Jacques.

So he was back. He was up to his usual tormenting games, games with people's lives. She hated him, standing there so exquisitely dressed, so coldly impassive; yet at the same time she wanted him desperately. She fled back up the stairs and lay on her bed in her darkened room as the wind moaned around the eaves and she burned with despairing need, the lock of hair and the message quite forgotten.

Monique, comtesse de Sarblay, could not believe her luck. She'd thought she was as good as dead when she'd been hauled from the great, communal cell that she shared in La Force with the other prisoners and dragged before the so-called Revolutionary Tribunal. They'd accused her of cruelty to her servants, and she'd pleaded, 'But it wasn't cruelty! Believe me, they loved every minute of it!'

Of course, they'd not believed her, those coarse buffoons, with their filthy red caps and their flasks of rough wine and their black, tobacco-stained pipes. But these people did. They understood. The magnificent dark-haired one, citizen Jacques, they called him, he understood her need. It was he who'd roughly enclosed her in these wonderful bonds, the collar and harness that encased her plump breasts, the cold smile never leaving his thin, wonderful mouth, obviously realising how the sweet kiss of black leather would chafe her soft, plump flesh and drive her absolutely wild.

And now the woman called Marianne was dangling a soft leather whip over her plump buttocks, trailing it tantalisingly down her sleek bottom-cleft. The comtesse shuddered in delight. Her nipples, thrust out by the straps of the harness, were hard and proud; she knew that her nether lips were plump and wet below the thick red tangle of her pubic hair, pleading for attention.

'So,' the woman called Marianne was saying softly, 'this is how you used to treat your servants, is it, madame Monique? Stripping them, tying them up so they were helpless and naked, and then beating them until they cried out.'

'Yes. Oh, yes.'

'Why?' Marianne struck her buttocks lightly with the whip, a whispered promise of pain. 'Did you enjoy hurting them, Monique?'

Monique looked up, aghast. 'Not hurt them, never!'

'Then why did you do it? It is part of our bargain, Monique, that you confess everything, every little detail. Don't you understand that?'

Monique swallowed, wildly excited. They were all watching her. The beautiful blond youth, the big rough man who looked like a peasant, and the dark-haired, masterful one that she would die for.

'I liked to see their reddened bottoms,' she whispered. 'I would stand over them sternly with my whip, dressed in my finest clothes, watching and drinking fine wine from my husband's vineyard. The women would get so excited. As they kneeled on all fours, like this, with their bottoms in the air, their secret parts would glisten and weep with longing until the moisture

157

trickled down their plump thighs. And the men – ' She broke off and licked her lips.

Marianne prodded her buttocks warningly with the whip. 'Carry on, Monique.'

'The men. Oh, their pricks would grow so stiff, so mighty as I gently lashed their tight, hairy bottoms! I would bend to cup the pouch of their velvety balls, and their strong shafts would thrust forward so hungrily.'

'And then?'

'Then, sometimes, I would allow the men and women to pleasure one another, at my instruction.' The comtesse felt the hungry throbbing between her moist thighs as she recalled it. 'I would watch as the men slid their great pricks remorselessly between the girls' cheeks, and I would watch as they rode them, wishing that it was me being filled by their hot shafts of flesh.'

'They were still tied up?'

'Still restrained, yes.'

'And what did you do, Monique? Apart from watch?'

Monique licked her lips. 'I – I used to pleasure myself.'

'How?' It was Jacques who spoke this time; she shuddered deliciously at the coldness in his low voice.

'With my fingers, monsieur. Or, sometimes, with the whip.'

The silence in that dark, heavily-draped room was almost unbearable. The candles flickered dimly, and she was aware of all their eyes burning into her, devouring her shame. Then Marianne was standing right over her, saying:

'Like this? You shameless wanton, Monique – you mean like this?'

And to the comtesse's horrified rapture, Marianne was sliding the inverted whip handle between her exposed bottom cheeks, using the rounded leather knob to stroke deep within her plump, honeyed lips, nudging gently but remorselessly into her moist, quivering entrance.

Monique moaned in delight, thrusting her hips back-
wards, trying to impale herself on the cool leather shaft;
Marianne slipped it in and out with tantalising lewdness
a few times, then withdrew it and used it to tap her
hard on her rump.

'Not yet! You have not grovelled sufficiently yet,
Monique!'

'What do you want me to do? I'll do anything,
anything you want!'

Marianne grinned softly. 'I think the men are ready
to take you up on that offer. First, you must pleasure
them with your mouth, Monique. Show them what you
can do.'

'Willingly, madame. Oh, willingly.'

Armand the big peasant kneeled down first, followed
by the boy Jules, both of them eagerly unfastening their
tight breeches. Panting, Monique crawled towards them
on hands and knees, her pink tongue already protruding from her generous mouth. The big one, the one
with the black beard, oh, she felt faint with wanting
him! His great, darkened penis reared up from his hairy
belly like the limb of an oak tree; tremulously she took
as much as she could into the moist, hot recesses of her
mouth, her own loins quivering shamefully as she
imagined that magnificent, veined length of flesh pulsing deep, deep inside her. He fondled her straining
breasts, grunting aloud his pleasure as her head
swooped and dipped.

'Both of them,' warned the woman Marianne behind
her. 'Remember you are to pleasure both of them, you
wicked, shameless creature!'

Obediently Monique released the big peasant's prick
and turned towards the slim blond youth, whose brown
eyes were alight with excitement. His cock was slender
and white, but it was still a pleasure, a different kind of
pleasure, to take it into her mouth, to lick and savour
its silky hardness, and the boy looked glazed with
rapture as her tongue snaked round it and sucked,

159

drawing the sweetness from the very depths of his body.

The comtesse de Sarblay had to admit to herself that she had never experienced such exquisite pleasure. To be exposed and humiliated like this, with all her perverted sexual hunger laid bare, made her shudder with excitement. All that was missing was the dark-haired one, who still stood back in the shadows. Lifting her head from Jules' throbbing cock, she gazed at the one called Jacques with tormented eyes, and whispered, 'You. Please – you?'

He laughed coldly. 'Why not?'

Yes, breathed Monique to herself. *Oh, yes.*

Already, the tall dark man who was in charge of them all was unfastening his breeches. Monique squirmed helplessly, feeling the sticky lovejuices running anew down her trembling thighs. She glimpsed his penis, and it was magnificent, long and dark and somehow mysterious, already pulsing with vigorous life as he released it from the confines of his clothing. 'Please,' she moaned aloud. 'Please, I beg you. Fill me, ride me with your beautiful cock, monsieur.'

With a grimly intent look on his face, he moved to crouch behind her. She was sorry, because she couldn't see him any more, and he was so beautiful. But then he gripped her bottom, pulling the cheeks apart, and she felt his hot, silky shaft prodding at her tight, aching anus, and she cried aloud, longing for the shameful penetration, yet fearing that her pulsing little rosebud hole would never, ever accommodate him. She felt him grip his penis in his hand, and slide it lower, dipping it in her love juices, anointing it with the honeyed liquid that oozed from her body. It rubbed along her cleft, slick and wonderfully exciting, and this time, when he pushed it against her bottom hole, it slid in, filling her with wave after wave of hot, heavy pleasure. Oh, the shame of his wicked violation! If he was one of her servants, she would have him horse-whipped for this; yet she was his prisoner, and he could do what he liked with her. She closed her eyes in rapturous submission, throwing her head back in her extremity of sensation, visualising with delight the lewd sight of his beautiful shaft penetrating her forbidden passage, feeling his heavy, full balls brushing tantalisingly against her buttocks. He withdrew his penis slowly, and she cried aloud in her disappointment, only to feel him slide back in, further than before, until a hot, delicious throbbing started up deep at the base of her belly, and she knew that ecstasy was near.

At that moment the man Armand leaned forward, his huge, empurpled penis still quivering hungrily against her cheek, and growled in a husky voice, 'Me as well, madame la comtesse.' He thrust his rampant cock into her open mouth and she welcomed him gladly, sucking and licking at the mighty shaft until she felt his hot seed gushing in floods into her willing mouth, vaguely aware that the man behind her who had captured her secret entrance was holding himself very still within her. Then Jules, the sweet blond boy Jules, knelt before her, and his slender penis slipped delightfully between her swollen lips. She tongued him generously, all the time aware of the strong phallus penetrating her rear, knowing that her own release, when it came, would be cataclysmic. Jules did not last long. After a few moments of her hot sucking, he gave melting little cries of delight and spurted feverishly down her throat, his slender hands all the time toying with her magnificent, pendulous breasts as they swayed within the black harness.

Then, as Jules sank to the floor, she realised that Jacques had slid his hands round to her churning vulva, and was finding her yearning kernel of pleasure, sliding his fingers round its throbbing base, rubbing and stroking until the exquisite pleasure was almost a pain. At the same time he thrust deep within her, filling her with such powerful, deliberate strokes that she could stand no more and exploded into violent, noisy rapture, writhing in her ecstasy and feeling him drive himself to his own racking orgasm deep, deep within her. She shouted aloud her incredible release, and collapsed onto the floor.

When she lifted her head some moments later, they were all gathered round the table in the corner, dressed and utterly composed, looking at some papers.

'Have I passed the test?' she whispered, her body still awash from the explosion that had seemed to melt every inch of her flesh in a furnace of pleasure.

The members of that strange little tribunal looked at one another, exchanging glances. 'You have passed, madame,' announced Jacques. 'Tomorrow you will be given all the papers necessary for a safe exit from Paris.'

'What a shame,' said Monique, comtesse de Sarblay, with a wicked glint in her eyes. 'I was rather hoping that I might have failed, and then we would have to do it all over again.'

Jacques laughed. 'You have been a worthy subject, madame la comtesse,' he said. 'But I think that you should save your energies for your journey to freedom. Jules, you too must leave tomorrow.'

'No!' The boy looked utterly crestfallen; Monique felt sorry for him.

'Yes,' said Jacques.

Nicole lay on her bed in the darkness. From below, she was sure that she could hear low cries, the tantalising sound of a woman reaching a long, shuddering climax of sexual release. She pressed her hands hard over her ears, but her cheeks burned and her mind was filled with tormenting pictures of the woman in the lewd leather harness, licking her pouting lips as she gazed at Jacques.

How he must hate the aristocracy, to go to such lengths to humiliate them. He was vile and hateful himself, and yet she wanted him, so much.

Even now, though she'd been lying alone up here for what seemed to be hours, she was hotly aroused, trembling with her own need. Her silken night robe seemed too tight, so feverishly she untied the sash round her waist and freed her breasts. They throbbed with arousal. Desperately she cupped them in her hands, trying to soothe the hardened, pouting nipples, but she only succeeded in sending renewed shafts of fierce desire burning down towards her already melting loins. The flesh between her thighs pulsed moistly, yearning to feel the thick, solid flesh of a man's erect phallus driving deep into its soft, secret depths.

Biting her lip in despair, she pulled herself up and brushed her loose hair back from her cheeks. Then she walked impetuously over to the chest of drawers and drew out the mahogany box of ivory love toys. Lifting out the thickest of the implements with trembling fingers, she walked slowly back to her disordered bed and lay there with her robe rumpled up round her waist, her legs drawn apart and raised at the knee as she drew the cold ivory shaft tantalisingly along her swollen vulva. The rounded tip of it just caught her hard little bud of desire, and she rubbed it again more purposefully, feeling the heat mounting in her love-starved body. She was ready to drive the ivory penis deep within herself, longing to feel its silken, satisfying caress, but she would tantalise herself for just a moment longer . . .

There was a light, urgent knock at the door of her chamber, and Marianne slipped in. 'Nicole! Monsieur Jacques is back, and he wants to see you immediately – *oh!'*

She stopped mid-sentence at the sight of Nicole lying there in her near-naked extremity, her tawny hair cascading wantonly across the pillow, her cheeks already flushed, her eyes hazy with sexual longing. Marianne's blue eyes fastened on the exciting ivory phallus, lying potently against the silky folds of flesh between Nicole's parted thighs.

'Oh, Nicole,' breathed Marianne passionately. 'How very beautiful you are, *chérie!* Please, let me come to you. Oh, how I have been longing to love you.'

And Nicole found herself rapturously submitting as Marianne's sweet little mouth found her yearning nipples, pulling and savouring them with exquisite delicacy, while at the same time Marianne's nimble hand closed round the big ivory penis, and stroked Nicole's soft thigh, and slid the love-toy gently but deeply up into her hungry vagina.

It was wonderful. Clutching at the cool shaft fiercely with her tense inner muscles, Nicole arched her hips to welcome its caress as Marianne drove it hungrily in and out of her slick, wanton flesh, at the same time nibbling at Nicole's aching breasts and sliding one moistened little finger quite deliciously along the base of her quivering bud of pleasure.

Gasping aloud beneath Marianne's loving attentions, Nicole felt the demanding onslaught of her climax. Clutching fervently at the ivory shaft with her inner muscles, so that every one of Marianne's slow, deliberate strokes pulled exquisitely at her swollen, sensitised flesh, she thrust her hips high to meet Marianne's caressing finger at her clitoris, and shuddered into long, melting rapture as the waves of sweet pleasure coursed through her heated body.

Then it was over, too soon, and she bit back her disappointment, because she wanted a man to fill her, not the cold stick of ivory. She wanted a man to hold her in his strong arms, to kiss her deliciously full breasts with his rasping tongue, to drive himself to his own release in her tender embrace, so she could feel his engorged penis pulsing and spasming deep, deep within her.

She wanted Jacques. Dangerous, elusive, powerful Jacques. Turning from Marianne with a sigh, it struck her suddenly that everyone wanted Jacques, and everyone got him. No doubt even that lewd woman down below, the one they called the comtesse, had had her fill of him. The only one he scorned was her, Nicole. All right, so Marianne had been sent to summon her to his sacred presence, but no doubt that was only to put her in her place about some new misdemeanour.

Marianne, as if sensing her silent misery, had softly removed the phallus and was sitting on the bed beside her, tenderly stroking her hair. 'Poor Nicole. *Chérie*, you look so pale and sad; whatever is the matter? Shall I tell monsieur Jacques that you are too tired to see him tonight, that you're already asleep?'

Nicole swallowed, her throat aching, and said in a low voice, 'Yes. I don't want to see him, Marianne.' Suddenly, drawing her robe around herself, she gazed at Marianne with dark, haunted eyes and whispered, 'Oh, Marianne, where has he been these last few days? Why will no-one tell me who he is? Why is everyone so secretive about him?'

Marianne sighed. '*Chérie*, as I told you before, I know very little about him, about his past, or his mysterious network of friends in the city. But one thing I do know, and this you must learn to accept. We are all of us nothing to him. We're just part of his scheme, and that is all.'

'You mean we're part of his revenge?' shivered Nicole. 'His revenge on all aristocrats, because of the way he was thrown into prison without a trial?'

Marianne hesitated. 'That is only the part of it. I think that what really drives him on is his quest to find the woman who was responsible for sending him to prison in the first place.'

'The woman who accused him of raping her? The mistress of the great nobleman of Marseilles?'

'Yes,' whispered Marianne. Her brow puckered in uncertainty, as if unsure how much more to say. 'They say that he's still obsessed by her, even after all this time, and he's heard rumours that she's in Paris. That's why he came here, in the spring, to find her.'

'And what will he do to her when he *does* find her?' breathed Nicole, her hands unconsciously twisting together in her lap as she thought of the whip scars that striped Jacques' back. 'What revenge could possibly be

165

harsh enough for the woman who nearly destroyed him?'

Marianne shook her head vehemently and laid her hand on Nicole's arm. 'No, Nicole, you don't understand. He's not looking for revenge – far from it. You see, he's still in love with her.'

Nicole's heart seemed to stop. The blood drained from her face. 'No. It can't be. Not after what she did to him!'

Marianne nodded sadly. 'Yes, it's true. She was so beautiful, you see; it's as if she cast a spell on him. Soon after we moved in here, Jacques and Armand got very drunk together, and Jacques told Armand that this woman would steal the heart of a dead man. It seems that he's still haunted by her, even after everything that happened to him because of her. Apparently he heard a rumour that she was in Paris somewhere, possibly in one of the prisons; so he's been using his network of secret friends to comb the streets and alleys, to get lists of the inhabitants of all the gaols, looking for her. She might well be dead, but I don't think he'll ever give up. It is his obsession.'

Nicole whispered, 'And what if he does find her?'

'Then he will leave Paris with her, I assume, and find some place of safety. I don't suppose it will matter very much to them where they go, as long as they are together.'

Nicole suddenly realised that she felt totally awake, and cold, and quite sick. She understood everything now, all of Jacques' cool yet intense nature, his clinical and dispassionate lust. He was thinking of *her* all the time.

Suddenly realising just how deeply she had been deluding herself, how strongly she had allowed her false hopes to form, she said in a low voice, 'Marianne, would you tell Jacques that I'm too tired to see him tonight?'

'Of course, *chérie!* I will tell monsieur Jacques that you were already asleep when I entered your room. I'll let

166

you rest now. Goodnight!' With that, Marianne pressed a light kiss to her cheek and turned to leave the room.

As soon as the door was shut behind her, and her light footsteps faded away down the passage, Nicole jumped from her bed and started to pull clothes frantically out of the armoire until, buried at the back, she found the clothes she'd arrived in, the remnants of the shabby finery that Gerard had given her. She would take nothing else.

She would leave with nothing, just as she had arrived with nothing. And it was absolutely imperative that she should get away from here quickly, before Jacques cornered her, and entrapped her once more with his seductive words and smile. Once she'd gone, she'd have nothing to remind her of him, except for the fierce, sweet memory of that first incredible night when he'd cast his dangerous spell over her.

Suddenly, she caught sight of the diamond necklace lying in its open case on the dressing table. She gazed at its cold, fiery beauty with longing. The price she would get for that would settle her in comfort for a long time. Her fingers reached out, then she hesitated. It was stealing, and she'd vowed to take nothing from him! Then she relaxed. It would serve Jacques right if she did take them, because after all, *he'd* stolen them from the St Maury family. They belonged to him no more than they belonged to her.

She picked the diamonds up and put them in a soft leather pouch, slipping them loosely into the pocket deep within the folds of her skirt. She would keep the gems as a kind of insurance, just in case things went badly wrong and she couldn't get work.

And now it was time to make her escape, in the lonely hours of darkness, and flee from Jacques and the St Maury mansion for ever, before they destroyed her.

Chapter Nine

*T*he next morning, Armand was up even earlier than usual, anxious to get all his jobs done because he wanted to speak to monsieur Jacques about Louise. He thought about Louise every moment of the time, even as he cleared out the grates, and brought in firewood, and swept the steps, and pumped bucketloads of water ready to be heated for monsieur Jacques' bath.

He had made very sure, of course, that Louise was safe and well-provided for in some quiet lodgings off the Rue de Sèves; but even so, after three nights there, she was beginning to complain, to say that she might have to go somewhere else if he wouldn't take her to monsieur Jacques. And Armand couldn't bear to lose her, not yet. It made him shudder with despair, to think of never again being subjected to all the lascivious delights she introduced him to with her mouth, and her lips, and her pretty, cunning fingers.

Frowning, he heaved up another load of logs from the woodpile ready to take inside, conscious that the weather was chillier now that October was nearly here. And when he took them inside, he wished that he hadn't bothered, because all hell was let loose. It seemed that madame Nicole had disappeared, just run off into the night without a word to anyone. Marianne was sobbing into her apron. What on earth would monsieur Jacques say, she wailed, when he came downstairs and was told the news?

Armand stroked her damp cheek, running his fingers through her dark, wavy hair. She was a good woman, his Marianne, and he felt a twinge of guilt at the thought of what he'd been doing every day with Louise when he was supposed to be shopping for the household. 'Perhaps she's just gone out for a walk,' he encouraged. 'She'll probably be back before he's up.'

Marianne stamped her foot in a temper, pushing his hand away. 'She's left for good, you stupid man! She's left all her clothes, everything, and gone off in her old gown and cloak, the ones she arrived in, even though they're almost threadbare! And the worst of it all is that the diamonds have gone! The diamonds that monsieur Jacques gave her – the case is lying there, empty . . .

Armand said a little less confidently, 'She'll be back soon, you'll see.'

Marianne slumped suddenly against his broad chest, her face pale with crying. 'Oh, Armand. I only hope you're right.'

Then they heard Jacques coming down the stairs, humming softly to himself as he walked into the kitchen.

Armand stayed close to Marianne, though he'd much rather have slipped away. Marianne was pouring monsieur Jacques his coffee, strong and hot and black just as he liked it, when Jacques said suddenly, 'Where is Nicole? Didn't you tell her, Marianne, that I wanted to speak to her as soon as possible?'

Marianne's face crumpled. She stammered out, 'She – she's not here, monsieur Jacques.'

Jacques frowned as he took his coffee and sipped at it. 'You mean she's still in bed? She's not ill, is she? That would be – inconvenient.'

Marianne looked urgently across at Armand for assistance, and got none. 'No, m'sieur, you don't

169

understand. I mean she's not here, not in the house. She's left.'

There was a moment's raw silence. 'Left the house?' said Jacques in a quietly ominous voice that Armand and Marianne knew only too well. It made them shiver.

'Yes, m'sieur!' stammered Marianne. 'I went up to look for her an hour ago, to take her some hot water, and there was no sign of her. Her clothes were all over the floor, her room was in a dreadful mess, and then I realised that the only things missing were the old clothes she arrived in. She's gone, m'sieur Jacques! And – and she's taken the diamonds with her!'

'The diamonds?' Jacques turned on her with an icy harshness in his voice that made her quail. 'You're quite sure?'

'Oh, yes, m'sieur! The case was lying there empty . . .' And Marianne burst into fresh tears, rubbing at her reddened eyes with the back of her hand. Never, ever had she seen monsieur Jacques so angry. She hadn't realised that the diamonds, precious as they were, meant so much to him.

Abruptly, Jacques put down his coffee cup. He looked at Armand, and said, 'For God's sake. Someone must know where she's gone. She can't just have vanished into thin air.'

Armand shrugged helplessly. 'I know nothing, monsieur.'

Jacques was already reaching for his greatcoat, which hung in the passageway. 'I'm going after her, Armand. Take care of the house while I'm away. No-one must be allowed entrance to this house without my permission, you understand? Absolutely no-one.'

Armand swallowed. 'M'sieur, when will you be back?' He wasn't thinking about Nicole or the diamonds; his mind was still full of Louise, because she obsessed him.

Jacques, already making for the door, turned back impatiently. 'When I've found Nicole Chabrier. However long it takes.'

'M'sieur, I wanted to ask you something – '

But Armand was too late with his question, because Jacques had already gone. They heard the heavy front doors slam behind him.

Marianne's sobs had gradually subsided, but she was still wringing her hands on her damp apron. 'I've never seen him like that,' she whispered. 'I never thought that dear Nicole was a thief. Oh, what made her do it?' Suddenly she turned on Armand. 'And what were you pestering him for, you great fool? What question did you have for him that was so urgent?'

Armand blushed a fiery red above his dark beard. He thought of Louise, waiting for him impatiently in the little flat off the Rue de Sèves, and muttered, 'Oh, nothing.' He poured himself some strong black coffee. 'It can wait.'

Morbleu, today he'd have to tell Louise that she couldn't come to the house, not yet anyway. But monsieur Jacques, with his many friends scattered around the city, would find Nicole and the diamonds very quickly, of that Armand had no doubt, and then things would settle down quietly again. And when Jacques eventually met Louise, he would be extremely pleased with Armand for rescuing her from the clutches of the mob.

For who, he thought dreamily to himself, could help but be pleased to meet such a delicious creature as Louise de Lamartine?

Nicole stirred and stretched out sleepily, at first thinking that she was in her luxurious bed at the St Maury mansion. Then she heard the raucous early morning cries of the streetsellers outside, heard the noise of carts rumbling across the cobbled streets, and remembered; she was wrapped in a blanket on a low couch in Anne-Marie's small, cluttered apartment. Glancing across the room, seeing Anne-Marie curled up still asleep in her bed, she threw her friend a silent prayer of gratitude.

When Nicole fled so impulsively last night, she'd not

considered just how very late it was to be out alone on the streets of Paris. It was dark and cold; the wind chilled her, and she'd been more frightened than she cared to admit, frightened of being on her own, of the looks people slanted at her as she hurried along the dirty cobbled streets towards the Faubourg St Victor. There had been a few ordinary people hurrying home from the theatre or from dinner with friends, but they were easily outnumbered by the grim-faced *canailles*, who slouched at every street corner waiting for trouble as dry tinder waits for a spark.

Somehow, she'd managed to get to her old lodgings without incident, but she received a hostile reception from the landlady.

'Your room?' old madame Rimaud had snapped, her hair and part of her face covered by a formidable nightcap. 'It's gone, of course, let out to those conscript soldiers from Marseilles. They pay well.'

'But my things!'

'What things?' sneered Madame, and slammed the door in Nicole's face.

It was then, as she stood in the cold, dark street in utter despair, that Nicole had thought of Anne-Marie. Anne-Marie was an old friend, only a little older than Nicole, but an experienced actress who had befriended Nicole when she first came to Paris. Fun and lively, she had always been one of Nicole's favourite companions. Perhaps, thought Nicole with sudden inspiration, Anne-Marie might even help her to find work again, in the theatre! Memories in Paris were short, and with the recent horror of the September massacres only too clear in people's minds, they might have forgotten about Gerard and her connection with him.

It seemed very late to Nicole, but to Anne-Marie, used to theatre hours, the night would still be early. Nicole remembered the way to her little apartment without difficulty, and prayed that her friend would be in.

It seemed that for once she was in luck. The friendly

landlady, no doubt used to Anne-Marie's many visitors of both sexes, showed Nicole up the stairs to Anne-Marie's door, and at the soft 'Come in!' that followed her knock, Nicole entered to see her friend sitting in front of her dressing table, carefully removing her stage make-up. She was dressed in a lovely green silk dressing robe that matched her eyes; when she saw Nicole's reflection in the mirror, she jumped to her feet, her silky dark hair tumbling round her shoulders, and hugged Nicole to her with the most blissful words of welcome. 'But of course you can stay, darling Nicole! For as long as you like!'

When Anne-Marie finally let her go, Nicole took off her cloak and gratefully accepted the brimming glass of warming red wine that was offered to her as she sat on the worn little settee in the corner of the cosy room. 'I haven't got much money,' Nicole warned her, thinking with sudden shame of the heavy gems deep in the pocket of her skirt. 'But I'll pay you for my share of the lodging just as soon as I can.'

'Nonsense, darling! Whoever cares about money?' laughed Anne-Marie. 'Whatever happened to your glamorous comte de Polignac? When you suddenly disappeared from theatre life, we all assumed that he'd taken you to Austria with him!'

'He went to Austria on his own,' said Nicole flatly. 'I had to go into hiding, because I had been denounced for *incivisme* – everyone knew that I was his mistress. He left me nothing.'

'The scum. 'Anne-Marie frowned fiercely, then her green eyes suddenly twinkled. 'Anyway, I bet he was useless in bed.'

Nicole gasped. 'He was. Oh, he was. How did you know?' They broke into intoxicating laughter, and it was just like old times as they gossiped and reminisced over their wine.

'Are you acting again, Anne-Marie?' asked Nicole after a while.

'After a fashion.'

173

'How wonderful. I wish I was!'

There was a slight pause, and then Anne-Marie said, 'Perhaps you could, Nicole. Are you really sure you want to work again?'

'In the theatre, you mean? Oh, yes!'

Anne-Marie sipped at her wine, regarding her thoughtfully. 'Well, this is almost like working in the theatre. There's this manager I know, who's all the rage, called Paul Vichy. I think he'd like to meet you, Nicole.'

Nicole leaned forward eagerly. 'That would be wonderful! When? Tomorrow?'

'Soon,' laughed Anne-Marie. 'Very soon, I promise you.'

After that they had talked late into the night, until at last Anne-Marie found a warm blanket for Nicole and they blew out the candles and wished one another good night.

Nicole was so exhausted that she expected sleep to come instantly. But just as she was drifting off into weary slumber, the thought of Jacques shot through her like a sharp stab of pain.

Had he realised yet that she'd gone? Would he even care?

She doubted it very much. Fighting back her despair, she decided that she was glad she'd taken the diamonds he'd stolen, glad! At least it was some kind of revenge on the man, damn him.

The pavements were crowded as people streamed out of the brightly lit theatre and swarmed, chattering and laughing, towards their carriages. News had come to Paris that very day of the great French victory against the Prussians at Valmy. After months of inglorious defeat, the threat of imminent invasion by the Republic's enemies seemed to have been lifted at last, and the Paris theatregoers were in a lighthearted mood, humming snatches of the new marching song, the

Marseillaise, which had been sung with patriotic fervour during the play's interval.

A tall, dark-haired man was making his way puposefully through the crowds dressed in an elegant brown frock coat and English tan jockey boots. More than one woman glanced at his handsome figure surreptitiously, and wondered who he was hurrying to meet; one of the beautiful actresses, no doubt.

Just then, one of the leading ladies of the company, Gabrielle de Chaulnay, swept out, surrounded by her giggling, chattering actress friends, and almost collided with him. As he turned to murmur some appropriate words of apology, one of her friends whispered swiftly in her ear: 'That's him, Gabrielle! That's the one who was asking about Nicole Chabrier!' and, Gabrielle, biting back the words of irritation that had sprung automatically to her lips, tapped her fashionable jewelled walking cane lightly on the cobbles and gazed up into the man's intriguing face. 'You are looking for someone, citizen?' she enquired in that low, husky voice that had made her the darling of Parisian society.

'Perhaps,' he said, assessing her just as she was assessing him. She was not surprised to hear that his voice was cultured and quietly elegant, like his clothes.

Sophie, still clutching Gabrielle's arm in excitement, whispered, 'It is him, I'm sure! He's the man who's looking for Nicole; he's been asking round all the theatres, Gabrielle!'

The man heard her and turned a ravishing smile on her. 'It's true, I am looking for Nicole Chabrier. Have you seen her lately, citizeness? She used to work at the *Comédie* with you, didn't she?'

'So you know me, citizen.'

He bowed politely. 'Who in Paris doesn't know you, citizeness de Chaulnay?'

She smiled, gratified. 'Why do you want to find Nicole?'

'Because she has something of mine, and I want it back.'

Somehow the man intrigued her. 'If you're looking for Nicole,' she said, 'I might just be able to help you.' Swiftly she handed him a gilt-edged card inscribed with her name and address. 'Perhaps you would like to call on me in, say, an hour?'

He hesitated only fractionally, then bowed his dark head. 'Citizeness, I would be honoured.'

It was exactly an hour later that the man climbed the stairs to Gabrielle de Chaulnay's apartment in the fashionable Rue de Chantereine district, where many of the actresses and theatre managers lived. As he knocked, someone quickly opened the door into a softly candlelit room that was opulent with ornate furnishings and deep rugs and silk hangings. At first the flickering candles dazzled him, and the rich perfumes of citrus and musk that hung heavily in the warm air almost stifled him. Then the door was shut firmly behind him, and he realised that there were four of them in here, including Gabrielle de Chaulnay herself; all of them beautiful with their tumbling hair and their diaphanous gowns, and all of them gazing at him with cold, glittering eyes. He could see immmediately that they meant him no good whatsoever, but by then it was too late.

'Your name, citizen?' It was Gabrielle herself who spoke; she was undoubtedly the most beautiful of them all, with her flowing ringlets of rich brown hair and her perfect complexion enhanced very subtly by rice-powder and red lipsalve. She licked those lips now as he replied.

'My name is Jacques.'

'Are you the one known as citizen Jacques? *The* citizen Jacques?'

'There are many men in Paris with my name, citizeness.'

'Don't play with me, my friend.' Her voice was silkily cold as she toyed with the slender jewelled cane she held in her ringed hand. 'You are the celebrated citizen

176

Jacques, are you not? We have heard interesting stories about you. We have heard of dissolute parties at your secret mansion. We want to know if these stories are true.'

'Oh, no.' Jacques was smiling, and moving slowly back towards the door. 'I fear you have been misled, ladies.'

His hand reached for the door; Gabrielle snapped out, 'Oh, no you don't!' and suddenly she'd pulled out a thin, rapier-like steel blade from her walking cane and was holding it at his throat. 'Let me tell you, citizen Jacques, that the door is locked behind you, and from now on you're going to do exactly as we say. Otherwise, we believe that there are certain members of the new National Convention who would be most interested to hear about your activities.' Still pricking his throat with the point of her blade, she looked round quickly at the rapt circle of onlookers. 'Now, girls, what shall we do with him? Why don't we start by throwing dice for the removal of his fine clothes?'

Jacques began to laugh very softly, holding out his hands in self-deprecation. 'I fear, madame, that you will be disappointed.'

'Oh, I don't think we will,' replied Gabrielle, smiling back, her blue eyes luminous with greed. 'Are you going to co-operate, or are you going to make things difficult for yourself?'

'Will you tell me where Nicole Chabrier is?'

'Such devotion! What she has taken from you must be very precious. If you do exactly as I say, I might just think about it.'

Jacques moved swiftly then, throwing up the rapier blade with his hardened fist and making for the door, but two of the women threw themselves at his legs and the rest of them clung to his body. Even then, he could probably have escaped, but he found himself unable to retaliate as viciously as if his opponents had been men, and thus they overpowered him, feeling no similar compunction about hurting him as they threw him to the floor. Someone had fetched a strong length of silken cord, and they ripped his coat off and trussed his hands behind his back. He still struggled, but Gabrielle somehow twisted her sheathed cane through his bound arms and wrenched them up high behind his back, so that every time he kicked out or tried to resist she was able to jerk the cane higher until the perspiration stood out on his forehead. Meanwhile the other women were carefully unfastening his white silk shirt and his skintight breeches; he struggled again when they started to fondle his vulnerably exposed phallus, but Gabrielle pulled on her stick and he closed his eyes with sudden pain.

'Do what you like with him, girls,' Gabrielle grinned. 'I do believe he's learning some sense at last.'

'Oh, he's beautiful!' cried out the youngest of the women, Sophie, as she cradled his heavy balls in her hands and watched avidly as his manhood jerked helplessly into life. 'What shall we do with him, Gabrielle? Take turns?'

Gabrielle pondered. She hated men. All her life they'd used her, humiliated her, and now that she was rich and successful she took every chance she could for revenge. But there was something about this one that was different. He seemed to accept everything, even pain, with a kind of stoicism that made her wonder what sufferings his past life had held. He was incredibly handsome, of that there was no doubt; as handsome as any aristocrat, with his fine, regular features and cruel yet sensual mouth; and his body was perfectly proportioned and honed into exceptional fitness. But there was something else about him, some deep inner reserve that she doubted anyone had broken through. He was a man, and of course she hated all men, but she was curious to find out for herself what he was really like, whether the stories about him could possibly be true.

She said, moistening her lips, 'We'll take turns, of course. And I shall be first.'

Carefully lifting her flimsy muslin skirts, she straddled him so that she could see his taut face. He tried to struggle at first, to draw up his legs and push her away, but she ordered two of her girls to crouch by his shoulders, ready to jerk at the cane that pinioned his arms, and after a few attempts at resistance he soon gave up. Her secret parts were already moist and wet, eager for the challenge; with delicious slowness she lowered herself inch by inch onto his jutting penis, enfolding him deep within her hungry, swollen flesh, while the other girls gathered round, watching enviously. He felt good, so good; hot and hard and strong. Gabrielle hissed out her satisfaction as he moved involuntarily inside her, and saw him shut his eyes against his own mounting excitement. The feel of him deep within her was unbelievable; so hard, so silky-smooth and warm, so pulsing with life and vigour. She felt her own juices flow richly, anointing his mighty shaft; and, reaching to toy ecstatically with her own clitoris, she slid up and down on his imprisoned phallus, closing her eyes and uttering tiny soft cries as she slipped easily into a sweet, delicious climax.

His hard-boned face was taut and strained, his eyes closed as she shuddered above him, her spasms finally dying away in languorous ripples of warmth. Suddenly, grateful for the unexpectedly acute pleasure he'd given her, she leaned forward, running her hands across his bare, muscled chest, and whispered, 'If you manage to satisfy us all, my fine citizen Jacques, if you give us good value, then I'll tell you where you can find your Nicole.'

His eyes opened to meet hers briefly. 'A challenge?'

'A challenge,' she responded, and chuckled softly as she saw the light of amusement in his fine dark eyes. He was different, this one. Gabrielle de Chaulnay admired courage, and he had it in plenty. He would need it by the time thay had finished with him. Slowly she raised herself from his warm, tense body, seeing that his penis was straining hungrily into empty air, glistening still with her juices, yearning for a soft female cavern to bury itself in. Turning round, she called out, 'He's all yours, girls. Do what you want with him.'

From then on she saw very little of him, because he was almost covered by females in various states of disarray. One of them crouched over his loins and drew his beautiful penis deep within her mouth, swirling and sucking at the fiercely engorged flesh; he exploded then, pumping his seed despairingly between the girl's avid lips, and Gabrielle saw the man moan softly in defeat; but then his face disappeared from view as another pushed her naked breasts into it, thrusting her straining nipples hard against his lips and teeth. Then someone else who'd already stripped herself toppled her off him and sat eagerly astride his head, displaying her ripe, bare bottom cheeks and rubbing her honeyed cleft against his face. 'Lick me, citizen Jacques,' she was urging. 'Stick your fine tongue up into me, lick my juices, ah, yes!' Yet another had roused his penis once more into rampant life by sucking on it hotly; she jumped astride him and was riding him hungrily, bobbing up and down at a furious rate on his helplessly engorged pillar of flesh and squeezing her own dark nipples in ecstasy as her face darkened with impending orgasm. The blonde girl Sophie, who had decided that she had fallen in love with him, lay dreamily on the floor between his legs, stroking his strong, hair-covered thighs and watching avidly as his massive, glistening penis was exposed time and time again by the girl who slid up and down on him so rapturously.

Gabrielle watched with narrowed blue eyes as one by one they all sated themselves on his pinioned body; yet he showed no sign of giving way again. He was good, too good. The stories were all true. She found herself almost regretting her decision to humiliate him like this, but she had issued her challenge and would stick by it.

The girls had rolled off him now, all sated in one way or another, smiling contentedly and stroking his beautiful body while his penis throbbed upright with stark need. He'd outlasted them all, damn him. Suddenly

Gabrielle reached into her bedside drawer and pulled out a well-worn, cylindrical object made of smooth black leather, a fat artificial phallus which she used occasionally herself. Holding it in her hand, she walked over to him. 'You still want to know where Nicole Chabrier is?'

The sweat beaded on his forehead, but he still sounded calm as he said, 'Isn't that what all this is about? Or is this how you usually treat your guests?'

Her eyes narrowed. 'Usually we charge a lot of money for this kind of thing. Turn over.' Already she was oiling the lengthy leather phallus and she saw his eyes fasten on it and grow dark. 'Turn over, I said!' She jerked on the cane to assist him, and the other girls gathered round raptly as Gabrielle ripped his breeches halfway down his thighs. Slowly, deliberately she ran her oiled finger down the dark cleft between his tight bottom cheeks and saw him flinch, saw how the heavy pouch of his balls jerked and tightened between his iron-hard thighs as she inserted her finger slightly.

'Still going to last out, citizen Jacques?'

He gritted his teeth. 'Try me.' He was on his knees, stooping uncomfortably because his arms were bound behind his back with the cord and the horizontal cane. He was utterly helpless, utterly in her power. With a hiss of pleasure, Gabrielle rammed the oiled leather shaft up into his tightly collared hole and the other girls gathered round, eagerly coating their hands in scented oil as they reached beneath him to fondle his testicles, his inner thighs, his lengthy, throbbing penis. Carefully, lovingly, Sophie made a circle with forefinger and thumb, and tightly ran it up and down over the rim of his swollen glans, while Gabrielle slid the leather penis faster and faster in and out of his tight bottom-hole; it was too much for him and with a hoarse shout Jacques shuddered and exploded, his semen jetting forth in great gouts of shameful pleasure as the girls gasped and fought one another to catch the milky juice on their bodies and faces.

Gabrielle saw how the man slumped at last in defeat.

181

Feeling an unaccustomed pity, she gently withdrew the black leather phallus and reached to unfasten his arms. As she did so, his sweat-soaked shirt slipped higher up his back, exposing his ridged scars, and the women drew back from him with horrified gasps. 'Oh, the poor thing!' Sophie murmured in horror.

'He's been in prison,' said another one swiftly, running her hands tenderly over the scars. 'Those are the marks of a flogging. And look, he's been branded.'

To Jacques, it seemed as if he suddenly had access to their sisterhood. They couldn't do enough for him. They untied him and bathed him, bringing him a tray of delicious food and wine. Normally, they told him, the charge for such an evening's entertainment was a hundred livres, but for him it was free, and he was welcome to return any time he liked. Jacques smiled, and told them he was honoured.

Finally, just before he insisted that he really must leave, Gabrielle told him that Nicole Chabrier would be at Paul Vichy's party in two days' time. He absorbed the news with no apparent emotion, and they all stood by the door to kiss him goodbye.

'Gorgeous. Quite gorgeous,' murmured one of them, leaning against her friend; and Sophie, the youngest, sighed, 'Lucky Nicole Chabrier.'

'I'm not so sure about that,' said Gabrielle de Chaulnay thoughtfully. 'I've met men like him before. If you're not careful, they'll destroy you.'

Chapter Ten

*B*right flambeaux burned outside Paul Vichy's
fashionable house in the Rue Chantereine, and the
carriages thronged the narrow street, jostling for space.
Nicole, hurrying to keep up with her friend Anne-Marie
as they made their way through the crowds to the
welcoming front door, still found it incredible that life
in Paris had returned to normal so quickly after the
dreadful prison massacres. But Anne-Marie had just
shrugged when Nicole had hesitantly mentioned it
earlier that day.

'Pooh,' she'd shrugged. 'The Royalist traitors and the
popish priests had it coming to them. They would have
opened the gates of Paris to the Austrian army,
wouldn't they, if they'd been allowed to go free, so
something had to be done with them. Remember we're
at war, Nicole. You should have heard Danton standing
up in the Assembly last week, making his speech about
how Paris is fighting for survival, and the people will
win; he was truly magnificent, and everyone, even his
enemies, applauded him. Now, where did I put my
gloves? I thought I'd wear this striped cotton gown for
Paul Vichy's party – what do you think, *chérie*?'

Now, they were here at last; and as they climbed the
steps to the front door, two tall, bewigged footmen in

silk frock coats came forward to greet them and took their cloaks with silent deference. Anne-Marie had generously lent Nicole one of her newest gowns, of the latest style, made of flimsy cream muslin with a wide sash and a full skirt. She smoothed it down, feeling instinctively for the leather pouch containing the diamonds which she'd slipped deep into the pocket. One of the footmen was black; Nicole wondered if he was one of the freed slaves from the French colony of St Domingue that so many of the fashionable liberals were taking on as servants. He seemed to be watching her with his dark, appraising eyes as she handed him her cloak; quickly she looked away and shyly followed Anne-Marie into the thronged house.

Anne-Marie hadn't been performing that night, but instead they'd gone to watch the opening night of a play. It had been a dull Roman tragedy, of the kind that was all too popular these days with its worthy Republican theme, and Nicole had found its speeches intolerably boring. She wondered why the frivolous, light-hearted Anne-Marie had chosen to go to it, but it was obviously the place to be seen. 'It's one of Paul Vichy's productions,' whispered Anne-Marie to her in the interval, guessing at her friend's perplexity. 'It would be very rude not to attend, when we've been invited to the party afterwards!'

The party. In her former life, Nicole had been used to parties every night, but somehow everything had changed, and she felt nervous about being part of normal society once more. 'Who will be there?' she asked.

Anne-Marie laughed knowingly. 'You would be surprised, *chérie*! Some of the greatest, most powerful men in Paris will be guests, but they prefer to remain anonymous – you will see!'

'And why are we invited?'

'You will see that too. The entertainment Paul has planned for tonight is a novel idea, truly enterprising.'

Nicole pondered, not understanding. 'Will monsieur Vichy offer me a job?'

'That depends, Nicole, on your audition this evening,' said Anne-Marie mischievously, and would say no more.

Audition. Nicole frowned at the memory of the word. This must be it, then, her audition to act in one of M. Vichy's famous productions. On their arrival at the Vichy house, she and Anne-Marie had been shown into a small back room, well away from the other guests, where there were four other beautiful girls who'd already changed into their costumes and were whispering excitedly in a corner.

Nicole recognised the costumes immediately, because they were the ones from the Roman play that they'd seen earlier; not the costumes of the main protagonists, the Republican heroes and their wives, but the brief, knee-length tunics of the slaves, with thonged leather sandals that tied around their ankles. The other girls' eyes were glittering with repressed excitement as they welcomed the newcomers. Anne-Marie obviously knew them all, and Nicole, though they talked to her kindly, felt shy and alone.

'What are we to perform?' she asked, puzzled. 'What about my lines?'

The others giggled. Anne-Marie said quickly, 'You'll soon see. Don't worry, you've no words to learn, Nicole.'

'Just make sure it's the best performance of your life,' put in another, and the girls went off into peals of laughter.

Somehow, without being able to say exactly why, Nicole began to feel uneasy. Somehow she was aware of a strange, heated atmosphere, of an air of expectancy that reminded her strongly of some of the dissolute parties she had gone to with Gerard. Something was about to happen, and she wasn't at all sure that she wanted to be part of it.

185

Reluctantly, she picked up her costume and started to get changed. She felt desperately worried about the pouch of diamonds, hidden deep in the pocket of her gown; but there was nowhere to conceal them in the flimsy tunic she was about to put on, and Anne-Marie, who of course had no idea about the existence of the necklace, assured her impatiently that their things would be perfectly safe in here.

Because she was thinking about the diamonds, she thought about Jacques, and she pushed the thought away suddenly because it was like a fierce stab of pain deep inside her, a pain that wouldn't go away. Hating him, because even here she wasn't free of him, she slipped on the flimsy cotton tunic and fastened the leather sandals at her ankles. The tunic came down barely to her knees; she felt shamefully conscious that she was wearing absolutely nothing underneath, but reminded herself that she was an actress, and that of course none of this would be for real.

Then the door opened and two big, burly men came in, dressed in short tunics that revealed their thickset bodies, their strong and muscular legs. Their physiques were made even more striking by the fact that while one of them was blond, with short cropped hair and smooth tanned skin, the other was as black as the night, and Nicole suddenly realised that they were the two footmen who'd greeted them at the door, divested now of their fine clothes and powdered wigs. They carried lengths of rope in their hands, which they held out threateningly, calling out, 'Come on, you sluts. Move!'

Anne-Marie shivered deliciously in mock fear, and the other girls giggled. Nicole, bewildered, said in a low voice, 'Is this really an audition, Anne-Marie?'

But Anne-Marie was dragging her impatiently towards the men, who were tying the girls' wrists and then roping them in a line together. 'Don't be tedious, dear Nicole! You want a job as an actress again, don't you? Well, things have changed slightly in the theatre

186

world, but you'll certainly get your chance to impress them all tonight! Oh, look at him. Isn't he beautiful?'

One of the other girls had sidled up to the big black man and was kissing him hungrily. He fondled her breasts casually with his big hand, and then thrust her away. 'Control yourself, slut!' The girl giggled and licked her lips as he roped her wrists behind her back, her breasts thrusting eagerly towards him still; and Nicole, watching, felt her blood become strangely heated. She felt only too vulnerable in her flimsy tunic, with nothing on underneath; her own nipples stiffened visibly, poking against the thin cotton, and she saw the big blond-haired guard survey the hard nubs lasciviously as he reached out to grasp her hands for the rope. 'So we've got a new girl tonight,' he said. 'Should be interesting.'

Nicole tried to pull her hands away, suddenly frightened. This was no play. This was for real. 'Get your hands off me!' she hissed.

The others watched her in admiration. 'She'll drive them wild,' one of them whispered appreciatively. 'What an actress!'

And Nicole suddenly realised the extent of the trap she was in. If she tried to protest about anything the men ordered her to do, they'd all think she was just putting on an act, and laugh at her . . .

They'd caught her by now, and roped her swiftly into line with the rest of them. In single file the girls were led out along a corridor and up some steps, into a dimly-lit room lined on one side by thick, full-length curtains. Then the curtains were swung back, and Nicole realised that they were on a small stage. The rest of the room where the unseen audience sat was in complete darkness, but she knew they were there, because she could hear the collective hiss of indrawn breaths, the salacious murmurs, as the half-dressed girls were revealed to their view.

Nicole gazed down blindly, gradually becoming aware of row upon row of intent faces, all male, gazing up avidly. She turned blindly to Anne-Marie, who was next to her. 'Oh, what is happening?'

Anne-Marie regarded her almost with impatience. 'Nicole, *chérie*. Don't tell me you didn't realise! That dry, boring Roman play we saw earlier was only for show. *This* is the real entertainment; this is what everyone pays for!' She flashed an eager, challenging look down at their audience. 'Some of the most powerful men in Paris are down there, Nicole. This is the most exciting play you'll ever be in, I promise you!'

'Silence, there! Get into line, you bitches, and stand still!' Roughly the two guards pulled them into line, and the girls hung their heads in submission; but Nicole saw how they continued to dart lascivious glances at their audience from under coyly lowered lashes. Then the blond guard strutted to the front of the stage, his hands on his hips, and said into the expectant silence, 'Now, my fine citizens. Here is your chance to survey what we have on offer for tonight. What am I bid for the first wench?' And swiftly he unfastened a tall, sultry-looking redhead and pulled her forward.

'What can she do?' roared someone suddenly from the audience. 'How can we pay for what we can't see?'

The guard grinned slowly. 'What do you want to see, citizen? Remember, whatever you ask for, you'll have to pay.'

'Fifty livres for a real kiss!' yelled someone else, and the audience shifted and muttered with repressed excitement. Nicole watched helplessly, her heart beating wildly as the guard nodded and turned with narrowed blue eyes to the redhead. 'Very well. Show us what you can do – bitch,' he said softly. The woman's wrists were still bound behind her back. Slowly he grasped her by her long thick hair and forced her to his knees in front of him. Then he pulled up his short tunic, and there were grunts of surprise from the audience, because he was wearing a black leather pouch to restrain his already bulging genitals. He fondled himself briefly there beneath the girl's hot, greedy gaze; she leaned forward suddenly, her mouth her only instrument, and with eyes alight with excitement she began to run her tongue smoothly up along the strong, hair-roughened muscles of his thighs, moving her lips softly over the black leather pouch so that the audience could see how it stirred and swelled still further. With a grunt, the guard untied the pouch and pulled it off; his penis hung thickly against the heavy sac of his balls, already stirring into vigorous life, and the girl gave a soft smile and fastened her lush mouth eagerly around his pulsing shaft.

The audience went very still as she began to suck and pull at the stiffening penis, running her tongue round it tantalisingly. The blond guard braced himself, planting his sturdy legs firmly apart and gritting his teeth at the fierce onslaught of pleasure as the girl's tongue and teeth worked over his rapidly hardening flesh. Softly the girl withdrew her mouth, smiling with secret satisfaction, so they could all see how the thick, angrily engorged shaft jutted out fiercely now, its swollen plum quivering blindly into the empty air; there was a murmur of appreciation from the audience, and an audible sigh of excitement as the girl once more opened her mouth wide and took the hot red member as far down her throat as she could, until her guard shuddered and closed his eyes in unbearable tension.

Nicole swallowed hard, feeling her own fierce excitement rising relentlessly at the lewd spectacle. Was this what she would have to do? In front of all these people? The idea repulsed her, and yet she felt her secret flesh grow moist and hot at the thought of such shameful pleasure. She couldn't tear her eyes from the guard's sturdy instrument of pleasure, revealed so deliciously in all its arrogant strength as the girl slowly drew her lips back down to the swollen glans, nibbling and licking enticingly. Nicole shuddered, longing to feel that great shaft sliding between her own slender thighs, nudging at her slick flesh lips, ravishing her with all its delicious masculine strength.

189

At a grated command from the guard, the red-head suddenly began to move frantically, sliding her full lips swiftly up and down the engorged penis, tormenting him with the hot sensuality of her velvety mouth. The guard threw his head back and shut his eyes, grasping her thick red hair in his extremity as his balls tightened and his buttocks pumped harder and harder against the girl's face. She lapped up his juices avidly, her throat working madly as he spurted his hot seed deep down her willing throat.

There was a tense, erotic silence, broken by lazy clapping from the audience. What next? thought Nicole despairingly.

She didn't have to wait long to find out. 'Fifty livres to see the big negro service a wench! That tawny-haired one who's hanging back!' called out a lecherous voice.

The black guard's eyes moved over Nicole lazily, and she shivered at the open lust in his dark eyes, her gaze drawn in apprehension to the already obvious bulge at his groin. But before she could even think of the words to voice her protest, Anne-Marie, her green eyes glittering with excitement, stepped quickly forward. 'Me – oh, please – me!' she whispered, her cheeks flushed.

Coldly nodding, he sauntered up to her and unfastened her rope. He led her with her wrists still bound to the very front of the stage, then forced her to crouch on her knees and elbows with her black, silky hair hanging like a curtain over her delicate face. Then he roughly pulled up her tunic so that her naked white buttocks were exposed, and gazed at her silently.

Nicole gasped at the sight of her friend's utter degradation, at the same time feeling her own sexual need pulling with deep, warm contractions at the base of her belly. Her thighs were damp and sticky with her own shameful desire. But not like this, oh, please! Not like this, in front of all these watching people! Then she actually stopped breathing, because the black man had slowly hitched up his tunic, and had ripped off the straining leather pouch that so inadequately constrained his own tumescent genitals. And his dark, pulsing shaft, exquisitely thick and long, thrust proudly out from his sleek loins.

He fingered his silky penis lovingly, his lips slightly parted in anticipation, and some of the girls moaned in longing, desperately envious of the crouching girl on the floor, who was about to be pleasured by that fine, glossy instrument. Anne-Marie, instinctively sensing their heated arousal, twisted round, and cried out in excitement.

The guard rubbed his hand up and down the massive shaft a few more times, proudly displaying his rampant manhood to his stunned audience, then slowly lowered himself to his knees behind Anne-Marie. Still gripping his heavy penis, he explored between her pouting bottom-cheeks with his other hand and gradually slid his fingers down her moist, crinkled folds, slipping about in her juicy wetness. She whimpered, shuddering with need; and with a slow smile he rubbed the dark head of his phallus down between her thighs then found her lush, melting hole and thrust in, deeply, as his dark face contorted in ecstasy.

Anne-Marie let out a high sob of rapture as his magnificent length slid deep within her loins. She was almost on the brink already, quivering and clutching involuntarily at the fleshy shaft that impaled her; swiftly the black man leaned over her, his buttocks still pumping vigorously, and ripped her tunic to her waist to fondle her soft, dangling breasts. As he squeezed and pulled lasciviously at her pouting nipples, Anne-Marie arched into climax, engulfed in shimmering ecstasy as his big penis continued to ravish her thoroughly until her last whimpers of sated delight faded away into the still air.

But it wasn't over yet. Not for nothing were the invitations to monsieur Vichy's parties the most fought-over in Paris. The audience sighed enviously as he pulled out of her, his stiff rod wet and shiny with her lovejuices, and, still on his knees, pulled her round gently to face him. Guiding her carefully, he made her take his penis in her hands, and Nicole saw how her friend Anne-Marie shuddered with renewed excitement as her slender white fingers fastened round his mighty stem. Then he encouraged her to masturbate him, slowly and sweetly in front of all those people, sliding the foreskin up and down over the rim of the swollen glans; until his balls jerked and trembled with the onslaught of climax, and he threw back his head in a rictus of despair, and the semen gushed hot and milky from his quivering penis, spurting over her exposed breasts and belly. Moaning softly to himself in the words of his own tongue, the negro rubbed his sensitive glans against her hard, semen-smeared nipples as the last of his seed seeped gently forth, his dark eyes glazed over with the extremity of his pleasure. With silent adoration Anne-Marie took the throbbing tip in her mouth, sucking and kissing it in utter gratitude for the ecstasy bestowed.

At last, her head bowed and her legs shaky, she drew her torn tunic together and returned to her place in the line, and the black guard, bracing himself, stood up and stepped back to join his colleague. A burst of spontaneous, appreciative applause broke the acute silence that had fallen.

Nicole closed her eyes, quite weak with longing. Half of her ached for it to be her turn next, while the other half shrank back in acute shame. If summoned to perform, she knew she couldn't resist for long, so great was her desire to feel a strong, pulsing male shaft sinking deep within her own heated flesh.

Just then a small man in the front row, with greasy black hair and a scarred cheek, whom she'd noticed staring at her earlier, called out suddenly, 'What about the tawny-haired wench? She's been hanging back all evening! I'll give fifty livres to see what she's hiding!'

'No!' Nicole's cry was instinctive but useless. It was impossible to struggle, with her hands bound tightly behind her back; coldly the powerful Domingan pulled her away from the other girls, and the stocky, blond-haired guard, with a sneering grin, ripped her tunic slowly down the front and pulled it away.

The shame of exposure before all these avid men washed over her trembling body like a shock wave. Nicole shut her eyes in despair, but she couldn't shut out the appreciative hiss from the crowd, couldn't help but feel their hot eyes burning her naked limbs, her high, trembling breasts, her slender thighs. Impatiently the Domingan pulled her forward to the front of the stage, and she stumbled, almost falling to the ground. Her long tawny hair had tumbled in loose swathes round her naked shoulders but it wasn't long enough to cover her breasts, with their sweet pink crests pouting in humiliating betrayal of her secret, shameful arousal.

'Stand tall, bitch!' The blond man put his big hand under her chin and jerked her head upwards, while the black man bent to pull her legs apart so that her pink nether lips, moist and swollen with desire, peeped through her tawny triangle of hair. There were groans of appreciation from the crowd; and the blond guard, suddenly realising that this beautiful new prize could prove to be the success of the night, called out over the noise, 'Five hundred livres for citizeness Nicole. Five hundred livres, and she's yours for the night, citizens!'

Nicole shuddered. She couldn't believe it. They were actually trying to sell her! She wrenched at the rope; the blond man jerked her close to him again and muttered in her ear, 'Damn you, bitch! What the hell are you doing here if you didn't want to join in?'

'I didn't know,' she faltered. 'I didn't realise what it would be like.'

'You mean you haven't heard of citizen Vichy's special after-theatre parties?' he growled in her ear, so the audience couldn't hear. 'You're either a stupid little innocent, or else a very fine actress. Either way, it's too late now!' He turned swiftly back to the crowd of onlookers; Nicole saw how their faces shifted

193

lasciviously in the dark, smoky room and felt sick. 'What am I bid?' repeated the guard. 'Who'll improve on five hundred livres?'

'Six hundred!' called someone else.

'Seven hundred, I'll give you!'

The guard grinned. 'Looks like this could be an interesting evening.' He pulled casually at Nicole's exposed nipples to stiffen them still further; she closed her eyes in despair as he called out, 'Seven hundred livres – is that all you'll pay, citizens, for this magnificent, tawny beauty? See her firm, delicious little breasts, her flat belly, her slender thighs!'

Then, with no warning, his big hand cupped her heated mound and as Nicole gasped aloud, his stubby fingers prodded and explored, sliding through the tangle of silken curls to caress her soft flesh folds. Nicole knew to her shame that her vulva was moist and swollen, for she was unbearably excited by the lewd displays that she'd seen; and as the man's forefinger curled round her aching pleasure bud and tickled it with a coarse grin on his face, she shut her eyes in despair while a hot tongue of desire licked relentlessly through her.

'One thousand livres!' It was the small, stocky man with the greasy black hair and the scarred cheek who spoke; he was leaning forward eagerly in his chair, his narrow face cruel and lascivious. His skin was dark and swarthy; he was from the south, perhaps from Provence like Jacques, thought Nicole dazedly, but, oh, the two men were worlds apart . . .

'One thousand livres? *Morbleu!*' someone was muttering sourly, 'your purse is fat, citizen Saltier. I can't afford that, not even for such a delicious, ripe little beauty.'

As the guard began to untie her wrists, the scarred man stood up and walked swaggering towards the stage to claim his purchase. Nicole recoiled in sick horror. No. This couldn't be happening to her. Yet the man was moving purposefully towards her, his small eyes greedy and cruel. This wasn't a play, this was for real. And he was paying one thousand livres for her, more than the artisans of Paris saw in an entire year. She shuddered with unbearable revulsion as the hateful little man reached up possessively towards the stage to claim his prize.

Then, suddenly, from the back of the hall, a low, clear voice cut like a knife through the lustful silence. 'Twelve hundred livres.'

The scarred man scowled ferociously into the darkness. 'Damn you, the bidding's stopped! She's mine!'

But the blond guard, his hands on his hips, pushed the man away from Nicole and said, flatly, 'It seems, citizen Saltier, that the bidding is still open.'

Saltier, his face twisted with rage, grated out, 'Thirteen hundred.'

'Fifteen hundred.' The same quiet, anonymous voice again.

Saltier swung round, staring into the black darkness at the back of the hall. 'Damn you, whoever you are!' he snarled in his bitter disappointment. 'Damn you to hell! No wench is worth that much. I wish you ill of her, citizen!' And he slunk off into the shadows, muttering angrily.

Nicole's heart was hammering in sick agony as it dawned on her that she'd been sold off for the evening as if she were indeed a slave. Her legs were trembling so much that she swayed and nearly fell to the ground as the guard reluctantly untied her naked body and handed her her tunic. Anne-Marie caught her eye and whispered, 'Well done, Nicole! You've probably found yourself a fine rich protector!' and Nicole shrank away from her former friend in blind disappointment. Anne-Marie, whom she'd thought she could trust, had led her into this, deliberately deceiving her with talk of parties and auditions. Though perhaps it was all her own fault, for being so stupid, so naive. The guard was helping her to pull on a fresh tunic and saying appreciatively, 'Fifteen hundred livres – well, well. Citizen

Vichy will be inviting you to a few more of his little parties, I should think, wench!'

Stark rebellion suddenly boiled up inside Nicole. Who the hell did they think they were, these vile men who treated her as a mindless sexual commodity?

Pushing her tangle of hair swiftly back from her eyes, she hissed out defiantly, 'Oh no he won't!'

And, shoving the guard violently to one side so he swore aloud in surprise, she made a dash for the door, before the unknown fool who had offered fifteen hundred livres for her should make his unwelcome appearance. Nobody, but nobody bought Nicole Chabrier!

She almost made it to the door, but suddenly a pair of strong hands grasped her from behind. She lashed out wildly. 'Let me go!'

Her captor swung her round, relentlessly gripping her arms; and she found herself staring up into the familiar face of citizen Jacques.

Nicole shook her head in sheer disbelief. 'Damn you, Jacques, let go of me. Let me get away from this hell-hole!'

His fingers tightened on her arms and she felt weak suddenly, her heart thudding at his unexpected near-ness, at his dark, mocking face so close to her own. He said softly, 'Let you go? When I've just paid fifteen hundred livres for you? Come, now, my Nicolette, is that fair?'

She moistened her parched lips, her amber eyes wide with stunned disbelief. 'It was *you*?'

He nodded. 'It was indeed. More fool I. Come on, we're going home.' And he pushed her out through the door into the dimly-lit corridor that led away from that stifling room.

Home. To the big house in the Faubourg St Germain. She knew it was stupid and illogical of her, but the relief flooded through her like a warm, enveloping tide. But she wasn't going to let him know that, not ever!

Once out of that hateful room she stood stock-still,

her eyes blazing up at him, and said with withering scorn, 'So you're reduced to paying for your women now, are you, Jacques? I'm not going anywhere with you!'

He laughed coldly, still gripping her arm. 'You'd rather stay here and go through that kind of fiasco every night, Nicole?'

'Anne-Marie says that citizen Vichy's parties are patronised by half the leaders of the new National Convention! She says she's found lots of powerful friends and protectors here!'

Jacques' thin mouth twisted bitterly; his eyes jerked back to the room they'd just left, from which came the noise of raucous cheers and claps as some new spectacle presented itself. 'I'm sure she's right, and the powerful people she speaks of are probably all in there. Drunken, ribald louts, the lot of them; worthy leaders of the Paris rabble.'

'How dare you criticise?' hissed Nicole. 'You speak like some high-born aristocrat, not the filthy, jumped-up convict you really are!'

Jacques' face tightened in sudden bleak anger and Nicole shivered in fear; because if he went now, if he abandoned her here, she would be utterly lost. He grated out, 'Perhaps I'm changing my mind. Perhaps there are worse things to be than an aristocrat in this fine city of ours. Come on, we're getting out of here.'

Gripping her arm purposefully, he started to lead her through the maze-like corridors of the big house, and this time she offered no resistance.

'How did you find me?' she asked in a small voice.

His eyes were expressionless as he said, 'I remembered that you were an actress. I've been making certain enquiries around the Paris theatres.'

She hurried along beside him, struggling to keep up. 'I can't imagine why you bothered!'

'I wanted my skilled accomplice back; remember our agreement? And also, my Nicole, I searched for you because from what I've observed of you so far, you're not particularly good at looking after yourself. Here, put my coat over your shoulders. It's raining.'

'I can look after myself perfectly well!'

He just looked at her, and she was utterly quelled as he wrapped his still-warm coat round her bare shoulders.

They were outside now. The main street, which had been so crowded with carriages on her arrival earlier, was dark and deserted; a fine drizzle was falling. Jacques hunched up his shoulders against the wet and started off down the street so quickly that she had difficulty in keeping up with him. Nicole, enveloped in his big coat, was hurrying after him, just preparing to dispute his comments on her ability to look after herself, when she heard a hoarse shout from behind.

'Not so fast, my friends! The wench is mine, I think!'

Nicole turned round with a gasp to see the scarfaced man Saltier coming up behind them out of the shadows, with a wicked knife in his hand. Jacques immediately thrust Nicole away from him, pushing her out of the way so hard that she bruised her shoulder on the wall of the nearby house and sank down against it, half sobbing in fear.

Saltier laughed and circled warily, tossing his knife from hand to hand, his knees bent like a cat ready to spring. Jacques was very still, but Nicole could see that his shoulder muscles were tensed like coiled steel beneath his white silk shirt. He said softly, 'You don't seem to understand the rules, my friend. I paid for her, not you.'

Saltier snarled, showing crooked yellow teeth. 'Filthy *aristo*, throwing your money around! Nothing's changed for people like you, has it?' And he lunged at Jacques, aiming the knife straight at his heart with a heavy, vicious thrust that made Nicole cry out in fear. But Jacques was even quicker; somehow he fended off the blow and knocked the cruel knife flying, following with a swift, hard punch to the man's stubbled jaw that had him sprawling winded in the rain-soaked gutter.

Nicole ran to Jacques' side, her face white with fear. 'Quickly – oh, let's get out of here!'

Already Saltier, spitting and swearing, was hauling himself up and wiping the blood from the corner of his mouth. His eyes were black with angry speculation as he gazed venomously up at Jacques. 'Hey,' he exploded in sudden amazement, 'hey, filthy *aristo*, I know you from somewhere!'

But Nicole heard no more, because Jacques had scooped her up in his arms, trailing coat and all, and was carrying her swiftly down the street, well away from citizen Vichy's notorious party.

Saltier lurched back unsteadily towards the door, cursing foully under his breath. One of his friends waited for him, grinning, a bundle of female garments over his arm. 'Here,' he said, 'the wench left all her fine clothing; I was rummaging around and found it in a back room. You might as well take it, because she certainly won't be coming back to claim it. You'll get a few livres for the cloak and gown; they're good quality.' Saltier grunted, taking the bundle without really looking at it. 'I know him from somewhere, I'm sure,' he was still muttering. 'I know him, and when I finally track him down, I'll make the bastard sorry he crossed me.' His stubby fingers tightened round the muslin gown as if it was Jacques' neck he was thinking of, and as he did so, he felt something hard and heavy in the deep pocket. Waiting till his friend had gone back inside, he drew out a small leather pouch, and as he looked inside it and saw the brilliant diamonds with the engraved golden clasp, his small eyes widened in disbelief.

Nicole shivered uncontrollably in Jacques' strong arms, her hands wrapped around his neck, her cheek burning against his silk shirt. He was so warm, so strong. She closed her eyes, and the helpless pain of wanting him as badly as ever swept through her trembling limbs. He had a carriage waiting in a darkened back street; he

199

handed her in first, and when he climbed in after giving orders to the coachman, he put his arm round her and held her close to steady her as the coach lurched away over the cobbles. 'Nicole. What is it?'

'That man,' she whispered. 'He was so awful. And he seemed to know you from somewhere.'

Jacques' rain-dampened face seemed to tighten imperceptibly. 'Nonsense,' he said, dismissing the subject. 'How could he?'

Nicole twisted round in his protective arm to gaze up into his face, unable to stop herself from snuggling closer to his warm, reassuring body. 'And that money, Jacques, fifteen hundred livres! You didn't actually pay it, did you?'

'Indeed I did. Otherwise you wouldn't be here, *chérie*.'

Fifteen hundred livres! It was a fortune. She gazed silently out of the window, watching the ominously empty streets of Paris spin by as the big iron wheels rattled over the cobbles, and said with an aching throat, 'I suppose you could always go back tomorrow night and claim a refund.'

He took hold of her by the shoulders then, and turned her so that she had to face him, had to look into his dark eyes.

'I have no intention whatever of claiming a refund, *chérie*,' he said softly. 'I intend to get what I paid for. Every damned *sou* of it.'

And, placing his hands at the back of her neck, his fingers twisting lightly in her thick, tousled hair, he drew her face towards him and kissed her.

Nicole reeled with the intensity of it. His kiss burned her into near-oblivion; it was heady, sweet, delicious as his tongue explored the moist voluptuousness of her yearning mouth, tangling possessively with her own tongue. The coat slipped unnoticed from her shoulders; clad only in the short, flimsy tunic, she stretched her slender bare arms helplessly round his neck, the blood leaping in her veins at the feel of his wide, hard shoulders beneath her fingertips.

Mid-kiss, so she had no chance to protest, he lifted her easily in his arms and sat her astride his thighs, facing him. Still cherishing her mouth relentlessly with his own, he was toying with her tunic, releasing its fastenings; she hardly realised as it slipped to her waist, until she felt his head move down to relentlessly capture her exposed nipples. Nicole was consumed by fire, throwing back her head in wanton delight as his hot mouth tugged and laved at her turgid crests. She was wearing nothing at all beneath her tunic; her naked thighs had been forced relentlessly apart as she sat astride his legs, and her soft secret flesh, already pulsing and moist with excitement, was being rhythmically rubbed against his groin by the motion of the carriage. Deliberately he clutched her buttocks with his cool hands, pulling her even closer against his all too masculine body, so that her soft, swollen flesh lips were parting and rubbing wetly against the firm fabric of his breeches. She gasped as she felt the upright, swollen shaft of his penis, imprisoned in there; the honeyed moisture spread shamefully from her sweetly aching cavern, trickling onto his dark clothing, and she writhed her hips helplessly against him, pressing her yearning breasts against his hot, sensuous mouth. Oh, but she could climax like this, very quickly, rubbing her parted lips and her throbbing, soaking pleasure bud hard against the thick, captive flesh of his swollen instrument . . .

He drew his face away from her nipples and she moaned in disappointment as the hardened buds leaped and thrust demandingly. 'Steady, my Nicolette,' he whispered huskily in her ear, nibbling at the delicate lobe with his tongue. 'Patience, my little wildcat.'

But he too was on fire for her, she realised exultantly. Sliding her hips back a little along his iron-hard thighs, she bent to fumble with his fastening, gasping in dizzy pleasure as she succeeded at last and was able to ease

201

out his erect, springing phallus. It was strong and proud as it reared eagerly towards her from its secret mat of dark hair, its purple tip glistening in hunger. Nicole felt her own inner flesh churning with the urgent need to enfold that solid pillar of male flesh, to feel it assuaging the hungry, primitive ache so deep inside her.

She bent forward raptly to kiss his beautiful mouth, her little tongue darting into its warm recesses and savouring the hot, masculine taste of him; her hands ran hungrily over his silk shirt, pulling apart the buttons, gasping as she found the hard buds of his nipples, rubbing them till he groaned aloud and she felt his penis strain hotly against her soft belly as she leaned against him. She writhed deliciously against it, feeling the silky upright shaft sliding lasciviously against her plump, juicy flesh lips, its solid length tantalisingly caressing her throbbing pleasure bud. Oh, God, she was near, so near.

Gasping with the intensity of her desire, she planted her knees firmly on the seat on either side of his hips and then slowly, trembling in exquisite tension, she lowered herself onto his hot, pulsing phallus. As the velvety tip slid deliciously between her soaking sex lips, she cried out with delight, throwing her arms around his neck, rubbing her pouting breasts wantonly against the hard, muscled wall of his chest. He was so beautiful. The feel of his strong, dark shaft sliding deep into the very heart of her, filling all of her hungry, wanton flesh, was so exquisite that she was moaning his name aloud, already almost at the brink. The sensations crowded hot and tumultuous in her heated blood; his wicked mouth at her breasts, his tongue and teeth rasping at her engorged nipples; his huge penis driving up deep within her, his hands coaxing her tautly clenched buttocks to work faster, faster as she writhed to meet his powerful thrusts, conscious of nothing except the delirious build-up of rapture.

Then one of Jacques' hands slid round surreptitiously to tangle in the soft tawny hair at the base of her belly;

and glided lasciviously down the hot, juicy flesh folds to caress the base of her helplessly quivering kernel of pleasure. With a choked cry, Nicole sank her fingers into his shoulders and threw herself wildly up and down on him, impaling herself with searing intensity on that hot, hard pillar of flesh, clutching at him convulsively with her whole being as wave after wave of the most exquisite sensations engulfed her yearning flesh. The pulsing went on, deep and hard and unutterably sweet as Jacques groaned and pumped himself into her. She pressed frantic kisses against his taut face as he too climaxed, and then slumped in his arms, the pleasure still washing through her limp, exhausted body.

He stroked her hair and held her very tight, his eyes closed, his penis still throbbing sweetly, languorously deep within her as her last melting spasms ebbed away; and Nicole buried her hot face against his shoulder, aching with love. Jacques had combed the streets of Paris, looking for her, wanting her.

Outside the carriage windows, the menacing Paris streets went by in a hazy blur; his arms tightened around her, and she took his strong, slender hand and kissed the long, sensitive fingers one by one. On his left hand was the delicate gold signet ring that she'd noticed before, and she saw, by the dim light of the passing street lights, that it was engraved with a tiny, five-petalled rose, just like the emblem above the doorway to the chateau. The crest of the mysterious St Maury family. No doubt, she smiled softly, he had helped himself to it when he moved in, just as he'd helped himself to everything else in the opulent mansion, including the diamonds . . . Her hand flew to her mouth, and she gasped out, 'Oh, no! The necklace, Jacques – your necklace! I've lost it.'

He smiled resignedly. 'I assumed, *chérie*, that you sold it to finance your adventures.'

'No! I didn't sell it. I wasn't going to! But I've left it back in that house.'

There was a silence; then he said slowly, 'Back in Paul Vichy's house?'

'Yes! It was with my clothes. Oh, Jacques, I'm so sorry.' Her face brightened. 'But after all, it wasn't really yours anyway, was it?'

He sighed, and stroked her hair. 'My Nicolette, you'll bankrupt me. You realise that?'

His tone was light, and she felt immeasurably relieved that he wasn't angry with her. Just for a split second, his eyes seemed shadowed and brooding, in stark contrast to his casual words, and her heart leaped in alarm; but then he kissed her again, and, dismissing all her stupid fears, she sank contentedly into his arms.

Chapter Eleven

Nicole lay basking sleepily in the golden sunshine of late October, reclining like a contented cat on a deep pile of cushions in the rose-scented arbour. It was just past noon, and the only sound in the beautiful walled garden was the faint, melodious trickle of the old stone fountain. Nicole sighed happily, quite replete after her lunch of luscious peaches and chilled white wine, and decided that she had never been so happy in her life.

She'd been back at the St Maury mansion for just over a week now, and all that time Jacques had been tender and close to her. He still didn't sleep in her room; Nicole was still aware of a strange detachment, an elusive quality about him; but her anxieties were allayed whenever they made love, which was often, and always with a passionate intensity that made her blood sing wildly in her veins just to think of it. And Nicole had noted with secret elation that Jacques hardly left the house now. It was as if the search that had obsessed him for so long was finally over.

He'd gone out today, though, and he'd told her, just before he left at noon, that he was investigating the possibility of leaving Paris and going to live somewhere in the country, somewhere rural and isolated, untouched by war or revolution. The new wave of violence in the city, which had been sparked off by the Convention's ferociously heated debate over whether or not the King should be executed, had made Jacques sombre. Last night, as they sat in the candlelit dining room over supper, Nicole had seen him brooding and she'd said softly, 'Some people think that the King deserves to die, Jacques, for all the suffering that he has brought on his people.'

Jacques had frowned. 'Oh, foolish and misguided he is, without a doubt. But if they kill him, Nicole, they will make a martyr of him. And who will lead France next? The army? Some power-hungry military dictator, who will bring all of Europe into the war against us?'

Nicole said in a low voice, 'It's not a game any more, Jacques, is it?'

'No, *ma chère*. The games are over, I fear.'

Seeing her worried face, he'd kissed away her fears and carried her to the velvet-covered couch, where he caressed every inch of her body until she moaned aloud in melting pleasure. Then he entered her in hard, piercingly sweet fulfilment that made her sob out his name, and cling to him as if she would never let him go.

She smiled softly as she basked in the garden, remembering, and she must have dozed in the sun, because when she heard the distant sound of people's voices she jumped to her feet, her heart hammering. Jacques back already? No, it was far too early.

Suddenly cold in spite of the sunshine, Nicole hurried round to the wide terrace at the front of the house. Coming up the path towards her was Armand, looking strangely bashful; and leaning on his arm was a young woman, a stranger, wrapped in a shabby grey cloak. Nicole instinctively smoothed down her crumpled cotton gown, her heart beating strangely as they approached. At a whispered word from Armand, the woman threw back her hood, and Nicole gasped, because here was possibly the most beautiful woman she had ever seen in her life.

She had long, silvery-blonde hair that cascaded in ringlets around her shoulders, and a perfect heart-shaped face dominated by wideset violet eyes that sparkled with unshed tears. She looked young, and pale, and completely overwhelmed. Nicole felt her soft heart go out to the lovely stranger and walked quickly up to take her hand. 'Who is this, Armand?'

An unaccustomed blush stained Armand's bristled cheeks. 'I found her, madame Nicole. Poor Louise was out on the Paris streets, being chased by the rabble, and I rescued her. I decided to bring her here, because, you see, she has nowhere else to go.'

Nicole said uncertainly, 'But Armand, you know the rules. No-one must be brought here without monsieur Jacques' permission.'

She saw the woman's face cloud over in distress, and saw how she slipped her tiny hand into Armand's great fist in mute, desperate appeal. Armand glanced down lovingly at her trembling figure.

'I know all that, madame Nicole,' he said in his slow, deep voice. 'But you can see for youself how Louise is desperately in need of our help.'

Louise gazed appealingly at Nicole. 'I am all alone in the world, madame, without family or friends. I have no papers, no money, nothing; my poor husband was executed some months ago. I had heard that citizen Jacques might be able to help me to escape from Paris. Otherwise, there is no hope for me.'

Nicole looked pityingly into her pale, tearstained face. 'Of course you must stay!' She stepped forward impulsively and took the blonde woman's small, trembling hands into her own. 'I'm quite sure Jacques will want to help you. Armand, please tell Marianne to find poor Louise a room, and see that she has everything she wants. And Armand, perhaps it would be better to let me explain to Jacques. I will choose the best time to inform him that we have an unexpected guest.'

Armand's face lit up in a huge smile of relief. 'Bless you, madame Nicole.'

'Thank you. Oh, thank you,' breathed Louise fervently.

Poor Armand's half in love with her already, thought Nicole suddenly. And who can blame him? She does look truly angelic, almost ethereal, with that glorious silver-blonde hair.

She watched as Armand led Louise protectively up to the main doors and then she stopped suddenly, the blood draining from her face. That glorious silver-blonde . . .

She, Nicole, had a tiny lock of hair like that, tied in a red ribbon and thrust away deep in a drawer in her bedroom. She'd forgotten all about it, and the message that came with it. *'Tell Jacques there's a woman looking for him and give him this, will you? He'll understand . . .'*

With an effort, she pushed the stab of unreasoning fear away. It was far too late now to give Jacques the forgotten message. And the hair, with its unusual colour; that must be a coincidence, surely. Why on earth would one of Jacques' helpers want to warn him about a poor, fragile young widow, who was seeking refuge from the rabble?

Neither Armand nor Nicole saw how Louise de Lamartine's eyes glittered with pure, malicious triumph as she walked up the steps and saw the St Maury crest engraved on the heavy stone lintel. 'I was right,' she breathed rapturously, gazing up at the distinctive five-petalled rose. 'It *must* be the right house. It *must* be him.'

Hours later, Louise lay back in the hot, scented tub of water that Armand had willingly hauled up to her second-floor room and laved her creamy breasts and sleek flanks with expensive, sweet-smelling soap. She couldn't believe it. They'd fallen for everything, even her story that she had seen her poor, noble husband guillotined in the Place du Carrousel.

Earlier, when they'd thought she was asleep in her room, she'd tiptoed round the wonderful house in a voyage of exploration. It was the house of her dreams; would its owner match it? She tingled at the thought of citizen Jacques, rubbing her thighs together lasciviously, feeling her lush inner lips pouting in wanton anticipation. Soon he would be here, and then she would know for sure if he was really the man she'd been seeking for so long.

She'd seriously begun to wonder if she would ever make it here, so long did she have to wait in those miserable, shabby lodgings Armand had found for her. She'd grown terribly impatient with the slow-moving, slow-thinking Armand, and began to wonder if he was lying about taking her to citizen Jacques' house, except that she didn't think he was capable of such deviousness.

But she was here now, and everything was going well, although the presence of the woman Nicole was a nasty shock. Armand said that citizen Jacques had been away for almost two weeks searching for her, and Louise was forced to concede that she was indeed beautiful, with her glorious tawny hair and gold-tinted skin, like a candle-flame. Louise was confident, though, that she'd soon eclipse her; and she, Louise, had the secret advantage that they all took her to be a sweet, innocent widow. Except for that dolt Armand, of course, and he'd never confess what he'd submitted to at her hands; never confess how he'd let her truss up his great naked body and let her torment him with little, burning switches on his hairy buttocks, and stick her fingers in his bottom-hole, driving them in lasciviously until his great penis jerked and quivered in its extremity.

Then, to torment his leashed body still further, she'd undressed slowly in front of him, letting his lust-maddened eyes feast on her latest surprise: her naked, hair-free mound. She'd slipped out to a chemist's shop near the Place de Grève and bought all the ingredients to concoct her own precious lotion, which she'd been taught to make long ago by an elderly but still beautiful courtesan at Versailles; and while she waited for Armand's next visit she'd amused herself by melting every trace of hair from her body until between her thighs she was as sweet and soft as a young girl.

She enjoyed the sensation herself of cool air on naked flesh, and the sight of her smooth mound, scented with sandalwood and musk, drove Armand wild. She'd played with herself in front of him, pulling her pouting lips apart to show him the glistening nub of her aroused clitoris; he'd almost howled, and tried to drag his bound body towards her, his great penis jerking hungrily against his belly, but Louise had frowned at him and said softly, even as her own moist finger slid deliciously down her juicy flesh folds, 'Armand, I'm disappointed in you. You've been very wicked. You said you would take me to citizen Jacques.'

'I can't,' he whimpered. 'He isn't there, I've told you. He's searching for madame Nicole.'

'I don't believe you.' She was using two fingers on herself now, and the pleasure was pulsing sweet and hot between her moist thighs. 'I don't believe you know citizen Jacques at all.'

'Dear God,' he moaned. 'As soon as he returns, I'll take you to him, I swear to you.'

She watched the bound man sternly. The big purple plum of his phallus jerked and throbbed, glistening enticingly; his heavy, velvety balls swung between his thighs as he tried vainly to control himself. She decided to take pity on him, mainly because she was almost at the point of no return herself. Slowly she leaned back against the narrow bed, parting her legs so that all her dark, honeyed inner flesh was revealed. 'You've been a bad boy, Armand,' she whispered. 'But I think you've suffered enough for now. Come. Take me, fill me with that great prick of yours.'

Armand, his eyes suddenly alight, struggled to his feet with difficulty because his hands were still bound and lunged towards her, his great phallus swaying heavily. Without a word he rammed himself into her sweet, soaking flesh lips, his mouth and tongue guzzling hungrily at her pouting nipples, and Louise sighed with pleasure as she felt that great, hot shaft slide deep within her hungry flesh. 'Oh, yes,' she breathed. 'That's it. Again, my fine Armand. Ride me, ride me . . .'

Gasping, he withdrew, so that she shuddered with longing; then drove it in again, his staff so lengthy, so thick that already she felt herself shudder on the very brink. Holding her breath, she slid her finger down to circle her own wanton bud of pleasure, caressing it lasciviously; then she glanced down again at the great, slick shaft as it slowly disappeared once more within her juicy flesh, pleasuring her yearning love-channel so magnificently with its hard, solid length. 'Oh,' she gasped – 'Oh, Armand . . .'

And she tensed all over, then furiously thrust herself towards him, impaling herself again and again on his wonderfully stiff penis, driving herself to ecstasy as the ripples of hard, grinding pleasure devoured her, engulfed her in a shattering climax. Armand exploded deep within her at the same time, his whole body shuddering with shameful release. 'Soon,' he whispered huskily. 'As soon as I can, I'll take you to citizen Jacques.'

And now, the day had come, and Louise was here at last. Soon, she would meet him, and finally know if he was truly the man she'd been looking for. The blood rose softly in her cheeks at the thought of him and her finger stole down to finger her secret flesh folds, so sweetly caressed by the warm water of the bath. She realised that she was hotly aroused already; her nipples ached and pouted longingly as she stroked her plump slit, and she knew that she could easily bring herself to a sweet little climax here and now. But no. She would wait for something better.

She'd really enjoyed herself exploring this wonderful

house earlier, when those fools below thought she was asleep in her room. She'd gazed with silent venom into the feminine disarray of Nicole Chabrier's room, vowing to oust her from this house within twenty-four hours, and then, her heart pounding with strange excitement, she'd peeped into the room they'd told her was citizen Jacques'. It was cool and spacious, and in meticulous order, with a high, damask-curtained bed that made her squirm in anticipation. There was the masculine scent of fine, clean linen and leather riding boots, with just a hint of the delicious toilet water he used, fragrant with citrus oils and bergamot. She shivered with pleasure and closed the door silently, rapturously imagining the dark delights to come. It was him. It had to be him.

She didn't dare to explore the ground floor, of course, because they were all down there: Armand, and Nicole, whom she already hated, and the plump, pretty dark-haired one, Marianne, who'd been wary of Louise, but watched her avidly when she thought she wasn't looking. Louise decided that Marianne looked very promising.

And so, still anxious to know this great house and all its secrets, she'd gone up further flights of stairs, carefully exploring all the shadowy rooms and corridors. There'd been empty bedrooms, junk-filled attics, and cobwebbed landings. It was late afternoon, and this upper part of the house seemed cold and dark; she wished she'd brought a candle and shivered uneasily, physically forcing herself to go up the last narrow stairase to a shuttered turret room.

And there, she'd gasped in delight at what she found.

Trembling with excitement, she wandered slowly round the confines of the secret chamber, her fingertips trailing lovingly over the darkly sinister objects that were displayed on the walls with such exquisite effect. This, above all else, even more than the crest above the entrance, confirmed that she was in the right house.

Remembering that room now, savouring the memory

of those various whips, the strange harnesses, the soft leather masks, Louise lay back in the warm water of her lavender-scented bath and closed her eyes in delicious languor. Soon they would all discover, too late, that Louise de Lamartine was not the innocent, sweet little widow they took her to be.

Marianne stood tentatively outside the door to Louise's room, carrying fresh bath sheets for the new guest to dry herself with. She didn't know quite why, but she felt uneasy about madame Louise. Maybe it was the way her Armand followed the little widow around like an adoring dog, his eyes full of blind devotion. Maybe it was the way she'd seen madame Louise's downcast eyes flash in sudden calculating interest as they'd passed m'sieur Jacques' room earlier.

Marianne knocked on the door and heard that low, sweet voice call out, 'Come in.'

Marianne put the linen sheets down on the bed, and was about to hurry swiftly out again, when Louise said imploringly, 'Please, Marianne! Would you help me to wash myself? I always think it is so much easier with someone else to help, don't you?'

Marianne hesitated. There was a lot to be done downstairs. But the sight of Louise lying back in her scented bath, with her high, ripe breasts just breaking the water, and her silvery-blonde ringlets cascading round her shoulders, held her transfixed. No wonder that fool Armand was utterly hypnotised.

'Oh, please!' murmured Louise, gazing up at her. 'It won't take you a minute, dear Marianne.'

Marianne, her cheeks burning, stepped forward blindly and tried not to look at those beautiful, pink nipples that bobbed so enticingly through the suds. She swallowed hard. 'If you lean forward a little, madame, I shall wash your back.' Louise sighed, her eyes half-closed, and cupped her full breasts, lifting them dreamily and letting her fingers play with their pouting crests. 'Wash my breasts first, Marianne,' she commanded silkily. 'Hold them firmly; stroke them and soap them well, really well.'

Marianne gasped and drew back, but Louise caught her hand and smiled at her and enfolded her fingers over one juicy globe; and Marianne, her blood seething with shameful excitement, ran the soap firmly over the rounded flesh of Louise's beautiful firm breasts and felt a surge of desperate longing licking at her belly as the taut, stiffening nipples sprang to meet her fingers. Blindly, feeling her own arousal course wantonly through her veins, she caressed the turgid peaks with the pads of her wet thumbs; Louise gave a soft moan and raised one knee a little higher, gently rubbing her slender white thighs together beneath the water and Marianne saw, with a gasp of amazed shock, that Louise was completely smooth and hairless down there.

Louise gazed up at her with those wide, innocent eyes and said huskily, 'You like my body, Marianne? Then explore it and make it your own with your lovely soft hands.'

Marianne swallowed hard, feeling her own breasts tingling and straining against her tight bodice. Lazily Louise reached up and caressed their aching fulness through the taut cotton; Marianne gasped aloud with fierce delight at the forbidden pleasure and Louise, laughing softly, drew Marianne's unresisting hand down to her water-laved thighs. 'Stroke me, Marianne. Oh, I burn for you. Stroke me, pleasure me with your gentle fingers.'

Entranced by the feel of those soft, silky folds of naked flesh unfurling like the petals of a flower between Louise's parted thighs, Marianne, her own breathing ragged, let her hand wander beneath the lavender-scented water. The flesh there was so soft, so delicate; she heard Louise's gasp as she brushed past her most sensitive parts. Taking a deep breath, Marianne rubbed her fingers tentatively up and down the warm, fleshy slit, remembering those nights of pleasure with her friend Jeanette, and the cruel madame d'Argency.

214

With an urgent cry, Louise grabbed her hand and held it there beneath the water, then ground herself against Marianne's stiffened fingers, writhing her hips in delight. Marianne, blushing hotly, wet with excitement herself, felt the woman's pulsing vulva clutch at her fingers and she obediently thrust them upwards into that wet, quivering flesh until Louise collapsed with delicious, melting little cries, her eyes closed, her beautiful face quite flushed with pleasure. 'Oh, thank you, dear Marianne,' she whispered ardently, 'thank you. I was dying of need.'

Marianne, suddenly ashamed at what she'd done, snatched her hand away from the woman's lewd flesh as if it burned. She felt uneasy again. 'You'll leave my Armand alone, won't you?' she asked anxiously as she stood up. 'He's a good, simple man and he's not used to women such as you!'

Louise, meanwhile, had drawn herself out of the bath and was rubbing herself tenderly with the fresh bath sheets. She smiled sweetly at Marianne and said, 'Your Armand has ravished me countless times already, dear Marianne. He is magnificently equipped, is he not?'

Marianne gasped. 'But that's impossible! You've only just arrived here.'

'Ah,' said Louise softly, 'but it was a long journey. Poor Marianne, your gown is all wet. I fear I must have splashed you. Here, let me remove your damp clothes.'

And Marianne stood there transfixed in the centre of the room as Louise unbuttoned her bodice, and slid her gown to the floor, and bent her head to lave and lick at her pouting breasts. Soon, she was moaning and gasping out her pleasure on the bed as Louise's plump, flickering tongue lapped avidly at her naked secret places, parting her flesh lips and pushing eagerly into her hot, moist depths.

Louise lifted her head affectionately, her face smeared with Marianne's juices. 'Your Armand,' she said affectionately, 'is a hungry, wicked man, with a prick like a stallion. You are so lucky, Marianne. Does he hold you

215

in his arms every night, and drive that great weapon in and out of you until you melt with pleasure?'

'Yes,' Marianne whispered. 'Yes, he does. Oh, please don't stop!'

Louise dipped her head, and once more Marianne felt the hot, hard point of her luscious tongue driving deep within her honeyed cavern. Then Louise reached with her hands to pinch and roll Marianne's burgeoning nipples; Marianne arched her hips, frantic with need.

'Do you mind sharing him, Marianne?' whispered Louise. 'Would you like to watch your Armand's fine great penis driving up into my secret parts? Would you like to see me writhing beneath him as he impales me with his magnificent shaft? Would you like to see me clawing at his back and wrapping my legs round his thrusting hips as he ravishes my sweet flesh and pumps himself deep within me?'

'Yes!' moaned Marianne, her face contorted with need. 'Oh, yes.'

'You promise to do exactly as I say? To persuade Armand to do exactly as I say?'

'Yes, anything! But please, please don't leave me like this.'

With a smile of satisfaction, Louise lowered her face once more to Marianne's churning hips and drove her long, stiffened tongue deep into Marianne's aching love-channel.

Marianne felt the sweet, longed-for pleasure surge and gather at every steady tongue thrust. She shut her eyes and imagined her Armand, his great cock jutting proudly, kneeling behind this woman's plump buttocks even as she bent over Marianne, and thrusting deep within her tight, puckered hole with strong, savage strokes. With a loud cry, Marianne arched her hips, grinding them wetly against Louise's face, and felt that delicious tongue, wriggling like a plump snake deep within her. She clutched in ecstasy at the moving flesh and felt herself tensing frantically into the moment of crisis; then she was over the edge, and the sweet, wicked delight throbbed through her as Louise's tongue contined to suck tenderly at her heated pleasure bud, extracting every last shred of sensation.

Louise lifted her head. 'Dear Marianne. That was so good. You will promise to do exactly as I say, to make Armand obey my every command?' Marianne lay back weakly, her dark hair curling about her damp face, her body still pulsing with the sweet aftermath of orgasm. 'Yes,' she said helplessly. 'Of course.'

Louise's eyes glittered. 'That room at the top of the house,' she said. 'Tell me about it. And then tell me everything you know about citizen Jacques.'

Heavy black clouds had built up during the afternoon, banishing the golden sunshine; and by early evening when Jacques returned the rain was falling relentlessly, tugging the crisp autumnal leaves from the half-denuded trees.

Nicole heard the front door open, heard his familiar footsteps in the hall and ran out to welcome him gladly. The big house seemed strangely quiet, and her spirits were unnaccountably low; of Armand and Marianne there had been no sign for some time, and Nicole assumed that the poor, exhausted little widow, Louise de Lamartine, was still resting up in her room.

Jacques was shrugging off his long wet greatcoat and running his hands through his glistening black hair. He looked tired; his expression was serious as he said, 'We'll be leaving Paris very soon, Nicole. I've got your papers ready.'

Nicole leaned her cheek against his warm chest and slipped her hands round his back, holding him tight. 'Where will we go to, Jacques?'

'Where would you like to go to, my Nicolette?' he smiled, stroking her hair.

'I don't mind,' she replied honestly, lifting her small face so that her amber eyes were held by his dark gaze. 'It doesn't matter at all, as long as I'm with you.'

For a split second, a shadow seemed to cross Jacques'

217

face; he looked as if he were about to say something; but then he shook his head imperceptibly and followed her into the warm kitchen, where a rich mutton and haricot stew simmered gently on the stove.

Thank goodness Marianne's such an inspired cook, thought Nicole in silent gratitude as she began to ladle out the fragrant meal. Food was really scarce now that the war against the Austrians was gathering momentum; but somehow they still managed to eat well.

Jacques seemed tense, preoccupied as he toyed with his food. Nicole watched him, feeling again that oppressive sense of unease. Something was worrying him, something he wasn't telling her about. Bad news about the war, perhaps, or some new trouble on the streets of Paris.

She'd just started to eat when Jacques put down his fork and said, 'Where are Armand and Marianne? I thought they would be eating with us.'

Suddenly, she remembered Louise, and wondered how she could ever have forgotten her. Putting down her spoon, she blurted out, 'Oh, Jacques! I almost forgot to tell you. Armand brought someone back today, a new guest.'

Jacques' face tightened. 'I've told him never to do that,' he said harshly. 'No-one should ever bring anyone here without proper safeguards.'

Something about his imperious tone brought the anger to Nicole's throat. 'She's a helpless widow, Jacques, who saw her husband guillotined! Armand rescued her from the mob this morning; what was he supposed to do? Leave her to be torn to pieces? Let's face it, you've rescued all kinds of depraved people from prison and helped them to escape from Paris. Why not her?'

He pushed his chair back and stood up. 'Nothing and no-one are what they seem in Paris, Nicole. No-one. Not even me.'

Nicole shivered, suddenly frightened, suddenly realising yet again just how little she knew about him. She whispered, her mouth dry, 'Are you telling me that I shouldn't even trust you, Jacques?'

He drew his hand tiredly across his forehead and said quietly, 'Yes. Perhaps I am. Where is this new guest?'

'We put her in the second-floor guest chamber,' Nicole said defiantly, though inwardly she was trembling at his ominous words. 'I assume she's still resting there, but I've not seen her for a while.'

His mouth thinned. 'So you've given her, in effect, the run of the house! I find this incredible.'

Nicole leaped to her feet herself, her eyes glinting with retaliating sparks of anger. 'What harm can a helpless young widow do to us all?'

'That,' he returned grimly, 'remains to be seen.' And he strode from the kitchen, slamming the door behind him so that the candles flickered and nearly went out.

Nicole sat down again, feeling sick with disappointment at his inexplicable anger. She couldn't eat any more, but just sat there, waiting for him to come back, because there was nothing else she could do.

Jacques strode up the stairs with a burning, inexplicable impatience. The second floor, Nicole had said. Nicole. Her eyes had sparkled with sudden tears as he rebuked her. He hadn't realised until it was too late how very vulnerable she was beneath that defiant exterior.

She hadn't learned the lesson yet that it was dangerous to trust anyone, even if you loved them. *Especially* if you loved them. No-one knew that better than Jacques; he had the scars on his back to prove it.

A candle burned low in one of the upper chambers; he flung wide the already open door and went in. This must be the room where their guest had rested, because already it was filled with that particularly feminine disarray which annoyed him intensely, unless it was Nicole's. The bed was rumpled and disarrayed, betraying that the woman must have slept restlessly, while a big wooden tub filled with rapidly cooling water stood before the dying embers of the fire.

Then he recognised the scent.

The room was filled with a soft, pungent aroma that stirred his deepest senses like a half-remembered pain, haunting him, filling him with the old, dark despair of those years in Toulon that he thought he'd shaken off at last. He drew his hand across his eyes, dazed. No. He must be mistaken. It must be a trick of the senses, a terrible coincidence. Yet still, the enticing, heady scent of sandalwood and musk filled his nostrils, bringing endless nightmares back to life.

One thing at least was plain; the woman was no longer in the room. All his senses on edge, he continued to search the big, silent house.

A flicker of light, like a will o' the wisp, glimmered from the little staircase that led to the topmost room in the house. Jacques stood at the bottom and listened, and heard a low, soft female laugh that somehow chilled his blood. Marianne, of course, and Armand, playing games up in the turret room, using its sinister playthings in some secret entertainment of their own. But where was the sad little beauty that Nicole had talked of so pityingly, with her fragile, innocent ways and her hauntingly familiar scent? She couldn't be up here with them. That was impossible.

Jacques climbed the stairs silently and eased open the door.

A candle burned low in one corner, casting long, flickering shadows that leaped across the walls like ghosts. Jacques saw Armand first, crouching on his hands and knees on the hard bed, wearing nothing but a black leather harness that encased his erect penis and scrotum, its straps running up through the deep cleft of his backside. His head was thrown back in a rictus of despairing pleasure, because Marianne was kneeling behind him, her breasts hanging out lewdly from her dishevelled gown, her face flushed with pleasure; and she was holding a big leather whip in her hands, driving the oiled leather handle in and out relentlessly between Armand's tight bottom cheeks as if it were a phallus, slowly caressing and savouring his tight anal ring with the butt as Armand groaned aloud. Jacques, whom they were too engrossed to notice, could see how his fiercely straining genitals thrust out hugely from the tight leather straps, while his forehead was beaded with perspiration.

And then, a low, agonisingly familiar voice came from the shadowy corner of the room, and Jacques saw her. 'Faster,' she was saying. 'Faster – see how quickly you can drive him to his extremity, dear Marianne.'

She was leaning almost casually against the stone wall in the near-darkness, a beautiful blonde woman, with her moonsilver hair cascading around her naked shoulders. She wore nothing but white silk stockings gartered at her thighs, and a boned black corset, laced tightly at the waist to push up her lovely firm breasts. At the top of her legs her sex lips, utterly devoid of hair, pouted obscenely, the soft silken folds already slick with arousal. And on her face she wore a black leather mask, with slits for her eyes and lips.

She saw Jacques standing there immobile in the doorway, and smiled like a cat, a little secret smile between the two of them. As if they were fellow-conspirators, she put her finger to her lips, indicating silence, then pointed to the two figures on the bed.

Armand was near to the end. His great phallus leaped and jerked in exquisite anguish as Marianne, with an intent expression on her flushed face, deliberately twisted and thrust the oiled leather whip deep into his tightly puckered bottom hole. Then suddenly she reached beneath him to clutch at the heavy, swaying bag of his balls. With a loud groan Armand clenched his buttocks round the hard leather shaft and jerked to his extremity, his hot seed jetting from his engorged penis in great, lascivious spurts as his face contorted with pleasure.

The blonde masked woman watched them, her eyes glittering, her nipples hardening with lust. Then slowly, deliberately, she reached down between her own legs and began to stroke her hairless flesh folds voluptuously, while her small pink tongue stuck out from the mask's mouth-slit and moistened her ripe lips. Jacques could see how juicy her finger was; she lifted it up to examine it and licked it, circling it suggestively with her soft mouth, sliding it in and out between her glistening lips; Jacques felt his own vile hardness throbbing relentlessly as he watched her.

She stepped daintily across the room towards him, her breasts swaying tantalisingly above her tight corset. He stood there immobile as she said, in that low, husky voice that turned his blood to ice: 'Oh, Jacques. I knew, somehow that it would be you. You see, I've been looking for you for such a long time.'

Instead of answering her, Jacques turned to Armand and Marianne, who had recovered and were watching him warily from the bed, afraid of his anger. He said to them, in a low, expressionless voice, 'Get out of here.' They grabbed their clothes and fled.

The woman had reached him. She rubbed her beautiful, high breasts briefly against the hard wall of his chest, and began to unfasten the pearl buttons of his silk shirt. He heard the hiss of her indrawn breath as she ran her fingertips lingeringly over his sinewy bronzed torso; then gently, very gently she eased the shirt from his immobile body, using her palms to caress the hard muscle of his chest, the dark nubs of his nipples. As she ran her hands around to his back, she felt the scarred ridges on his shoulders and turned him, very gently, to look.

'My poor Jacques,' she said in pity. The tears sparkled in her violet eyes. 'What have they done to you?'

'You ought to know, Louise.' He said it through clenched teeth and continued to hold himself very still, even though she was now unfastening the placket of his breeches and caressing his savagely erect penis with loving fingertips. He only moved when she bent her masked head to kiss its proud, velvety tip, so that her

222

hair fell like a shimmering curtain around his groin and his thighs.

She gazed up at him. He could see her tender, tear-jewelled eyes through the slits in the leather, could see the soft, tantalising rosebud swell of her mouth.

'You're strong,' she whispered. 'Even stronger, even more beautiful than before. Oh, Jacques. I have such memories, my love.'

He gripped her white shoulders with a sudden, fierce passion; she loved his harshness, rubbing her upthrust, naked breasts against his hard chest, her breathing coming short and fast as her nipples stiffened deliciously.

'So have I,' he grated out. 'Memories of two years spent in the Toulon *bagne*. Where you, Louise, put me.'

Then he ripped off her mask and threw her back on the bed, parting her moist, willing thighs so that he could thrust his rampant penis deep, deep within her, burying himself in her wantonly lush flesh, easing the hard pain of memory.

Oh, but she was beautiful. As beautiful as ever. Witch. Blonde witch. . . Already her hands were tangling in his thick hair and she was pulling his head down to meet hers, kissing the very soul from him, arching her full, delicious breasts up into his hungry mouth. Her inner muscles contracted round his penis, her warm, melting flesh caressed him, squeezed his hot shaft with a mind-searing sensuality until he felt his seed surging helplessly in his groin.

With a low cry of despair he arched his taut body high above her and drove his dark, rigid penis again and again between her luscious, juicy flesh lips.

She quivered and squirmed, clawing at his back, moaning out his name as he pounded into searing orgasm. 'Oh, Jacques. My beautiful Jacques, my only love, do what you want with me.'

'Anything?' he grated between thinned lips.

Her eyes glittered. 'Anything . . .'

Chapter Twelve

When Jacques showed no sign of returning to his unfinished meal, Nicole got up slowly to clear the half-eaten food away, then sat listening to the rain drumming against the high windows. It was as if everyone had vanished, swallowed up in the vastness of that mysterious house. Suddenly she felt as if she couldn't sit there alone any longer. She had to find Jacques.

What drew her upstairs, to that dark, sinister room at the top of the house, she never afterwards knew. But for some reason she climbed those narrow, twisting stairs with a painfully thudding heart. The door was ajar, and a single candle gleamed fitfully, barely illuminating the room for her sickened eyes.

On the bed was the woman Louise, naked except for her obscenely tight bodice. She was crouching on her hands and knees, with her glorious silver-blonde ringlets all but concealing her face and shoulders. She was making little moaning sobs of protest because, handling her roughly, pushing her about with the kind of brutal detachment she'd never, ever seen in him before, was Jacques. She had found him.

He was dressed only in his slim-fitting breeches and boots; his shirt lay discarded on the floor, and Nicole could clearly see the white, ridged scars on his brown back. He was working busily, tying poor Louise up, fettering her wrists and ankles with leather bonds and securing them tightly to the bedposts so that her white, firm bottom, raised high in the air, was utterly at his mercy. He was saying in a low voice that was smoky with sexual passion, 'This is what you like, isn't it, Louise? Now you're my prisoner, Louise; how does it feel?'

Nicole clenched her hand to her mouth in horror as she saw him take a phial of scented oil from the nearby table and trickle it down the girl's luscious bottom cleft; Louise moaned aloud as the cold liquid caressed her heated flesh folds and slid achingly towards her throbbing clitoris. Jacques waited, watching her writhe in her bonds; then he began to knead and stroke at her bottom cheeks, pulling them apart so that the tight, shameful hole was exposed, delving and probing into the resisting puckered orifice with his fingers until Louise groaned with despair and pulled helplessly at the leather strappings.

Never had Nicole seen Jacques look so savage, so bitter. Her fingers clutched with painful indecision at the edge of the door. She wanted to run and stop him, wanted to throw herself at him, tear at his hair until he stopped, because he had no right to torment poor Louise, who was an innocent, grieving widow!

Then the blood drained from her face as she realised the truth.

Louise, innocent, demure Louise, was in the throes of sexual ecstasy. Her swollen nipples were dark and stiff with pleasure; she lowered them eagerly to rub them against the rough woollen rug he'd draped over the hard bed. As Jacques stroked and fondled her buttocks, she thrust violently towards him, parting her thighs to bare her ripe sex; she was sweet and juicy down there, her moisture glistening lewdly on her silky flesh folds as she begged for Jacques' caresses.

No innocent, but a wanton, lascivious creature with

perverted needs. And Jacques was not going to disappoint her. As he probed the tight little rosebud hole with one hand, he was reaching towards his breeches with the other, and she saw that his phallus was already huge, springing like a monster from the dark cradle of his testicles, rearing up, eager for its juicy prey.

Nicole thrust her knuckles against her mouth, knowing she should go, and yet unable to. She leaned faintly against the wall as the candlelight revealed how the man was gripping his throbbing penis with his fist, and pushing it firmly against the woman's oiled orifice. Louise herself was ready and waiting; she let out a low, delirious moan as Jacques slowly eased the slick, long length of hardened flesh into her secret passage.

Louise bucked frantically against him, impaling herself desperately on that iron-hard shaft, moaning out her dark, impossible pleasure as he drove himself into her again and again, his balls slapping against her buttocks. She writhed in her bonds, rubbing her breasts ecstatically against the rough blanket beneath her. 'Oh, yes,' she whispered. 'Drive it up me, all of it, please, I beg you!'

With a grim smile, Jacques obeyed; then he slid his hand along her hairless flesh to find her soaking clitoris, pinching and kneading that hot tiny bud; with a series of little, yelping cries, Louise shuddered her way to climactic orgasm, calling out Jacques' name with savage abandon as he pumped himself to his own powerful release deep within her.

Slowly, his teeth still gritted against the extremity of his own degrading pleasure, he drew himself from her ravished orifice; and Nicole, the secret observer, slumped back against the wall with her eyes closed, feeling sick.

How little she really knew him. How right he'd been to tell her earlier that she was never, ever to trust him. She'd thought the games were over; but she'd been wrong. Nothing had changed.

The woman Louise (how had Nicole ever thought she

was sweet and innocent?) had twisted round to face Jacques, her limbs still imprisoned by her leather bonds. With her tousled hair and her flushed, smooth skin, she looked as sleek and satisfied as a beautiful cat, licking the cream from her lips. Jacques was slowly untying her, his eyes black and expressionless.

Then Louise was free, and she clutched Jacques to her, and Nicole, with incredible shock, heard her whispering, 'Oh, Jacques! Still as magnificent as ever, perhaps more so, my dear, for you have such terrible strength after those years in prison. I don't think I ever stopped loving you, because, Jacques, there's never been anyone else like you. They *made* me denounce you, all that time ago, Phillippe and his horrible aristocratic friends; they forced me to say that you'd raped me! I panicked, didn't know what to do; I didn't think what it would mean, until it was too late. Oh, my love, I never guessed that they'd treat you so cruelly. Your poor back. How you must have suffered.' And with soft, loving fingers she drew her fingers along his scars, over the brand on his inner wrist.

She drew him down towards her, rubbing her ripe breasts against the hard wall of his chest, and still Jacques said nothing, but his phallus was beginning to stiffen again, and Louise fondled the thick velvety flesh, catching her breath.

'Oh, Jacques,' she breathed contentedly. 'I knew I'd find you again some day. Have you been looking for me, just as I've been looking for you?'

Then Nicole heard Jacques speak for the first time, saying in a low voice that burned with intensity, 'Believe me, Louise, I've never stopped looking for you.'

It was enough. Somehow Nicole bit back her cry of anguish and turned to run down the stairs, away from that hateful room, away from Louise, away from Jacques.

So this was the woman Jacques had loved so desperately; the mistress of the great nobleman called Phillippe;

the woman whose false, panicky accusation of rape had condemned him to two years of living hell, the woman he and his men been searching for through the prisons and slums of Paris, his search expressing all the private obsession of his mind and body. The lock of silvery hair had been not a warning, but a clue, a promise that his long quest was nearly over.

He still wanted her. Marianne had been right. Everything else in his life, the inquisition of the aristocrats, the whole game of revenge, was just an extension of his mission to find this incredibly desirable woman; and now his mission was complete, because he'd got her back. Nicole realised with a stab of numb despair that every other woman he made love to must have been nothing but a shadowy substitute for Louise's devastating beauty, a temporary palliative for his addiction.

Blindly, feeling like some sordid, useless little eavesdropper, Nicole stumbled back down the stairs, her legs shaking, heading instinctively for her own room like a wounded animal to its lair. She hated him for what he had done to her.

Then, suddenly, she remembered.

He'd told her earlier that he'd got her papers, the *certificat de civisme* that she needed to get out of Paris. There was no need, then, for her to stay here and be humiliated any longer. She would find the papers, which were no doubt secreted in his room, and take a little money, and run. Last time he'd found her, because she hadn't run far enough.

She wouldn't make the same mistake this time.

Louise lay back on the bed, purring with contentment as her fingers traced the hard sinews of Jacques' arms. Neither of them had heard the swiftly fading footsteps. 'Oh, Jacques,' murmured Louise, 'if only I'd known earlier where you were and how to find you. It's taken me so long.'

Jacques, his wonderfully handsome face somehow taut and inscrutable, said, 'What a pity, then, that it's been such a waste of time. Because you're not going to stay.'

'You mean we're leaving Paris, my love?'

'No. I don't mean that at all.'

Louise's violet eyes flickered in momentary alarm. Then she relaxed and ran her fingers in sensuous delight down the taut muscles of his chest and belly, lingering in the soft, delicious pelt of hair at his groin from which his phallus was thickly stirring. 'My Jacques. You were magnificent before, but prison has somehow made you truly formidable.' She smiled lazily up at him. 'I don't think you quite understand yet, my darling. I don't mind where I go. Because, you see, I'm going to be staying with you.'

Deliberately Jacques lifted her hand from his hardening flesh. He began to fasten his breeches, carefully buttoning up the placket over the swollen shaft while Louise watched him in bemused puzzlement. 'No, Louise,' he said, 'I'm afraid it's you who doesn't understand. As I said earlier, you're not staying here. In fact, you're leaving. Now.'

Louise's face became suddenly drained of colour. Gone was the softness, the dreamy content. Her eyes became as hard and cold as purple amethysts. 'What do you mean?'

He was fastening up his shirt now, with a cold deliberation that frightened her somehow more than any words. He stood towering above her, and Louise realised that never before had he looked more magnificent, more desirable, this strange scarred man on whom she'd placed all her hopes.

His thin, wide mouth twisted cynically. 'I mean, my little *poule*,' he said dryly, 'that you've passed your audition, and therefore will, like every other successful applicant who passes through this house, be given your exit papers and sufficient help from my men to enable you to leave Paris. I'll even give you some money if you like.' He turned towards a drawer and pulled out a heavy leather purse, which he threw so it landed on the bed beside her; it jingled as it fell. 'There. Is that the correct amount for your services? Or do you charge more these days?'

She knocked the purse from the bed and lunged towards him, her eyes spitting venom. 'Damn you, Jacques! I don't believe this. How dare you insult me so?'

He opened his eyes wide in feigned innocence. 'Ah, so it isn't enough for you? My apologies, Louise. Of course, prices have gone up everywhere.' And, reaching in the drawer again, he pulled out another bag and threw it on the floor beside the first.

Louise felt really frightened now. There was a cold, empty bleakness in the man's eyes that she'd never seen before. Fighting down her panic, she slid from the bed and moved towards him, the candlelight gleaming on her wonderful, pearly skin. Lifting her arms slowly round his neck, she pulled down his dark head and leaned into his strong, hard body, kissing him, clinging languorously with her own warm lips to that cruelly sensual mouth.

There was no response. Feeling cold all over, she whispered, 'Oh, my Jacques. Nothing left for me?'

'You nearly destroyed me before, Louise. Don't you think that's enough?'

He pushed her away, not cruelly but casually, as if she were just a piece of furniture in his way. Then he walked towards the door, turning to say, 'You'd better get dressed. I'll send Armand up in a few moments with your papers, and he and some friends will escort you through the barriers. If you take my advice, you'll get as far away from Paris as possible.'

'Damn you, Jacques!' All pretence gone now, Louise crouched on the bed and hissed out her anger. 'Damn you for your insufferable arrogance. Some day, you'll regret this.'

'Louise,' he said, 'I spent two years in the Toulon *bagne* regretting the day that I met you. Isn't that

230

enough?' Then he walked out through the door, leaving her spitting with impotent fury.

Of one thing Louise was quite sure. If she wasn't going to have him, then neither was that tawny-haired slut, Nicole Chabrier.

Nicole had never been in Jacques' bedroom before. It wasn't locked, but it might as well have been, because to her this austerely masculine chamber was a forbidden sanctum, yet another part of him that she'd never been allowed access to.

She was beginning to realise that she didn't really know him at all. What other secrets was he keeping from her? *'Nothing and no-one are what they seem in Paris, Nicole. Not even me.'*

Perhaps Louise would sleep in here tonight, in his arms. The thought knifed her. Blindly rubbing at her aching eyes to banish the stupid tears that threatened, Nicole lit another candle and began her search. Once she'd found the papers he'd said he'd got for her, she could escape from this house, from Paris, from the destructive magnetism of Jacques himself.

Taking deep breaths to calm herself, she looked around and saw that there was an inlaid walnut *secrétaire* in the corner. Guessing that this was where his papers were kept, she wrenched it open and started leafing anxiously through. A paper fluttered to the floor; she picked it up in agitation and was about to thrust it back with the others when the writing caught her eye.

It was a letter, addressed in beautiful script to the marquis de St Maury, and dated May this year. She frowned. That was impossible, because the St Maury family had fled long ago, abandoning the house and everything in it; Marianne had told her so! And Jacques, the secret intruder, had been here since April. This letter must be a mistake: a letter from a creditor, perhaps, or an old family retainer. She hesitated, unsure where it belonged, seeing as all the contents of the *secrétaire* were in neat, docketed files. She had absolutely no idea where to find the precious papers that would enable her to leave Paris. She stood there in near despair, looking round the room, seeing how everything in the room was so neat, so orderly, with all the clothes folded away and the bed as smooth as if it had never, ever been slept in.

Suddenly, as she stood there, the blind hurt, the despair, the longing boiled up inside her in an explosion of helpless rage. Damn Jacques, oh damn him! He was impervious, invulnerable. This room was the very expression of cold orderliness, just like him. His cool, mocking voice echoed in her ears: '*My Nicole. Domesticity isn't exactly one of your virtues, is it?*'

Her fury erupting, she wrenched open some drawers, revealing his white, neatly folded shirts. Hissing, she seized an armful and dragged them out, and threw them on the floor. The silks and fine lawns pooled around her feet; gritting her teeth, she grabbed one with both hands and ripped it, then started on his lace-edged cravats, ruining them with grim concentration. Panting with the effort, she muttered, 'Let's see, shall we, just how domesticated your beautiful Louise is! Let's see if she can clear up this mess, and launder your shirts, and do your sewing!'

Then suddenly, the scent of him, the perfume of the lemony, masculine toilet water he used floated up to her from his heaped-up shirts. As abruptly as it had come, her wild rage evaporated, leaving her weak and distraught.

She sank onto his bed with one of his shirts pressed against her cheek and sobbed her heart out.

At last, Jacques had finished what he had to do. Conscious of a bitter taste in his mouth, like bile, he grimly ordered Armand and two of his silent assistants to escort Louise de Lamartine out of Paris. Marianne went with them as well, to act as her maid; it was Jacques' intention that Armand and Marianne should leave Paris for good this time, because they were no longer safe here. None of them were.

He'd had to conjure up Louise's papers within two hours; it had cost him a small fortune, but it was worth every livre.

Before the little escort set out along the dark, rain-soaked streets to the West Barricade, well armed with papers and bribes for the guards, who would probably all be drunk by this hour, Jacques had spoken quietly to his men, warning them about Louise and her tricks. He'd seen the deep, shameful blush in Armand's cheeks as he spoke, and knew that Armand at least needed no warning about Louise's capabilities.

Jacques had watched them leave, with Louise still spitting hate at him. He knew that Louise was a real danger to him now, capable of a much more venomous revenge than merely sending him to a convict hell for two years. As soon as they were out of sight, he turned back towards the moonlit house and went over to the pump in the courtyard. There, in the dark seclusion, he stripped himself completely and sluiced himself again and again with the icy cold water, washing Louise's touch from his body. The water was good on his scarred back, on his chest, on his genitals, running in glittering rivulets down his strong thighs. For a moment he watched it running over the indelible scar of the brand on his forearm; then he pulled on his clothes and went back into the house.

Where was Nicole?

She was never far from his thoughts now. All the time, he was trying to bring himself to tell her that she must leave Paris as soon as possible, but without him. He began to search for her with increasing urgency, and when he found her, lying asleep on the bed in his unlit room, he felt his heart wrench, because she looked so vulnerable, curled up on the coverlet with her glorious tawny hair spreading about her face and shoulders in wild disarray. Moving a little closer, he thought he saw the mark of tears on her cheeks, and

233

frowned. She couldn't possibly know about Louise, and what had happened up there in that turret room, could she?

Frowning into the darkness, he went outside to get a candle and set it in a holder beside the bed.

Then he saw the state of his room. And he realised that she did know about Louise.

It took some moments for the flickering light of the candle to penetrate Nicole's disturbed dreams, and even longer for the presence of someone else in the room to register.

'Nicole,' she heard him say, and she jerked upright, still clutching his shirt like a talisman against her breast. He was standing at the foot of the bed, his hair sleekly drawn back, his face inscrutable.

'Go away!' she hissed.

'It's no good telling me to get out of here,' he pointed out reasonably, 'because it's my room. At least, I thought it was my room.' He gestured at the debris on the floor, where his clothes were strewn in wild abandon. He walked towards her as she crouched panting on the bed, treading heedlessly on the crumpled garments. 'You have something to tell me, *chérie*?'

Nicole gripped at the shirt until her knuckles were white. 'You're always telling me how untidy I am. Well, I thought I'd give you the satisfaction of seeing how right you were, as always!'

Jacques eyed the ruined clothes in some wonder, tentatively digging at the mess with his booted foot. 'I'd have taken your word for it, Nicolette; no need to go to quite such lengths. But then, you never did anything by halves, did you? This time, you've really excelled yourself.'

'Get your precious Louise to sort it out,' she hissed ferociously.

His dark eyes seemed to gleam in understanding. 'Ah, I see. Been doing a little eavesdropping, have you?'

234

'How could I help it? It's her, isn't it? She's the woman you've been looking for . . .' She drew a deep, shuddering breath. 'You weren't exactly subtle about your precious reunion, were you? I want to leave, Jacques, as soon as possible. That's why I came here, to try to find those exit papers you said you'd got for me. I'm quite sure that Louise will want me to go as well.'

He frowned, mildly perplexed. 'You mean you're leaving me with all this mess to clear up?'

She drew herself to her feet and put her hands on her hips, trying to stop trembling, trying to forget that she hurt so much inside. Somehow she forced a shaky laugh. 'It will do you good! What a true bourgeois you are, my poor Jacques; you'd never get used to living like the nobility, would you? If you were a real aristocrat, instead of a sordid impostor, you'd be quite used to flinging everything around, because there'd be servants at your beck and call, clearing up after you!'

He nodded sadly. 'So the comte de Polignac was a true aristocrat, was he? Leaving everything around, forgetting things. After all, he forgot you, didn't he, when he left Paris so hastily – '

Nicole hissed and sprang at him. He caught her easily, laughing openly now. 'Oh, my delicious little wildcat. How utterly exquisite you are when you're angry. Shall I tell you what I'd like to do now?'

'What?' she spat, still struggling.

'This.' And he gripped the lace-edged bodice of her gown with strong fingers, and tore it apart with steady, gentle strength, exposing all the pink-tipped glory of her high, rounded breasts. 'Time for my revenge now, *ma chère*.'

She gasped aloud, the colour rushing to her pale cheeks. He began to fondle her, his sensitive hands cupping the firm globes, pulling gently with his lean fingers at the rosy crests until the agony of wanting him spasmed through her.

'Oh, why do you have to hurt me so much?' she whispered brokenly. 'Haven't you done enough?

Haven't you finished your games with me now that Louise is here?'

'Louise isn't here.' He said it very calmly, his dark gaze on her upturned face, his fingers working deliciously all the time over her taut, exposed nipples until she thought she would faint with need.

'I know she isn't here, in this room! I'm not blind! Where is she? Don't tell me she's had enough of you! From what I saw of the two of you earlier, it would take several days for you to get enough of each other!'

His jaw tightened. 'Nicole, enough of these games. Listen to me. Louise isn't here. She isn't even in the house. I've sent her away, out of Paris, under armed escort.'

Nicole had almost stopped breathing. 'You sent her away?'

'Yes. Is it so very hard to believe?' he replied softly. 'She wrecked my life once. I've no intention of letting her do so again.'

White-lipped, she stammered, 'But you've been searching for her! I heard you say to her earlier that you'd never stopped looking for her. Why?'

'For revenge, Nicole.' The cold bleakness in his voice suddenly made her shudder. 'I wanted to find her so I could make her suffer as I did. Now, I just want her out of my life.'

Nicole shook her head slowly; Jacques' hands rested lightly on her naked shoulders. 'But she's so beautiful,' she whispered brokenly. 'I saw you up there with her, Jacques. She had you spellbound.'

His face tightened. 'Exactly. And tonight was an exorcism; I've washed her from my mind and my body for good. Oh, Nicole.'

With tender hands, he slipped her torn gown from her body, and she stood there, her eyes wide and dazed, trembling with need. Swiftly pulling off his own garments, he gathered her in his arms and laid her on the bed, sliding his fingers along her hot, melting flesh, drawing her pouting breasts into his mouth and savouring the yearning nipples deliciously with his tongue and teeth, awakening all her dark inner core of need. Nicole felt his hard thigh parting her yielding legs; with a gasp she felt the velvety tip of his manhood slide deep within her moist, welcoming flesh, and then he stopped, holding himself very still, leaving her trembling on the brink of fulfilment as the waves of pleasure coursed through her sensitised body.

She moaned helplessly beneath him, clutching convulsively with her inner muscles at the hard, silky length of his magnificent penis, savouring it, engulfing it with her honeyed juices. When Jacques started to move again, very slowly, teasing her, she gasped aloud her need and clutched him to her; wordlessly he rolled over onto his scarred back, pulling her with him, and she sat astride him, riding him gloriously as he caressed her quivering breasts. She tried to make it last, but her need was too great. Throwing back her head, she shuddered in delight as she drove herself onto that exquisite rod of flesh time and time again, feeling it filling her, impaling her; he reached to caress her clitoris and she exploded in a cataclysm of shimmering sensation and collapsed into his strong arms, her flesh still pulsing with sweet, incredible pleasure.

He smiled softly in the candlelight, stroking her sweat-darkened hair, breathing in the scent of jasmine from her skin. 'Did you do that with Gerard?'

She stirred sleepily, gazing up at the lean planes of his familiar face, and smiled. 'No. Poor Gerard wouldn't have lasted a minute like that.'

'So your aristocratic lover had his failings, then?'

Nicole nuzzled her cheek against his hard chest, listening to the steady beat of his heart. 'In bed,' she murmured wickedly, 'he was useless. Absolutely useless.' Her hand slid down along his flat belly to caress the pulsing, silky flesh of his penis. With a mischievous smile she crawled down the bed and took the somnolent length in her mouth, wrapping her tongue round the glans, sucking and caressing with her saliva-moistened lips until it stirred deliciously into life once more. Then she took his full testicles into her mouth one by one, savouring and tasting their heavy masculine pungency, before settling down to enfold his swollen penis with her velvety lips and slide them tantalisingly up and down the silky, stiffened shaft.

He groaned aloud as his member jerked hungrily against the roof of her mouth, and Nicole smiled.

He was hers. Hers at last.

Nicole fell into a deep, blissful sleep, held tight in his arms. She woke only once, because Jacques was muttering in his sleep, his face dark and tormented. She cradled him and stroked his hair. His skin was damp with perspiration and she knew a sudden spasm of fear, seeing him like this, almost vulnerable. He didn't wake, and she held him until his dream subsided and he was peaceful again.

She wondered if he dreamed like that often, and what it was that haunted him so.

It was dark outside when she awoke, but she knew that dawn couldn't be far away because Jacques was already up and pulling on his clothes. She drew herself up, her arms clasped round her knees, and watched him by the light of the solitary candle, her face soft with love.

He saw her, and said softly, '*Chérie*, today you must leave Paris. I've made all the arrangements.'

Fear clutched at her heart again. 'But you? You're coming with me, aren't you, Jacques?'

She saw him hesitate, and wanted to cry out. But then he smiled. 'I won't be far away. Nicole, do you think you could restore this room to some kind of order, while I go and make us some coffee?'

He came over to the bed to take her hand and lightly kiss it, and then he left the room.

Nicole sat in bed for a moment, collecting herself, pushing away the strange apprehension. He'd said he wouldn't be far away. He wouldn't leave her, not now.

Pulling herself up, she tiptoed first down to her own room to wash and dress, then returned to Jacques' chamber and started to gather up the carelessly strewn clothes, hoping she hadn't damaged too many of them beyond repair.

When she saw the letter lying on the floor where she'd dropped it last night, she wasn't going to look at it. She was only going to smooth it out and fold it up, and slip it back quickly into the *secrétaire* before Jacques should return with the coffee.

She smoothed the letter out, and her eyes were drawn helplessly to the carefully written text.

'To Jacques Lamont, *ci-devant* Marquis de St Maury. 15 May 1792.

My dear Jacques,

Owing to the tragic death of your older brother Phillippe while fighting for the Royalist army at Verdun, it is my duty to inform you that the property and titles of St Maury now pass on to you.

However, I fear that in the present circumstances, your inheritance has diminished greatly in value. As you know, the St Maury chateau in the province of LeVar has been rased to the ground during a rebellion there. The town house in St Germain des Prés remains intact, for your brother secured it carefully before he left for Austria to join the Royalist army. However, as the property of a declared émigré, it is forfeit to the Republic, and I fear it is only a matter of time before it is ransacked.

I have the keys to the house in the bank's vaults, along with the St Maury diamonds and a considerable sum of gold, should you care to collect them from me in the near future.

Yours, etc.,
Giles Campan
Gauthier's Bank, Faubourg St Honore.

Nicole sat rather suddenly on the edge of the bed, the letter still clasped in her hand. The words danced before her eyes.

No. It couldn't be. It couldn't be that Jacques was the marquis de St Maury, owner of this magnificent house, of those wonderful diamonds that she, Nicole, had accused him of stealing from their rightful owner. It couldn't be.

She stared blindly at the shuttered window, watching the cold grey light of dawn stealing in. A future marquis of France who'd spent two years in prison?

But such things happened, she knew. The comte de Mirabeau, one of the most prominent of the leaders of the new National Convention, had been denounced by his own father for criminal debauchery and sent to prison without trial, by the infamous *lettre de cachet* system. Just like Jacques.

She shut her eyes in new-found despair. This house, then, had belonged to Jacques' older brother Phillippe, who'd enjoyed cruelty in the midst of his pleasure; hence the erotically charged atmosphere of this strange house. And – the knowledge came to her painfully, because it was almost too much to take in – Jacques had been denounced and thrown into prison by his own brother.

She held the letter so tightly that her knuckles were white.

She understood it all now. Louise de Lamartine had been the mistress of Phillippe, marquis de St Maury, and had lived with him in the family chateau in Provence. Louise had foolishly begun a secret affair with Jacques, Phillippe's younger brother; and when discovery seemed imminent, she'd grown frightened and accused Jacques of rape. So Phillippe had proceeded to have his brother sent to gaol. She could imagine the bitterness, the rage that must have infected Phillippe de St Maury's soul; how desperately he must have wanted to believe Louise's tearful story of rape, because he

240

wouldn't want to believe that his beautiful mistress had betrayed him with his handsome younger brother . . .

After that, Phillippe and Louise must have parted. Had Louise tested the marquis's loyalty just too many times? Phillippe had come north to Paris, but had been forced by the Revolution to abandon the magnificent family mansion and had fled to Austria, like so many other noblemen.

And now Jacques, freed from prison at last, was the marquis de St Maury. His brother had died fighting for the royalists, and therefore Jacques, his heir, was a proscribed enemy of the people, under automatic sentence of death should he ever be captured.

Just then a strange, muffled noise from the garden outside penetrated her numbed brain. Slowly, she went to push aside the shutters and rubbed her eyes, still dazed by the enormity of what she had just learned. She gazed out into the cold, grey expanse of the garden, and saw the soldiers.

Chapter Thirteen

*I*n the wraith-like mist of dawn, they looked like ghosts, as grey and insubstantial as the shadows. Only the garish tricolour cockades on their red caps and the shining barrels of their muskets seemed real. They were climbing the steps to the house now; she clutched the window-sill, faint with fear. They had come for Jacques, for the marquis de St Maury.

She flew down the wide staircase, and he was there, gripping her shoulders, shaking her as they heard the thumping of musket barrels against the door.

'Nicole,' he gritted out. 'If you have any sort of trust in me, then you must listen to me now, and do exactly as I say.'

'I'm not leaving you, Jacques. I'm not.'

He shook her again. 'Just this once, *ma chère*, you're going to obey me, like it or not. You know the cellars, beneath the kitchen? Down there, behind the wine casks, there's a bolted door.'

She nodded dumbly, her eyes wide with fear as the battering at the door increased. Jacques went on, in a low, urgent voice, 'The door leads to a secret under-ground passage that will get you well away from here. Just behind it, you'll find some things; your papers, and a pistol, and some money, together with the directions

242

to a safe hiding place outside the walls of Paris. Now go, quickly!'

Already the big doors were shaking with the force of the soldiers' blows. Nicole clung to him, her face white. 'No! I won't go, Jacques! You must come with me!'

'There's not time for both of us, damn you! If I hold them off for a few moments, you can get away! Run, Nicole, run!' He wrestled with her, trying with all his might to push her away; but at that very moment the stout door splintered, and the hall was suddenly filled with the rough, menacing presence of a dozen soldiers, their muskets raised ferociously. Nicole froze trembling at Jacques' side.

Their sergeant, a short, stocky man with an eyepatch, stepped forward.

'Perhaps you can help us, citizens. We're looking for Jacques Lamont, *ci-devant* marquis de St Maury, wanted for crimes of *incivisme* against the French republic.'

In utter despair Nicole threw herself in front of Jacques and cried out, 'He's not here. The St Maury family left France a long time ago.'

'One of them did, citizeness,' sneered the sergeant. 'Phillippe de St Maury, enemy of the people, joined the traitorous Royalist army and met a well-deserved death. We're looking for his heir, and we think we've found him.'

Jacques gripped Nicole's shoulders tightly in warning and pushed her to one side. 'What if I deny it?'

The sergeant put his hands on his hips and gazed insolently up at Jacques. 'You'd have trouble denying it, because you've been formally denounced to the Vigilance Committee, citizen Lamont.'

'By whom, may I ask?'

'By a lady, name of Louise de Lamartine. She proved most co-operative with my men at the West Barricade last night.' He laughed. 'Seems you were trying to send her packing, were you? One wench too many, citizen, though I must say I vastly admire your taste.'

He leered insolently at Nicole; Jacques said calmly,

'Denunciation by one person is not enough to prove that I'm the marquis de St Maury. You must produce more evidence.'

'And I have it.' Exultantly the sergeant pulled forward a man from the back of the group of soldiers. Nicole recognised him with a sick jolt as the scarred Provençal, Saltier, who'd bid for her that night at Paul Vichy's party, and had sworn to get even with Jacques afterwards.

'That's her,' Saltier cried excitedly. 'And him, the marquis. Stole the little beauty right from under my nose, he did, the arrogant bastard. It was then that I recognised him, and I've been looking for him every day since! You see, I used to work for his father, the old marquis, years ago on their estate in Provence, and I remember those two brothers as if their faces were engraved on my brain.'

Jacques said scornfully to the sergeant, 'You'd take mere hearsay as evidence?'

'Not hearsay!' shouted Saltier exultantly. 'Remember the diamonds, my fine marquis? Well, when I discovered them in your fine mistress' gown and saw the St Maury crest on the clasp, I knew beyond a doubt that it was you. Gave the family diamonds to your whore, you did – '

He broke off, his jaw suddenly slack as Jacques drew out his pistols from his pockets and then balanced them lightly in his hands as he turned them on the cowering soldiers. 'All right,' he said, 'I am the marquis de St Maury. And the first one of you to lay a finger on me or my companion won't be leaving this house alive.'

The sergeant snarled, 'You can't hope to hold all of us at bay with just two pistols, citizen!'

'Perhaps not. But I'll take two of you with me first.' The soldiers cowered back uncertainly against the door; keeping his eyes fastened on them and his guns poised, Jacques grated out under his breath, 'Nicole. For God's sake, run. Can't you see you're only making things worse?'

One of the soldiers lunged towards them, and Jacques fired; Nicole saw the bright wet blood on his jacket and fled, horrorstruck, along the hallway to the kitchen, stumbling blindly down the stone steps into the dark, cold cellars. Gasping for breath, her eyes struggling to cope with the gloom, she wrenched open the door hidden behind the winecasks and slammed it shut behind her.

She leaned back against the door, and the tears spilled blindly down her cheeks. Jacques was right. She had made everything worse. His foray into the Vichy house on the night of that vile party had been the start of his undoing; he'd been noticed, and she'd even left his beautiful diamonds where they could be found and recognised by his enemies. Then, as if that wasn't enough, she'd allowed Louise into the house, to lay the seeds of ruin for them all.

In this cold, stone-enclosed gloom, she could hear nothing; but she imagined the shouts, the gunshots from above, and couldn't bear it.

It was dark in La Force, except for a meagre shaft of light stealing through a tiny grating set high in the stone wall. The smell of filthy straw was indescribable; in fact Jacques was convinced that it was the foul stench that brought him round. They'd beaten him till he was unconscious with their muskets, because of some of the things he said to them, which perhaps hadn't been sensible of him, but it seemed worth it at the time.

He drew himself up, and looked around properly.

It seemed that he'd been thrown into the common cell, along with all the other new prisoners: the thieves, the common murderers, the men and women who'd had the misfortune to bear noble names, or even to associate with proscribed aristocrats such as himself. A true levelling out of society, he mused as he gazed at the rich assortment. *Liberté, Egalité, Fraternité.*

He sat in the dark corner with his back against the damp stone wall, trying to ignore the many furtive glances cast in his direction. There was a huddle of women in one corner, Paris fishwives, they looked like, who were eyeing him up and chuckling. He wondered how they'd managed to fall foul of the law. They looked more like the sort of women who'd be leading the mob, or sitting gleefully round the guillotine in the Place du Carrousel as it claimed its latest victims.

A group of grim-looking men played dice in one corner, and just beyond them a couple fondled one another furtively, their eyes hot. Jacques pondered absently on how the threat of approaching death seemed to sweep away any last restraints on human carnality. He thought suddenly of Nicole, and the wide distress in her beautiful eyes as she realised that it was she who had exposed him to the denunciation that had been the end of him. He wanted to tell her that it didn't matter, that they would have found him anyway sooner or later.

One of the women, handsomer than most of her friends, with curling black hair and dark eyes like a gypsy, came sauntering over to him with her hands on her hips, her gold earrings glinting. 'My name's Thérèse,' she said. 'Fancy a fuck, citizen Lamont?'

'I certainly would, if I could see anyone remotely resembling a female in this place,' he agreed, smiling benevolently up at her.

She hissed out a stream of filthy invective. 'You'll be sorry for that,' she breathed. 'Oh, yes you will.'

After about an hour, they brought in another prisoner, a young woman with dark curling hair and big blue eyes, whose pretty face was white with fear. When the guards began to pull at her torn clothes and fondle her full breasts under the pretext of searching for hidden weapons, she began to shake, and looked to be on the verge of physical collapse.

Jacques looked up and saw her. Marianne. He swore softly under his breath. They must have caught her when they took Louise. He raised himself softly from

246

his corner and drew himself up, saying in his quiet voice, 'Let her go, citizens.'

An appalling silence fell over the grim, lofty cell. Marianne cried out, 'No, monsieur Jacques, you mustn't,' and then she was dragged aside by one of the guards, who laughed aloud and gripped the shuddering girl closer, thrusting his hips at her in a brutal parody of copulation. 'She's only a common little housemaid,' he sneered. 'Let's see how well she serves her new masters.'

Jacques gripped his shoulder to swing him round and felled him with one blow to his stubbled chin. The other guards fell on Jacques with curses and brutal fists, and dragged him across the straw to some iron rings set in the wall, to which they chained up his wrists and ankles so that he was standing helplessly spreadeagled.

And then he saw that the woman Thérèse, whose black eyes glittered with malevolence, was sidling up to the guard he'd felled and whispering, 'Let's have some fun with this one, citizen, eh?'

The gaoler grinned, rubbing his bruised chin. 'A good idea. What do you suggest, Thérèse?'

Thérèse turned to gaze thoughtfully at the figure chained to the wall as her friends gathered avidly round. 'I think,' she pronounced at last, 'that our friend the marquis de St Maury is a little too well dressed for this place. Let's see, my friends, what he looks like without his fine clothes.'

Marianne looked on in helpless horror as Thérèse and her friends moved in towards their prey.

Nicole had found everything, just as Jacques said: the money, the papers, the pistol, even an old cloak in which to wrap herself. And there was a map, with an isolated farmhouse marked with a cross, eight miles from Paris. She twisted it in her hands, realising that he must have been getting all this ready for her that morning, while she was still up in his room. He'd known that she would have to leave. He'd also known that he wouldn't be coming with her.

All she wanted to do was go back and be with him, wherever he was. But she'd only make things worse for him, she always did; so with a sorely aching heart she forced herself to follow the twisting passage that led from the cellar beneath the house and came out eventually in a dark little alley near to the river. Screwing up her eyes against the daylight, she paused to get her bearings and then set off towards the barricade. There, her fear nearly stifled her at the sight of the red-capped guards leaning nonchalantly against the barrier. What if they were the same ones as those who beseiged the house earlier? Her throat was dry with fear as she pulled her hood over her hair and joined the long queue of those waiting to get out.

They were mostly farmers, people from the outskirts of Paris who'd brought in produce at first light to be sold in the markets, and were now returning with empty carts. One of them, a kindly old woman with a shabby cart pulled by a worn out nag, took pity on the uncertain girl. 'Come up here with me, my dear,' she said. 'I'll wager we can outface those grim red-bonnets between us, can't we? You have your papers?'

'Oh, yes,' breathed Nicole, scrambling up eagerly. 'Thank you so much, citizeness.'

The guards knew the woman, it seemed, because she passed through every day at the same hour. So they barely glanced at Nicole's papers when madame said she was a niece of hers, and soon the old cart was rumbling through the barriers.

Towards freedom, thought Nicole, towards her rendezvous with Jacques, the marquis of St Maury. But she couldn't really believe that he would ever make it.

The old woman, glancing at her, said, 'Courage, my child. While there's life, there's hope.'

But Nicole doubted very much that Jacques was even alive.

* * *

They were stripping Jacques slowly, unbuttoning his coat and his shirt with lascivious glee, exclaiming over the fine quality of the materials, the handsome buttons, the delicate stitching of his shirt. He was unable to move, being shackled by ankles and wrist to the wall; but he was able to speak, and he made the most of it, keeping up a steady stream of calmly filthy invective until one of the guards impatiently pulled the voluble *aristo*'s lace-edged cravat from around his neck and started to tie it around his mouth.

Before he could complete his task, Jacques said politely, 'Perhaps, citizen, you'd do me the favour of blindfolding me as well, so I don't have to look at these filthy fishwives.'

Thérèse struck him hard across the face, so her fingermarks showed as red weals on his lean cheek, and hissed, 'Very well. Blindfold him.'

Marianne watched white-faced as they systematically set about Jacques' humiliation. So he was a marquis! It didn't surprise her in the least, because he'd always behaved like one of the nobility. She didn't suppose a brave, strong man like him would mind dying, but oh, to be humiliated like this, in front of these rats from the sewers of Paris who slunk closer to gaze open-mouthed at his ordeal, must be a thousand times worse than actual death to a man like him. She cursed Armand and Louise under her breath, remembering how they'd got away together. Armand deserved the cunning blonde bitch. She'd lead him a merry dance, the great fool, and then she'd kick him into the gutter when she had no more use for his sturdy prick.

The woman called Thérèse, the one with the glinting earrings, had unfastened poor monsieur Jacques' shirt, and was running her long, sharp fingers up and down the smooth bronzed skin of his thickly muscled chest. Her hands strayed low, to where the beginnings of dark, silky hair shadowed his belly; with a little hiss of indrawn breath, she began to unfasten the placket of his breeches.

The silence was intense, stifling. In that high, dank dungeon everyone was waiting with baited breath as Thérèse parted his breeches and pulled them roughly apart. A sigh went up from the onlookers. Between the iron-hard columns of his thighs, his phallus hung thick and lengthy from its cradle of springing black hair. Thérèse hissed in pleasure at the sight.

'Well, my fine marquis,' she drawled, 'let's see if you fancy that fuck after all.' She turned quickly to the guard he'd hit, and said, 'Your turn first though, citizen. Give us all a spectacle to enjoy, eh?'

The gaoler reached out his big, hairy fist and grasped at the chained man's genitals. A hiss went up from the rapt circle of onlookers. Jacques had visibly flinched at the first touch, but then he held himself very still, his blindfolded head held high, as if willing resistance. Marianne watched from the shadows, pity filling her eyes. Oh, what were they doing to the beautiful, handsome monsieur Jacques?

The brutal guard was fingering Jacques' testicles now, weighing them carefully in his hands, fingering their velvety fulness. Marianne found herself breathing more raggedly and moistened her lips, remembering the beauty of his manly parts herself, which she'd pleasured so many times herself. But this was different. This wasn't pleasure. She bit back a low cry as she saw that the guard was rubbing his stubby fingers along the length of the man's stirring penis, gripping its sturdy thickness, pumping slowly up and down as the heavy shaft stiffened with the onrush of blood and swelled relentlessly within the gaoler's relentless fingers. Marianne felt the warm colour flood her own cheeks and saw how monsieur Jacques' face tautened in anguish at what was happening to him.

The woman Thérèse and her cronies were laughing aloud. 'What a fine specimen! I wouldn't mind having that stuck up me,' breathed one excitedly.

'Let's all have him,' breathed Thérèse. 'Share and share alike.'

The guard was still pumping and stroking, and now Marianne could see how the thick, veined shaft was standing proudly out from his body. She caught her breath at the magnificent, quivering length of it. Oh, she had almost forgotten that he was so strong, so big. She longed to touch that hot flesh, to run her fingers over the soft, velvety tip that swelled like a ripe plum at the guard's rough ministrations, longed to feel the thick shaft within her own tender flesh lips, which were already moist and pulsing with need.

Then Marianne gasped in horror, because Thérèse had pulled her own gown apart, and was pushing the gaoler's hand away. To appreciative shouts from her friends, she bent over the man's blindly thrusting penis and thrust her heavy breasts against it, rubbing her big, dark nipples to and fro across the swollen glans, then cupping her ripe globes together so that the plump flesh squeezed tightly on the helpless shaft. 'Oh, but you have a fine prick, monsieur le marquis,' she laughed gloatingly. 'I wonder how many eager little serving girls you've pleasured in your time, eh? Let's make the most of him, girls, before Madame la Guillotine puts an end to this fine plaything.'

At this encouragement, one of her friends eagerly kneeled beside her, almost knocking Thérèse out of the way, and shaped her lips into a lush pink circle; then she took that frighteningly big shaft into her mouth, sliding down the solid flesh so far that Marianne held her breath, thinking it would surely choke her. The woman ran her lips up and down, nibbling with her tongue, swirling deliciously round the hardened stem, until the marquis's whole body was rigid as he braced himself against the onslaught of shameful pleasure.

Marianne watched longingly. Oh, how she wanted to do that, as she had so often before! To taste him, to feel that incredible hard flesh with her own tongue, to lick and caress him into oblivion . . . Her own excitement churned at her loins; her nipples were hard against her thin dress, and she was aware of the almost unbearable ache down at the very pit of her belly, a kind of sweet, dark pain that gathered and grew as she watched poor monsieur Jacques' degradation.

Then the gaoler was loosening his chains; not to free him, but to thrust him on his knees, fastening fresh chains round his wrists to bind them together behind his back.

'Here you are, citizeness Thérèse,' he grinned. 'Reckon our fine marquis is ready for you now. That's a sturdy great weapon he's got there, though. Reckon you can take it?'

'I'm sure I can,' breathed Thérèse, her ripe breasts still hanging loose from her bodice, her nipples stiff and hungry as she continued to play with them. 'Make sure he services me well with his fat prick and I'll reward you later, my friend.' Then, her eyes glazed with lust, she pulled up her shabby skirts and crouched on all fours, lifting her plump bottom cheeks in the air and positioning herself carefully so that Jacques' blindly thrusting member was nudging against her flesh.

Marianne gazed in anguish at the sight of the proud, blindfolded monsieur Jacques vainly trying to draw away when he realised what was happening. But the brutal gaoler swiftly gripped his throbbing, lengthy phallus and guided it inexorably towards Thérèse's exposed cleft, to prod against her glistening flesh folds. 'Oh, no, my fine stallion,' the guard muttered, 'you don't get away that easily. This is what you're here to do. See?'

And he thrust the helpless marquis's rampant shaft between Thérèse's hungrily parted thighs and up against her juicy vulva, where he rubbed it swiftly to anoint it with her glistening moisture. Then he guided it into her yearning love channel, and Thérèse cried out, 'Yes! Oh, yes,' as she thrust her hips back against him and enfolded all of his hot, throbbing length within her greedy flesh lips. A roar of appreciation went up from the other prisoners at this lustful display. Marianne hated them for it, but she herself could hardly bear to watch, so intense were her own emotions as she watched how Jacques' heavy penis was so eagerly engulfed by Thérèse's ripe flesh. Even now, she was writhing to and fro on his wonderful instrument of pleasure, moaning out her delight; and Marianne again felt the urgent tightening at her own loins, the intense, burning desire to to be impaled by that massive weapon.

Then she gasped, because Jacques struggled suddenly and twisted himself away, completely withdrawing his glistening shaft, so that the woman Thérèse howled out her rage and diappointment.

The guards leaped to jerk at his chains, forcing him back into position again. One of them ripped Jacques' breeches down the back, completely exposing his taut buttocks, roughly pulling his thighs apart so they could all see the dark cleft that separated his bottom cheeks, the loose-hanging, heavy balls filled with his hot seed. Marianne sobbed aloud in pity for his shame. But worse was to come, for then she heard the guard whisper huskily, 'So. Maybe you prefer it this way, do you, my fine marquis? Why on earth didn't you say?'

And, swiftly pulling out his own thickly erect phallus from his rough homespun trousers, he spat in his hand and rubbed it swiftly up and down the hot shaft, bringing it swiftly to its full, glistening length; then he spat again and moistened the swelling purple plum of his gnarled penis with special, loving care.

Jacques knew, Marianne could tell that he knew, what was in store. He writhed and twisted with almost superhuman strength, but the other men, guards and prisoners alike, held him down; and when the guard knelt behind him, and slowly pushed his penis up into the secret, dark orifice that had been laid bare, Jacques went rigid. Then his head slumped, as if at last he'd given up. But Marianne could see that his penis jutted out yet further with the unexpected stimulation, throbbing blindly against his belly.

The woman Thérèse saw it too. With a crow of

triumph, she once more crouched before him and bared her buttocks, imploring a friend to seize that massive, glistening shaft and thrust it deep within her greedy flesh folds.

The onlookers cheered and clapped at this fresh spectacle. While the guard, his face grimly intent, gripped Jacques' buttocks and drove himself slowly in and out of his tight anus, Thérèse slid herself up and down on his jutting phallus, jerking faster and faster and crying out, 'Oh, yes, yes, my fine marquis. That's it – that's what I want,' as her orgasm drew near.

And Jacques too, Marianne could see, was almost on the verge. His head was bowed in despair as the guard behind him pumped deeply into his tight passage, and the woman Thérèse squirmed on his penis in delirious ecstasy. Marianne could see how his tormented balls grew tight and thick, could see the fat stem of his beautiful, glistening penis as, in spite of himself, he began to move, to join in that lustful tableau, to slide his aching shaft lasciviously in and out of Thérèse's juicy flesh. Suddenly his whole body went taut; and then he drove himself, hard, deep within the climaxing woman and pumped himself in hot, shuddering spasms that drained his entire body, just as the man gripping his buttocks gave a shout of triumph and bucked rapidly to his own release between his clenched bottom cheeks.

Marianne felt the longing shudder through her own body, the deep, aching void of her own need. With a little moan of despair she let her tightened fist slip to the apex of her thighs, and pressed hard, grinding herself softly against her knuckles, feeling the hot slippery dampness even through her cotton skirts. Catching her lip betwen her teeth, she rubbed swiftly as the hot pleasure melted through her loins, imagining Jacques' strong, beautiful shaft driving up and up into her own yearning inner flesh, as it had so often, imagining the sweet, hard pleasure of her own velvety sex lips closing round the stiffness of it, sliding on it, clutching at it. She felt hot and breathless and ashamed

as the fierce desire licked like fire at her belly; then all
her being was concentrated in her tight, quivering bud
that throbbed urgently against her fist, and she pressed
hard against it, bracing her thighs against the sudden,
racking delight as her body spasmed into silent orgasm.

She felt faint and dizzy, and had to lean back against
the wall as the intense waves of pleasure coursed
through her. She wasn't alone in her frenzy; by now
several of the onlookers, demented by lust after what
they'd seen, were openly masturbating, while some had
retreated into the shadows to find swift release with a
partner.

Then Marianne gasped and cried out, because
another of the guards was advancing on the poor,
broken monsieur Jacques, with the others cheering him
on, and she didn't think she could stand it. Because she
couldn't think of anything else at all to do, anything
else to distract them, she flung herself on that bitch
Thérèse, kicking and scratching and screaming a thin,
high-pitched scream that penetrated the thick walls of
the prison itself. People turned round to stare at her,
forgetting their immediate prey, Jacques; she drew a
quick, deep breath and began screaming again, until
the guards grabbed her, still kicking and struggling.

Then the big doors of the cell clanged open, and the
chief gaoler appeared, roaring out, 'Diable! What the
hell is going on in here?'

The chief gaoler was a big, formidable man of whom
even the guards were afraid. As he strode into the cell
with his lantern held high, everyone sprang back into
the shadows, clustering in muttering groups. Only the
half-naked prisoner, forced to his knees by his chains,
was still. His dark, blindfolded head was bowed in
degradation, and with a sigh of exasperation the gaoler
walked across to him and held the lantern over his
crouching body. 'Who in the name of God is this?'

One of the guards faltered out, 'Jacques Lamont,
ci-devant marquis de St Maury, citizen. Arrested for

incivisme, crimes against the republic. Also a returned *émigré*, and therefore under automatic sentence of death.'

But the gaoler didn't reply, didn't even hear it all, because he was gazing at Jacques' exposed back, where the brutal guard had pushed up his shirt around his shoulders as he used his body so shamefully. Marianne saw it too, the familiar sight of those awful striped scars that ridged the firm brown skin with white, marking him for life. The gaoler's face tightened, changed.

'By God,' he breathed at last, 'you say this man is a marquis? A convicted felon, more likely. Turn around, citizen marquis!'

Jacques lifted his head slowly, tiredly, his body braced for fresh blows.

The gaoler ripped off the blindfold, and gazed down at him. 'Well, I'll be damned,' he said. Jacques gazed up at him steadily; there was a long, unnatural silence. Then the gaoler roared out, 'Put this scoundrel in solitary. Tomorrow, he'll be first for the guillotine!'

Marianne rushed forward in utter despair and flung her arms around his neck. 'Monsieur,' she whispered, 'monsieur Jacques! It was all my fault, what happened to you; I should have stopped that great fool Armand bringing madame Louise into the house! I'm so sorry – can you ever forgive me?'

She reached blindly to kiss him; the burly gaoler gripped her arm. 'You,' he snarled to Marianne, 'you can go into solitary too! For being a damned troublemaker!'

Nicole gazed despairingly out of the window of the deserted old farmhouse. It was late afternoon; darkness was falling, and with it, her hopes. She'd already spent one cold, lonely night here and it looked as if she would be spending another.

Tomorrow morning, she would have to leave, because of the note from Jacques scribbled on the edge of the map. *'If I don't turn up within twenty-four hours, then go. Obey me in this if in nothing else.'*

The old woman in her cart had given her a welcome if painfully slow lift well beyond the walls of Paris, past the scattered cottages and solitary farms and poor, mean villages that were all too clear evidence of the people's poverty. Where the road forked to Beauvais, Nicole had checked her map in the weak autumnal light and parted from her good friend, with grateful thanks. The wind blew sullenly from the east, carrying ragged leaves and wisps of straw in its wake and chilling her to the bone. Wrapping her cloak tightly around her slender frame, she'd struck off on her own, by foot, along a stony track that was almost overgrown.

She'd found the farmhouse that Jacques had marked on her map, just beyond a clump of trees about a mile from the road. It was surrounded by miserable, rain-blackened fields that had been harvested bare of their meagre crops of rye and potatoes, and then left to grow weeds. The farmhouse looked as if it had been empty for some time; its low, sombre rooms were dark and chill, the meagre furnishings stained with mildew.

Looking around dispiritedly, Nicole found flint and steel, and dragged logs in from the back yard to make a fire. She found some tallow candles too, at the back of a dusty cupboard; she'd lit several of those in the back kitchen, so they wouldn't be visible from the track, and sat down at the big wooden table to eat the food the old woman had pressed on her: stale cheese and hard bread, and a flask of rough wine.

She wasn't really hungry. She couldn't think of anything except Jacques. Abandoning her meal because it was choking her, she paced the stoneflagged floor, her thoughts torturing her. It was all her fault. She'd been so stupid, wilfully misunderstanding all the clues as to Jacques' real identity. If it wasn't for her, he'd never have been recognised and denounced by that vile man Saltier and the treacherous Louise. He might even have escaped from those soldiers yesterday, if it hadn't been for his responsibility for her.

And now, she faced her second night here, knowing

her hopes were forlorn. Tomorrow, she would set off on her journey again. There was a sum of money in the bag which would see her on her way. Where she went, she didn't much care.

Suddenly, in the gathering gloom, she heard the distant sound of hoofbeats. Her heart thumped painfully against her ribs, and she flew once more to the front window. The sound came from the main road; there were several horses, she guessed, travelling fast. She couldn't see them yet, because of the trees, but it sounded as if they had left the main road and were coming up here.

She grabbed the pistol that she'd left on the table and ran to another window, her breathing ragged and shallow. She felt the blood draining from her face as she saw them.

In the fast-failing light she could just make out soldiers, four of them on worn-out horses, with the all too familiar red jackets and tricoloured caps and gleaming muskets. They were riding their lathered mounts up here, up the track to the deserted farmhouse; one of them led a spare mount by its bridle.

Perhaps they were coming because they knew she was here. Perhaps the old woman had talked. Nicole bit back a sob of terror as they clattered into the cobbled yard and began to dismount, their voices gruff and sinister. In the darkness she couldn't see their faces, but they looked rough and menacing. She thought of locking the front door, and remembered that there was no lock, and no earthly way of securing it against these ruffians.

Her body was shaking with fear as she watched them stride up to that unlocked door. But somehow she forced herself to hold her head high; somehow she lifted the pistol with both trembling hands, and made herself walk slowly into the darkness of the narrow hall.

This was the end, she knew. She wished that she'd thought to light a candle out here, so that she could see her enemies. She hated the darkness, not to see properly what was happening. But better to die quickly here, she told herself, than to be dragged back to Paris to undergo the long, humiliating farce of justice there.

Even so, her hands shook almost uncontrollably and her throat was dry as the sturdy door crashed open and the soldiers burst in.

She held the gun as steadily as she could, pointing it at the first of those figures and hoping desperately that the darkness would conceal the shaking of her hands. Her lips were almost numb with fear as she breathed, 'Stop, or I'll shoot. I swear I'll shoot the first one of you to come near me.'

The first soldier stopped, and she saw his teeth gleam white in the darkness as he smiled. 'Then it's to be hoped, my Nicole, that your pistol's not loaded this time either.'

Her senses swam. She was trembling terribly now. Somehow, through the haze of her confusion, she saw the dark, gleaming eyes, narrowed in mockery; saw the loose dark hair concealed by the filthy red cap; saw that twisted, familiar smile.

'Jacques!' she screamed. 'Oh, Jacques.'

And she was in his arms, crying and laughing all at once, pummelling his chest and gasping, 'How? How did you get away?'

He held her gently, stroking her hair from her face. 'You'll never believe this,' he murmured, 'but the gaoler was a friend of mine.'

'No! I don't believe it!'

'It's true, *ma chère*. He, too, was a prisoner in Toulon; his name was Julien. Because he was unable to read or write, I wrote letters for him, to his family. He recognised me, and smuggled me and another friend of mine out of Paris.'

'Another friend?'

'Yes. Let me introduce you.'

One of the soldiers, smaller than the others, stepped out of the shadows, pulling off his hat so that a tumble of dark curls fell about his face; Nicole gasped out, 'Marianne!'

Marianne's cheeks dimpled in joyful response, and she ran into Nicole's arms, holding her tightly and kissing her. 'Dear Nicole! Aren't these clothes fun? We have some for you as well, and a spare horse, so we can all escape together!'

Nicole gazed suddenly up at Jacques, her heart stirring uneasily. 'Where are we going, Jacques? Austria? England?'

'No.' He gazed down at her calmly. 'We're going to Lyons.'

'*Lyons!* But why?'

'That, according to my informers, is the way Louise went.' Nicole noticed then that he was fingering the brand on his inner wrist, as if he could still feel the red-hot iron scorching his flesh. 'You see, I'm rather regretting letting her go earlier. I have a particular reason to find her again.'

With a sudden chill at her heart, Nicole realised that he had changed. His eyes were cold and bleak and empty; the only time she'd seen them like that before was when he was forced to recall his time in the Toulon *bagne*. What had they done to him in prison this time? she wondered desperately.

Marianne broke the heavy silence by tugging at Jacques' arm and saying, 'You want to find Armand too, monsieur Jacques!'

'Of course.' He smiled down at Marianne. 'Armand too. You're coming with us, Nicole?'

Nicole hesitated as a thousand thoughts and pictures ran through her mind. She gazed up at him in the ragged soldier's uniform, saw how his eyes glinted in a renewal of secret amusement, and a fierce stab of longing shot through her. There was no-one like Jacques, and there never would be. She took a deep breath.

'Yes,' Nicole said steadily. 'I'm coming with you.'

His inscrutable eyes glinted in approval. 'My Nicolette. What fun we shall have when we find our prey. What opportunities for revenge.'

'So the game goes on?' responded Nicole, her heart thudding.

He smiled at his accomplice. 'Indeed, *chérie*. The game goes on.'

The small fires of the gypsy encampment twinkled like fireflies in the forest clearing. Somewhere overhead an owl screeched, startling the grazing horses.

The women were busy with Armand. Louise smiled contemptuously as she watched them in the firelight, saw the pretty gypsy girls playing with Armand's ever-willing organ as it rose like a great staff, darkly engorged, from the silky mat of hair at his groin. The girls were giggling and backing off in mock terror at the sight of it, daring each other to touch the swaying pillar of flesh, fantasising about how it would feel poked up inside their hot, luscious love-holes. One of them daringly leaned forward to take the juicy, swollen glans into her soft mouth; her friends gasped in amazement as the great veined shaft throbbed anew and Armand sprawled back in the bracken, his eyes squeezed shut in rapture.

Louise frowned. What a fool he was. Soon, she would get rid of him. He'd been a useful enough bodyguard on their journey, but he had a tendency to dwell on the fate of Jacques and Marianne. Now that they were travelling with the gypsies, south towards Lyons where she had friends, she might contrive to lose him.

But then again, perhaps they still weren't far enough from Paris. Not yet. Perhaps she still needed his protection, because sometimes, she thought she heard light footsteps behind her, though when she turned there was no-one there. And sometimes, at the dead of night, she thought she heard soft voices in the black stillness.

She was being fanciful, stupid. She was safe now.

Sometimes, when she remembered Jacques, she felt a stab of desire so intense that it physically hurt her. But then, like a steel knife twisting in her belly, the pain of desire would turn to icy rage because he'd rejected her for that tawny-haired slut, Nicole. He'd be dead by now, of course. Another gift for Madame la Guillotine.

The gypsy youth lying sprawled beside her on the coarse blanket stirred sleepily, and she stroked his dark head. He wriggled his way down her body to nudge his face between her thighs, gently lifting her skirts; she felt his tongue, hot and sweet and rasping, strongly licking her velvety folds. Oh, but he felt good. Louise moaned softly and spread her legs further, arching her hips and clasping at his curly hair as he nibbled and sucked. His long, sensitive fingers probed her vulva and she thrust harder against him, the sweet sensations of pleasure starting to gather and build in her churning abdomen.

Wordlessly, he drew out his long, slender phallus from his breeches and stroked her glistening folds with its smooth head; she gazed at him dreamily. He was lithe and slim, with a silky, smoothly-tanned young body; his penis was smooth and powerful and delicious. Smiling, she reached down to stroke the firm shaft, feeling how hot it was; silently he gripped the slender stem and began to guide it between her hungry, swollen sex lips.

Suddenly, she thought she heard something; a twig crackling in the trees behind her, a foot crunching softly on the dried leaves. Knocking the youth aside, she whirled round to face the darkness. 'There's someone there!'

The gypsy smothered his annoyance and soothed her, patiently stroking her thighs. 'There's no-one,' he said calmly. 'No-one.'

Turning back to him, she quickly drew him back into her arms, though her heart was still thudding. Gently he slid his brown hand along her juicy cleft and eased his rigid penis into her. She grasped it eagerly with her inner muscles, savouring its delicious, bone-hard length, while he unfastened her bodice and kissed her stiff pink nipples. His shaft was good, long and firm and satisfying as he slowly ravished her, arching his tightly muscled buttocks and driving himself deep within her soaking flesh as she thrust eagerly against him. The hunger burned in Louise's womb; sensing her nearness he plunged faster, and she clutched at his hardened phallus until the explosion of pleasure tore through her, engulfing her loins, her breasts, her belly in sweet, spasming ripples.

He shouted her name and started to race towards his own feverish climax; she held him tightly, savouring every thrust of his eager penis as he cried, 'Oh, yes!' and started to jerk convulsively deep within her.

Then she heard it again. A footstep, then the soft echo of a whisper, somewhere behind her in the darkness. She wrenched herself away from the youth's pounding body, her heart hammering with nameless fear. Someone was watching her . . .

The gypsy had toppled off her, but his seed was still spilling from his lengthy organ; angrily he gripped her and rubbed his climaxing penis against her ripe breasts, his face hot and tight as the milky semen spurted over her nipples. 'There's no-one here!' he gasped out at last, his face flushed with exertion. 'No-one – you understand?' Then he pulled himself up, and walked dismissively away to rejoin his companions.

Louise wanted to call him back, but she still felt as if someone was watching her, laughing at her. 'Damn you, Jacques,' she whispered. 'Oh, damn you.'

Slowly she straightened her clothes and drew the blanket about her, because she was cold. Already, the stars were twinkling in the clear, velvet-black sky; there would be a frost tonight.

She lay there, shivering and waiting.

Visit the Black Lace website at
www.blacklace-books.co.uk

**FIND OUT THE LATEST INFORMATION AND TAKE
ADVANTAGE OF OUR FANTASTIC FREE BOOK OFFER!
ALSO VISIT THE SITE FOR . . .**

BLACK LACE